I0708467

Doors & Windows
A Novel

TC Kennedy

For my mother

When the Lord closes a door, somewhere
He opens a window.

Maria, *The Sound of Music*

| ONE |

It's not like the door was locked. I could've left at any time. And yet, I didn't. I didn't want to face what was out there, and not just what was beyond the heavy door—my blind date— but what was waiting for me when I went home. Nothing.

I waved my hands under the faucet again, leaning toward the mirror letting the water run, as I stood in the empty, dimly lit restroom of an upscale Italian restaurant. I knew the restroom was empty because the first thing I did was check the stalls as I walked in. I couldn't pee with anyone else in the bathroom. The medical term for my condition was "shy bladder."

While staring at my face in the large mirror spanning the wall, I grabbed a couple of paper towels to dry my hands. A dull ache had settled in the back of my head, no doubt from the scintillating conversation about my date's BMW. It's not technically a conversation if only one person does the talking, which is why I excused myself between the appetizer and the entrees to seek refuge in the ladies' restroom. He should date the car, he talked about it so much.

I ran my fingers through my dark brown hair that fell a few inches below my shoulders, fixating on the small freckles that splattered my cheeks and the bridge of my nose. The concealer I used this morning didn't cover them or the lightly shaded half-moons under my eyes, and I wished I had some of that concealer now. When Henry, my best friend, had moved out, quiet filled the house. Most nights, I laid in bed listening for something that was no longer there, finding sleep elusive and fleeting.

Startled by the restroom door opening, I glanced at the woman who entered. She walked straight to the furthest stall, a phone glued to her ear, her voice interrupting my train of thought. She didn't suffer from shy bladder.

Turning my attention back to the mirror, my eyes fell on the shiny, thin chain around my neck and the small silver cross dangling from the middle. I held it up for a second before tucking it back beneath my shirt. I unzipped my purse, fishing around for some lip gloss. I came up empty.

With one last glance in the mirror, I checked my teeth to make sure there weren't any remnants of basil from the bruschetta, but I knew I was stalling. Taking a deep breath, I opened the restroom door and found my way back to the table. And to Todd.

As I approached, I noticed that our entrees had been delivered. Todd, staring at his phone, had waited to start eating until I had returned. As I sat, he placed his phone on the table and picked up his fork, looking up and smiling. I was grateful there would be more eating and less talking about cars.

I felt I needed to say something first. "Sorry I made you wait. I hope your food isn't cold." As far as apologies go, it was on the weak side. There was no good explanation for my extended absence. Placing my napkin back on my lap, I picked up my fork.

"This looks delicious," I said. My plate was filled with creamy risotto with wild mushrooms. The side of roasted vegetables looked equally appealing. Definitely better than my usual microwaved meal.

The soft-lit restaurant was busy and the twenty or so tables draped in red cloth were all occupied. We were seated in the middle row at a small table for two, exposed to the scrutiny of the other diners but I was glad we weren't hidden in a dark, intimate corner where couples made too much eye contact and forked food from each other's plates.

My gaze moved to Todd's face rather than the wall behind him where I had earlier counted the number of exposed bricks as he talked about his BMW. It was easy to look at Todd's face. The first thing I noticed when he introduced himself were his blue eyes and easy smile. His facial features were proportional, and his sandy-colored hair was neatly styled. He was what our looks-obsessed culture would consider good-looking. Was that why Daniel set us up? Daniel, the mastermind behind this date, was the owner of the Straight & Narrow, a bar where I spend most Friday nights after work. Where I should have been instead of here.

I did very little to prepare for our evening out. I had stuffed some mascara in my purse before I left for work this morning. After I had turned off my computer this afternoon, I brushed my hair and popped a mint in my mouth before heading out of the office to meet him. Sarah, my friend and coworker, was a little dismayed that I didn't make more of an effort. She made me promise to tell her everything on Monday.

Since we both worked downtown, it was decided that we would meet at the restaurant. Al Tavolo, located in Pike Place Market, was the opposite direction of my building. The afternoon walk was a nice way to unwind from a busy workday. It helped that Seattle's typical June weather of drizzle and gray was on hiatus, and we were experiencing a dry, warm patch of late spring weather.

"Have you eaten here before?" I asked as I grasped my glass of water.

"Once. A few weeks ago. We brought a client here. I don't think it's been open very long." He took a bite of his ravioli stuffed with short rib, meeting it halfway as he bent his head forward toward his fork.

As we ate, I racked my brain for a new topic of conversation. Normally I was fine with silence but for some reason I felt the need to say something.

"So, you're an accountant. I guess you come by that honestly." I smiled, but he stopped chewing, his brow furrowed. Apparently, my comment confused him. "Your mom. Isn't she Daniel's accountant?"

He swallowed and his face relaxed. "Oh, yeah. She does his deposits and payroll, but she's not a CPA."

Genuinely curious, I asked, "How long has your mom worked for Daniel?"

"Ever since I can remember. She kind of came with the place," he said as he put another bite in his mouth. I noticed that his plate was nearly empty, and I was only four or five bites in. I didn't want to drag dinner out any longer than necessary, so I focused on my food, no longer worried about finding something to talk about.

"How long have you known Daniel?" he asked after he finished off his glass of moderately priced cabernet.

"About seven years. There's a group at the office that hangs out at the Straight & Narrow after work on Fridays. I guess you could say we're regulars."

As I ate, my shoulders relaxed and I no longer feared car talk as we had moved onto other superficial topics like favorite restaurants. After making a sufficient dent in my risotto and roasted vegetables, I wanted to check my phone to see what time it was but couldn't figure out a discreet way to do it. It must have been close to six-thirty. Everyone from work would probably be leaving the bar for home about now. Henry would still be there though, leaving with Daniel at the end of the night.

Our young, personable server removed our plates and dropped off dessert menus. I briefly looked over the options and then lowered the menu to look at Todd.

"Have you ever had the chocolate cake at the Straight & Narrow?"

"It's my mom's favorite."

"Do you maybe want to go there for cake instead?" It was true I wasn't eager to extend the date, but I did have ulterior motives for going to the bar for dessert. Henry and Daniel, for one, and there was a small possibility a few people from work still might be hanging around. Maybe Todd and I would do better in a group setting, and it would avoid the awkward end-of-date scenario of the two of us standing outside the restaurant trying to figure out if someone should ask for a number.

"I'm up for that." He put his menu down on the table. When the server returned, I reached for my purse on the floor while Todd politely declined the dessert offer and asked for the check.

With a cheery voice, the server informed us that the bill had been taken care of. As she picked up our menus and cleared our remaining glasses, Todd and I both looked at each other, confused.

"Daniel?" I guessed.

"Or my mother."

"Maybe they were in on it together," I said. "We can ask Daniel when we get to the bar." I scooted my chair back and set my napkin on the table.

As I grabbed my jacket from the back of the chair and hung it over my arm, I realized the one problem with this plan. Todd would insist on driving us to the bar. I mentally prepared myself for round two of an in-depth explanation of why the BMW was the greatest vehicle ever made.

His eyes brightened, as he was visibly excited that I would get to experience "the ultimate driving machine," especially after I mentioned that I had never ridden in a BMW. I was less excited. Normally, I would never get into a car with a guy I just met, but it was less than a mile to the bar, and technically he had been vetted by Daniel. Daniel would never set me up with a sociopath.

We walked two blocks to the lot where the black sedan with tinted windows was parked. Using his fob, he unlocked the doors, and I slid into the front passenger seat. It had that new car smell. Is this what Germans smell like? I thought about saying it out loud, but Todd might not think it was funny. They should make new car smells different for each brand. A new Subaru would smell like earth and wet dog.

I had the time to contemplate new car smells because Todd was messing around with the center console, which resembled the cockpit of a plane. He started the car, while continuing to look around the dash, searching for something.

"How long have you had the Beamer?" I asked Todd, repeating the term he called the car several times at dinner. He looked to the ceiling as he continued to push buttons.

"This is the first day I've driven it," he said, finally opening the roof window. He put the car into first gear, and we rapidly turned onto the street. Within the first four blocks, he changed lanes five times, weaving in and out of traffic.

As he sped down the one-way street, shifting gears while narrowly avoiding cars, my body tensed, and I braced myself against the back of the black, leather seat. When a white Tesla in front of us slowed as the light turned yellow, Todd tried to go around it. Forced to stay in his lane as a car sped by us, he hit the brakes hard, shifting into a lower gear to avoid hitting the Tesla in front of us at the now red light. Frustrated that he wasn't moving, Todd found the center of his steering wheel with the palm of his hand.

"We could have made that light," he said raising his voice over the sound of the car horn. With my back pinned to the seat, I watched him find first gear again, dismayed that my imaginary brake didn't work.

My hands trembled as I fumbled to unbuckle my seatbelt while I swung my head toward Todd. Maybe I was being impulsive—or maybe it was self-preservation—but I jumped out of the car, slamming the door behind me, and headed toward the sidewalk. Within seconds, I heard Todd call out of the open window of the passenger side.

"What's going on? I thought we were getting dessert?"

Still in the street, I turned around and bent my head down so Todd, leaning over the empty seat, could see me.

"Really? The date is over, Todd. We're not even halfway there and my stomach is in my throat. It's just a car. It gets us from point A to point B, preferably in one piece. Oh, and by the way, it's not called a Beamer. It's called a Bimmer." I turned and stepped onto the sidewalk. Thankfully, the light turned green, the walk sign appeared, and I started to cross the street.

A honk from behind, followed by the angry screech of Todd's tires, let me know he wasn't happy, as he drove passed me. Shaky from the brief ride, I pulled out my phone and started to text Henry. After three attempts, I deleted the typed words and put my phone back in my purse. By the time Henry borrowed Daniel's car to pick me up, I would already be at the bar. I decided the walk would do me good. Taking a deep breath in, I slowly exhaled, trying to calm my mind and body.

I glanced at the sky and noticed a few clouds moving in from the water. They weren't the white, fluffy kind.

The residual rush hour traffic still clogged the streets, but nothing like two hours ago. The street noise was more of a hum than a clash of horns and engines and even though I was still a little shaken from my sudden departure from Todd's car, I could still think clearly.

I should have never agreed to the date, but Daniel was persistent when I expressed my doubts about having dinner with his bookkeeper's son. And Maxine, my boss, had expressed concern that for the last few weeks, I seemed stuck, a little distracted. She made her point, as probably most lawyers would, with the evidence she had in front of her. Her observations were still rattling around my head when Daniel brought up the blind date.

All this speculation about my predicament was preceded by one event with which I was still struggling—Henry's decision to move out of my house. Henry. I conjured his face in my mind, his big smile, and his thick mop of black hair that matched his dark eyes.

After he moved out, it was work, home, microwave a frozen meal, some television or a few chapters of a book, and then bed, where actual sleep was hard to come by. I had Friday nights at the Straight & Narrow to look forward to, but that was about it.

Thinking about Henry made me think about Hawaii—a trip we planned months ago. In less than two weeks, Henry and I would be enjoying island life, sitting on the soft sand, sipping drinks in the warm sun. I saw the trip as a way for me and Henry to reconnect and get our friendship back to the way things were before he moved in with Daniel. I've accepted that they are serious and have a solid future and I want to be part of their lives together.

I checked the time on my phone. I should be eating cake by now. A raindrop fell on my arm, and I glanced up at the sky. The forecast said nothing about rain, but here it was.

| TWO |

By the time I reached the bar, my clothes were damp and limp, and the sunny thoughts of Hawaii were gone, replaced by disappointment at how the evening had turned out. I did a quick check up and down the street in front of the narrow building in search of the BMW, realizing that Todd might have decided to show up anyway. I didn't see the car. The brick façade of the Straight & Narrow was sandwiched between two less-assuming buildings. Its formidable glass door was deceptively easy to open, and my eyes immediately adjusted to the dark interior.

I nodded at the host, who still recognized me, even though I was sure my hair was a frizzy mop and mascara was dripping from my eyes. I walked to the back passing the impressive bar with its abundance of glass, mirrors, and dark wood that stretched along most of the left side of the narrow, high-ceilinged room.

Henry was sitting in the booth by himself. Everyone from work was gone, apparently home to start their weekend after a head start at the Straight & Narrow. Removing my jacket, I flung myself down across from Henry, who was typing something on his phone. I let out a soft sound, somewhere between a sigh and a groan. "I'm going to kill your boyfriend."

Henry, oblivious to my distress, was focused on his screen, intent on whatever he was typing.

"But he's my ride." He stopped staring at his phone, and looked up at me, seeing the spectacle that I imagined I was. He opened his mouth to say something when Daniel appeared.

"I take it the date didn't go well?" Daniel asked as he looked at his watch. "I mean it's only seven and from your appearance it looks like the date ended abruptly." He glanced around the bar. "Unless Todd is around here somewhere."

As I looked up at the tall, thin man, dressed in a dark suit with one of his on-trend ties, I was acutely aware he was the reason I had to walk ten blocks in the unexpected rain shower.

"He better not be here," I said, my mouth tight. "And no, it did not go well. It was a disaster."

Henry looked at me and then Daniel. "Nature's calling." He slid out of the booth heading down the hall in the direction of the restrooms and Daniel's office. Daniel sat in Henry's vacant seat, directly across from me. Grace, our usual Friday night server, came over and put Henry's drink in front of Daniel and asked if we needed anything, which momentarily broke the tension.

"I'll have a piece of cake, Grace. Thanks," I said, still staring, maybe glaring, at Daniel.

"You and your cake," she said with a light laugh. "You look like you need a drink too." She nodded at me. "How about an old fashioned?"

"Perfect," said Daniel speaking for the both of us while looking at the tall, tattooed woman holding a tray against the side of her hip. "Bring two. I'll take care of all of this, so you don't need to open a tab." He glanced around the bar. "Actually, the after-work crowd seems to have called it an early night. Why don't you close out. Marcus can take over any of your tables."

"Okay, I'll grab your drinks and cake first."

"Thanks."

As Grace headed toward the bar. Daniel turned back to me. "For some perspective, on a scale of one to ten…" He pushed Henry's drink out of the way as his gaze stayed on me.

I opened my mouth to say a one, but I knew I was overreacting. I let out a sigh as I sunk into my seat. "I'm not ready to date anybody, Daniel." Another thing I figured out on the walk over.

He smiled knowingly. "Just got out of a long-term relationship, huh?"

My eyebrows inched up my forehead and I let out a little snort. "Is that what it was? Maybe so. I know this sounds pathetic, but part of me thought Henry and I would always live together."

"Really? Don't you want to meet someone, get married, have a family?"

I wanted to tell Daniel that I thought Henry was my family, but I didn't say it out loud. It wouldn't change anything. "Henry doesn't want to get married."

"But Jane…"

I sat up straight and looked Daniel in the eyes. "I know what you're saying. Henry calls me the queen of romantic comedies after all. But happily ever after isn't real."

"But you deserve something close to that, more than living with your gay best friend."

As I lowered my head, he leaned toward me and tapped the top of my hands. "It will get better. I promise. Change is hard. For everyone." He leaned back in the booth, removing his hands from mine. He continued when I didn't respond. "I guess I feel responsible for your current situation, which is why I thought I needed to fix it with Todd. Seriously, I thought you two had a lot in common. Nancy is always talking about him. She's a proud mom."

"You've never met him." With my voice flat, it sounded more like an accusation than a question.

"Met him? I've known him since he was in high school. I just saw him on Monday when Nancy stopped by to show me her new BMW."

My head jerked up and I slammed both my palms down on the table, startling him. "I knew it. I knew that wasn't his car. He drove it like he stole it, which is why I look like this." My voice was louder than I intended.

"Well, I can't help it that you got in the car with him," Daniel said emphatically, recovering from my reaction. "Maybe he was nervous and wanted to make a good first impression and it just got away from him."

I leaned back in the booth. "Maybe. But the reality is I don't need a boyfriend." I hesitated before finishing my thought. "I think I need a roommate."

Just then, Grace placed a slice of dark, dense cake with a quarter inch of wavy chocolate frosting in front of me. I caught a glimpse of the ink flowing up her right arm and disappearing beneath her crisp, white shirt at the elbow. A vine of roses, pink and red. Henry, right behind her, slid into the seat beside me, picking up his drink and taking a gulp.

"Where's my cake?" he asked to everyone.

I noticed Grace staring at me, her eyes a little bigger as she ignored Henry. "Hey, I'm looking for a place." She looked at me like I was the person who could make all her dreams come true. "Actually, I'm desperately looking for a place." She placed a drink in front of me and one in front of Daniel.

"Oh, I don't know if you want to live with Jane," Henry said, inserting himself into the conversation while sliding my cake toward himself before I slid it back. He gave me the side eye and then looked at Grace. "I did it for almost ten years.

She's a bit of a slob, which you wouldn't think by looking at her. And obviously she can't share." He squeezed in this last observation, no doubt based on my refusal to give him my cake.

"I'm good with slob." Grace couldn't get the words out fast enough. She sounded so desperate I wondered if she would move in with a serial killer if he had a spare room. Glancing at Daniel, I tried to figure out what was going on. First, I was on a date with Guy Who Tries Too Hard. And now there was Girl Desperate To Live Anywhere. And somehow both of these were my problem.

"I can vouch for Grace," said Daniel. "She's a great employee, even though she's looking for another job."

She scoffed. "I can't even get an interview, so I don't think you have to worry about me leaving just yet. Besides, I can still work here on the weekends."

Henry looked at me and his face brightened. "Actually," he said, pondering, "I think this is a good idea, Jane. I mean it's almost been a month since I moved out." Henry turned to Grace. "Did you know that Daniel and I are now living together—in sin?" Henry's eyes darted in my direction when he said this. I didn't think Grace was aware of her boss's new living arrangement. Daniel shifted in his seat as he looked away. He was close with his staff, but he was also a private person. I could sense Daniel's discomfort, but Henry seemed oblivious.

Daniel pushed his old fashioned in front of Henry and slid out of the booth. He took Grace's tray from her hand. "I'll take this. Why don't you tell Jane a little bit about yourself and Jane you can share what you're looking for in a roommate."

My eyebrows lifted as I looked at Daniel. "Can I trust your judgment after the Todd fiasco?"

"I thought we decided it was more of a misunderstanding." Smiling, he turned and vanished into the crowd around the bar.

Grace slid into the booth taking Daniel's place. I picked up my fork and stuffed a big bite of cake in my mouth to buy some time. There was no need though. Grace launched into her life story without hesitation.

She had studied business at the University of Washington before dropping out and moving to Colorado with some guy. They eventually broke up, but she stayed in Denver for eight more years, mostly working in restaurants. She decided to finish her degree at UW so she moved back home. After recently graduating, she was looking for a job, but living at her parents' house was suffocating. They were constantly asking about the job situation and they didn't think she should still be waiting tables after earning her degree.

With my plate empty at the end of Grace's story, she said, "Parents, right?"

Neither Henry nor I responded, and Henry's face turned downward. Grace's smile faded, no doubt wondering what she had said to cause the sudden silence. I didn't enlighten her, and my facial expressions didn't change. Henry finished his drink and was working on the drink Daniel left behind. He must have decided someone should say something to alleviate the awkwardness and suggested a game to determine if Grace could fill his giant roommate shoes.

"Well," said Henry, trying to sound serious and shifting his weight in the booth, "let's start with a few questions to determine if you're suitable roommate material."

"Ask me anything," said Grace. "I have no secrets."

Well, that's one for the plus column, I thought. Honesty was something I used to take for granted.

Henry looked at Grace and in his best game show voice said, "A hot guy comes into the bar and waits until you get off work and then he asks if you want to go back to your place. Do you A, say that your roommate is sick and suggest his place, B, say sure, that sounds like fun, C, make out a little at the bar and then send him home alone or D, tell him you would never pick up a guy at the bar?"

Grace looked a little stumped. I didn't know if it was because of the randomness of the question or because she didn't know what she would do in that situation. And then she asked, "How tall is he?"

My smile widened. I wouldn't call Grace a friend, but I did spend most Friday nights in her company, even if it was just chatting with her while she brought us food and drinks. She was always upbeat, friendly, and she knew all of our names. If there were new faces, she made sure to learn their name as well. Still, I wasn't sure about roommate. But right now, the warmth of the alcohol and the satisfaction of the thick, rich cake created a Zen feeling throughout my body and all I had to do was listen. Cake made everything better. I let Henry play his game, one he was taking seriously. He expected an answer, so he gave her a clue.

"This is an easy question, Grace. There's only one wrong answer here."

"I'm going with D, final answer!" she shouted, but with the surrounding noise from the other bar patrons her voice didn't carry across the bar.

I wasn't convinced this was what Grace would have done in this situation, but at least she knew she should never bring some random guy to my home.

"Correct," said Henry, confirming the contestant's answer and moving on. "Next question. In order of worst to best, rank these three classic movies. *Clueless*, *The Breakfast Club* and *Ten Things I Hate About You*. You have sixty seconds." Henry decided to add another element to the game.

I thought about the question and decided I didn't even know the right answer. *The Breakfast Club* was the least but *Clueless* and *Ten Things*, I would have to toss a coin. Both great movies, based on great books.

Grace seemed to enjoy this game and clearly had a sense of humor. She talked her way through her answer. "I have never seen *Ten Things I Hate* and only part of *The Breakfast Club*. I guess *The Breakfast Club*, *Ten Things*, and then *Clueless*?" Her eyes narrowed as she looked concerned that she didn't answer the question correctly.

Henry looked at me.

I shrugged my shoulders and drained the last bit of liquid in my glass.

"That's an acceptable answer. Last question. You have a few hours to do anything you want. Would you A, read a book, B, watch a classic eighties or nineties rom-com or C, scrub the bathroom?"

Grace's shoulders slumped and she looked stumped, probably because she would do none of those things. She hesitated a little too long as she thought about it.

I decided to let her off the hook. "They're all acceptable answers, Grace. Look, I will definitely think about it, but work is crazy right now. Maxine—you know Maxine, she shows up on Friday nights occasionally—she's leaving on a two-month sabbatical, and we've been trying to tie up all the loose ends before she goes. Henry and I are going to Hawaii for two weeks and I haven't done anything to get ready for the trip. I don't even have a swimsuit yet. I guess I haven't given the roommate situation too much thought. Henry just moved out a few weeks ago and he's right, I am a bit of a slob. If you haven't figured it out already, I'm also a homebody and live a rather dull life. Friday nights at the Straight & Narrow are as crazy as I get." I finished my speech thinking it was probably too much information.

Before Grace could say anything, Henry had an epiphany, "Hey, if Grace moves in, we won't have to worry about Prince William when we're gone."

"That's true," I admitted, fiddling with the corner of the napkin my empty glass was sitting on. We weren't quite sure what to do with Prince for the two weeks we were gone.

"Who is Prince William?" asked Grace, puzzled. "I mean, I know who Prince William is."

I was about to answer, but from behind Grace's head I saw Todd walking down the aisle toward us. Our eyes met. With his lips tight and his jaw tense, that calm cake feeling left my body, to be replaced by a pit in my stomach.

| THREE |

When Todd was a few feet from the table, Daniel appeared out of nowhere and placed his arm around Todd's shoulder, steering him toward the bar with his head bent low, talking as they walked. Daniel must have seen him walk in and moved to head him off before he found me.

Henry sensed that something was up. "Is that your date from tonight?"

"Yes," I said as I craned my neck to get a better view of the two men. "I wonder why he's here." My eyes stayed fixated on the pair.

Grace turned her head around to see what we were talking about. "How did you meet him?"

I explained that Daniel had set us up and that he was Nancy's son. I assumed Grace knew who Nancy was since she also worked at the bar.

Daniel and Todd headed toward our booth and Henry, Grace, and I pretended we hadn't been watching them.

Daniel still had his arm around Todd. "Hey, Henry and Grace, can you grab your drinks and move to the bar?"

Reluctantly, they slid out of the booth, glancing back at me as they walked to the far end of the busy bar where there were a few open places to sit. Todd's eyes were cast to the floor, and I couldn't read his face, but since Daniel brought him over to my table, I assumed he came in peace.

"Jane, Todd would like the opportunity to apologize and explain. Is that okay with you?"

"Uh, sure, have a seat."

"I'm going to go somewhere else, but I won't be far," Daniel said, clearing my plate and the empty glasses in front of Todd before he left.

After a few seconds, Todd looked up at me. "Hey, I didn't mean to scare you. I'm sorry," he said, hesitating before continuing. "The BMW is my mom's, and I convinced her to let me drive it tonight. She picked it up from the dealership on Monday. I actually drive a Toyota Corolla. It's blue. Has a dent in the back where I hit a pole."

"Clearly not the same driving experience as a BMW."

He gave a little laugh. "Not even close. I have no idea why my mom bought it. I, on the other hand, have always wanted one," he said shaking his head. "I was nervous about our date and then excited to drive the car and I guess I got a little out of control when I was behind the wheel."

Daniel was right again. It was becoming more clear why he set us up. On paper, Todd checked a lot of boxes.

"And just so you know, I dropped off the Bimmer at my mom's." He tilted his head as he stared at me. "Hey, how did you know that a BMW is also called a Bimmer? I only call it a Beamer because most people don't know that it's really pronounced Bimmer." He sounded impressed by my very limited car knowledge.

"Our old next-door neighbor collected cars and he had a gray BMW that he would wash almost every Sunday morning in the summer. Sometimes he would let me wash the wheels.

It was a pet peeve of his when people would call his car a Beamer. He said that was a motorcycle."

"Yeah," Todd said as he confirmed what I was told as a child. "Well, that surprised me as much as you getting out of the car in the middle of the street."

"That might have been an overreaction on my part. I don't doubt that we would have made it here in one piece."

"Did you get caught in the rain?"

I wondered if he was asking because of how I looked or because he felt bad. I was so mad at Daniel that I didn't check to see what I looked like when I made it to the bar. My hand went up to my head and I ran my fingers down the side of my hair. "Yeah, I was surprised by the rain. I didn't see that in the forecast."

"Well, sorry about that too."

We stared at each other, waiting for the other to say something.

"Are you still up for dessert?" Todd asked.

"Sounds good." Who am I to say no to another piece of cake?

Todd and I talked, ate cake, and had a couple of drinks. The conversation, casual and natural, was vastly different from the conversation at the restaurant. We talked about books, music, and movies. We had a similar taste in music, but not so much in movies.

"Where did you go to college?" I asked, digging deeper.

"Loyola Marymount. I was accepted to Notre Dame, but it would have been a huge financial stretch and LMU gave me a substantial scholarship."

Now it made sense why Daniel thought we would have something in common, and a little smile appeared on my face as I came to the realization. "Well, I would think California might trump the Midwest when it comes to weather. And it's a little closer to home."

"Yes, both those points made the pro list. Where did you go to college?"

"I graduated from Seattle University with an English degree." I didn't mention that I went to community college for two years first. I understood that sometimes money, or the lack of it, can make decisions for us. I also had a scholarship, which helped.

I excused myself to use the restroom, making a mental note not to take too long. I was relieved to find my hair was just moderately wavy in a way reminiscent of an eighties hairstyle. My makeup managed to survive the rain and I didn't look like a raccoon. Staring in the mirror, I realized that I had judged Todd too quickly. There was nothing wrong with being passionate about something, even if I didn't share the same enthusiasm. I could have made more of an effort at dinner rather than slinking off to the restroom.

When I returned to the booth, it was exponentially more crowded. Grace and Henry decided it was a perfect time to return from their previous ouster and were sitting with Todd. He looked overwhelmed by the pair and grateful that I had returned.

When Henry saw me, he slid out of the booth so I could sit across from my date. Grace smiled at me with a nod toward Todd. I guess she approved of Daniel's matchmaking skills.

We ordered more drinks, and the conversation grew louder. Henry must have been considering a side gig as a game show host because he came up with a lightning round of questions for Todd.

"So, Todd, let's see if you have any chance of a second date with my best friend." He swung his arm around me. He was a few drinks ahead of me and I glanced at Todd when he mentioned second date. Todd seemed amenable to Henry's game.

"Pie or cake?" Henry started.

Todd knew the answer to this one, as the remnants on our plates made the correct answer obvious.

"Cake."

"Tea or coffee?"

He hesitated. "Tea?"

"It sounds like you're not sure, but I'll accept it anyway. Here's a hard one. Jane Austen or Charlotte Brontë?"

Henry didn't know that Todd and I had discussed literature earlier. I mentioned that I was a fan of Jane Austen but preferred the Brontë sisters. Todd said he wasn't much of a reader, but his mom took his Xbox for a month during the summer he turned fifteen and he read a series of books called *The Belgariad*. I looked them up on my phone while he was talking about them. They were highly rated on Amazon.

"Charlotte Brontë," he said confidently.

"Three for three. Impressive." Henry looked at me and I waited for him to say something inappropriate, but he didn't.

"Hey, I was also three for three if we're keeping score," said Grace. She had caught up to Henry in drinks.

"Now it's time for feats of strength," said Henry. "Todd let's see how many push-ups you can do." He moved to get out of the booth.

"Uh, no, there will be no push-ups." I put my hand on his arm to stop him from moving. He sat back in the booth, and his smile slipped from his face.

During the game portion of the date, the bar had filled up again. Some event must have ended, and people didn't seem to want to go home. Daniel probably regretted letting Grace go early, but she was in no condition to wait tables now. Eventually, he stopped by the booth to pick up all the empties.

"You guys seem to be having a good time," he said, his eyes on me. I waited for the wink but was grateful when it didn't come.

| FOUR |

It wasn't often, at least not lately, that I woke up next to a man in my bed. Or in this case, a man curled up at the bottom of my bed. It was Daniel who had suggested that Henry spend the night with me since he was going to be later than usual. He also figured we could talk about our upcoming trip.

Before he moved in with Daniel, Henry would occasionally fall asleep next to me. We'd put on our matching pajamas that we found at Costco and make smoothies while moisturizing with a mud mask. Then we'd pile up all the pillows on my bed, and I would read aloud from whatever book I was reading at the time, giving Henry a SparkNotes rundown first unless I had just started something new. If he wasn't in the mood for a read-along, we'd watch a rom-com from the eighties or nineties. When Henry first moved in, he had no idea who Amy Heckerling was.

Rubbing my temples, I tried to remember everything that happened last night, but the details were fuzzy. We had to Uber home since no one was capable of driving. I haven't had that much to drink in a long time, and I was glad I had that second piece of cake. For an evening that started out terrible, it turned out better than expected. Todd redeemed himself with his apology. Most guys wouldn't have done that. And while I didn't specifically ask and the topic didn't come up, I assumed that Todd was Catholic because of his college choices. Something we had in common and something that was important to me.

I didn't go to church very often growing up, but my mom considered herself to be a religious person, even though the patriarchy of the church bothered her. She didn't think it was good for women or men. She prayed the rosary every day usually sitting me in front of the TV with some cartoon on, probably *Blue's Clues* or *Dora the Explorer*, while she sat at the kitchen table with her rosary beads.

Henry and I had some philosophical discussions about religion when he first moved in. He considered himself agnostic and I respected that. On a few occasions, he would go to church with me. His questions afterward weren't to better understand what he had just experienced, but to question me why I believed any of it.

As I continued to dissect the evening, I thought about Grace. She was one of the funniest people I had met; an extrovert to my introvert and everyone needs a wingman. Staring at the ceiling, I mulled over the thought of calling her to see if she wanted to talk more about moving in. It might be what I needed to get out of my rut. Daniel would have her number, or he could give her mine.

The clock on my nightstand told me it was close to ten and I thought about getting up, when Prince William jumped up on the bed. The gray and white cat had started hanging around five or six years ago and Henry started feeding him. The next thing I knew he was living in the house. I wasn't a cat person, but he grew on me. We couldn't decide on a name though. I finally agreed to "Prince William" because I could call him "Prince" after the musical genius. Henry had this weird fascination with the royal family that I'd never understood and only referred to him as Prince William or my Darling Prince William. Unfortunately, Daniel was allergic to cats so when Henry moved out, Prince stayed with me. And despite Henry's assurances that he would come by and clean the litter box regularly, it had only happened once since he left.

The doorbell interrupted my thoughts, and I sat up surprised by the sound so early-ish in the morning. I listened for a second and then nudged Henry with my foot. "Hey, did you hear the doorbell?"

He shifted onto his back, wiping his eyes with the back of his hand, and mumbled, "What?"

"The doorbell. Someone is at the door," I explained, speaking slowly and enunciating my words.

"It's probably Grace," he said as he rolled back to his previous position.

"Why would it be Grace?" Confused by his answer, I leaned forward so I could get a better look at the lump at the bottom of my bed.

"Because I texted her last night after I looked in your fridge for something to eat and saw only pickles and soda. I told her to pick up some food and make us breakfast this morning and if it was good, she could move in." He said all of this with his face in his armpit, his voice muffled and raspy. Somehow, I managed to understand it.

I kicked him this time. "Well, go answer the door. I'm hungry." After a few seconds, Henry dramatically rolled out of bed and, while hunched over and groaning, stumbled in the direction of the front door. Prince jumped down and followed him, thinking he was going to get something to eat. Pulling the covers off, I strolled to the bathroom singing to myself as I pulled a washcloth from the shelf.

A smile spread across my face. It was like it used to be, having Henry here. It was hard not seeing him most days, and even though we texted every day—usually about our trip—it wasn't the same as sitting across from him at the table. I missed him so much, but I couldn't tell him that. I wasn't sure he missed me.

For some reason, I combed my hair, brushed my teeth and changed into some leggings and a long sweatshirt. When I wandered into the kitchen, which was next to my bedroom, I could smell freshly brewed coffee. I remembered Henry's slob comment from last night and I glanced out into the big room to see how I had left it.

I had always called the large open living area the "big room." There was a bank of windows opposite the front door of the big room with a panoramic view of the backyard. A stone fireplace with a wooden mantle backed up against the wall of my old bedroom. On either side of the fireplace were two bookshelves stuffed with books. Oversized, comfortable furniture filled the room. Fortunately, there were only a few empty glasses on the coffee table and my jacket was lying on a chair but for the most part, it just looked lived-in.

I noticed Henry was sitting at the long, wooden table that was in front of the kitchen island. His back was to the big picture window that faced the backyard. He was holding his head with his hands. A coffee cup was in front of him with the fumes wafting up toward his face.

"Hey, Grace. It smells delicious." I said.

"It's just French toast. There's more coffee." She nodded her head toward the coffee maker near the sink. Instead, I grabbed the tea kettle and filled it with water from the sink. Grace stood in front of the cooktop in the kitchen island as I placed the kettle on the burner next to her, turning the knob on the stove to ignite the flame.

"Thanks, but I'm a tea drinker. Henry's the coffee drinker. I was a hardcore Jane Austen fan in high school, and I acquired a taste for tea." I grabbed a cup and some tea from the cupboard and stood by the island waiting. It looked like Grace had everything under control.

"*Pride and Prejudice* is a solid book. I had to read it in tenth-grade English. Your house is great. The backyard is awesome." She briefly looked out the window behind Henry before returning her attention to the hot pan.

"Yeah, it's a bit of a jungle back there. The neighbor kid mows the front yard when he mows his, but the back hasn't been touched since Henry moved out," I explained.

"I told you I would come mow it," Henry sputtered.

When was the last time Henry had a hangover? I wondered. "I know you did. I also know how to mow grass, but I thought maybe I would let it revert to nature. I've never been a fan of manicured lawns."

"Or manicures," Henry said.

I knew he couldn't be that hungover if he could still manage one of his not-so-clever quips. I ignored him as I watched Grace flip over a piece of French toast.

"I'm sorry that Henry asked you to buy groceries and make breakfast. I wasn't expecting company, so I haven't been to the store." I felt I needed to explain why there was no food in my house.

"Henry sent me a picture, Jane. I've never seen a fridge that empty, even in college."

"Yeah, I guess my Pop-Tart diet isn't really working for me. Friday night at the bar is the only day I can say that I eat a real meal." I didn't mention that I had lost four pounds since Henry left.

"All right, I think we're getting close. Plates?" Grace asked as she looked around the kitchen.

Walking to the cupboard to the left of the sink, I grabbed a couple of plates. I handed one to Grace, and as she piled up the French toast, I took the bowl of fresh fruit and we set everything down in the middle of my worn table. Henry hadn't moved. The kettle whistled and I stretched across the island to pull the teapot off the burner. Henry clutched his ears and groaned.

"Why is everything so loud?"

"How much did you have to drink last night?" I glanced at him as I poured the steaming water into my cup.

"I don't remember. All I could find when we got back here was that nasty peppermint schnapps. What happened to all the alcohol?"

"You didn't really drink that, did you? We've had that forever."

"You could have told me." Henry was still holding his head.

Placing my tea on the table, I sat and reached for the bowl of fruit, spooning some onto my plate. "You drank all the other alcohol before you moved out or else you took it with you." I tried to pass the bowl to Henry, holding it in front of him, but he didn't take it.

"I don't think I can eat. I'm going to go lie down." He didn't move.

"Fine. More for us then." I put the bowl down and reached for the plate of French toast. He slowly stood and shuffled back to my bedroom.

"That's rough," said Grace. She sat at the table with a new bottle of syrup she had pulled out of a grocery bag. It took several attempts to get the tab off the opening of the plastic bottle.

"Is it?" I said as I plucked a fresh strawberry from my plate, putting it in my mouth. "He's a lightweight." My stomach growled and I turned my attention to the food in front of me no longer thinking about Henry. "Thanks again for making breakfast." Stabbing a bite of French toast, I stuffed it in my mouth.

"No problem. Last night was interesting," said Grace as she reached for the fruit. "What do you think of Todd?"

"I had a good time after he showed up at the bar. He didn't ask for my number though. I guess he can ask Daniel for it, or he knows where I am most Friday nights."

"That's true," said Grace hesitating before continuing. "After Todd showed up and Daniel asked us to leave, I asked Henry some more questions about the roommate situation. I hope you don't mind."

My mouth was full, so I shook my head.

"I was thinking an apartment, not a house. Since you guys didn't mention a landlord, I was confused. Henry told me that you own the house and that your parents passed away. Your mom when you were in high school, and your dad when you were little. That must have been hard."

I chewed slower, not sure where this was going.

"I mean I complain about my parents, but I can't imagine not having them around. Maybe not living with them. They weren't thrilled with the tattoos or when I dropped out of school, which I still hear about, although now, all the parental concern is focused on why I haven't found a job yet. But still..." She trailed off and took a bite of French toast.

Secretly relieved that I didn't have to explain my orphan status, I did wonder what else Henry told her. Did he tell her about my aunt? I decided it didn't matter and I thought Grace would have mentioned that too if Henry had filled her in.

"Yeah, I'm lucky that I have the house. There are a lot of memories of my mom here, and some of my dad. He passed away when I was four." I instinctively looked through the big window to the backyard. "He built the treehouse."

"It's awesome." Grace turned around in her chair and looked out the window to view the sturdy structure.

My dad didn't live with us, but he insisted that the big oak was a perfect tree for him to build me a little house of my own.

It was large enough for a grown man, a little girl, and a few stuffed animals. It was always special when he stayed over. For the most part, I had his undivided attention. After he died, I spent hours up there. Most of my memories are of us in the treehouse. It's a constant reminder of him.

I decided to change the subject.

"How's the job search going?" I asked, but then thought it might be a sore subject. "Unless you don't want to talk about it." I added.

"Fuck, I thought it would be easier," she said as she looked down at her plate, her shoulders caving inward.

She sipped some of her coffee. "I had a great internship at a startup, and I expected a job offer, but the company imploded. The two founders fighting. Total shit show. I came to work one day, and HR walked us out, one by one. So, on to plan B, which is to apply to anything I might have a shot at. I've had four interviews in the last four months. The worst part is, I have an interview and then nothing. I don't know if it's because I'm thirty-one and just now graduated or the tattoos or the lack of real experience or a combination of the three."

She sounded exasperated as she barely took a breath. Leaning back in her chair, she poked at a piece of French toast with her fork. "I don't know, but it's bumming me out." She looked at me. "How did you get your job?"

"Pity," I said, and it was true, but I didn't elaborate. Grace seemed like an open book and I envied her willingness to share her stories.

Her eyes brightened. "Then, hell, I should've had a job a long time ago. Maybe I wasted too many years waiting tables."

"Well, you have a lot of experience working with the public. Employers are probably looking for people with customer service experience."

"Yeah, I guess. Who knows where I would be without my job at the Straight & Narrow. I walked in there right after I was told my internship was ending six months early, and I planned to drown my sorrows in rum and Cokes. Daniel was behind the bar. I had no idea he owned the place, but he could tell something was wrong and he took an interest."

"Sounds like Daniel."

"After I told him how humiliating it was to be walked to the elevator with a small box of my belongings, he said I could work there, and it didn't matter if I didn't have any experience. I laughed, but he was serious. I told him I had waited tables before but wasn't sure he'd want to hire me after my previous employment horror story and my other last day of work when I walked out instead of someone walking me out.

"Was this in Colorado?"

"Yeah."

I guess I was paying attention last night. "What happened?" I asked as I wiped up a pool of syrup with the last piece of French toast.

"It was this crazy-busy night at the restaurant. There were these three middle-aged guys waiting for their table and one of them kept checking to see when they would be seated. When we finally had a table, I found them in the bar and I picked up a tray to carry their drinks, but the guy sitting was surprised when I grabbed his glass. The guy standing closest to me said—and I'll never forget this—'she's aggressive.' I gave him a look but didn't say anything. But then, staring right at me, he said, 'Be nice.'"

"What a jerk," I said shaking my head.

"Yeah, and that's when after working ten days straight, I was done being nice to asshats like him. I took the drink on the tray and threw it in his face and said, 'Fuck you.'"

"You did not." My eyes widened as I stared at Grace.

"Yeah, I did." Grace paused, taking a drink of coffee. "I grabbed my purse from behind the front desk and left. I ended up at Lucky's, a bar down the street, where the drinks were stronger and cheaper. Later, everyone from work showed up and bought me a bunch of drinks. My manager said that while she understood what I did, I was out of a job, which I sort of knew before she actually said anything. Anyway, everyone pitched in and gave me like five hundred bucks. It was pretty cool. I took the extra money, bought a plane ticket home, and moved back in with my parents. Where I still live," she added.

She wasn't subtle.

Prince found Grace's leg. He arched his back, rubbing his fur against her as his tail snapped back and forth.

"I see you've met Prince. Or Prince William, as Henry calls him," I said as I watched the cat.

"So, this is Prince William." She looked down at the cat at her leg. "I'm not sure he looks like a Prince William."

"Thank you," I said, feeling vindicated at the stupid name. "That's why I call him Prince. But you could call him 'Cat' because he's a cat and he doesn't know his name. I assume you're not allergic?"

"Nope. I'm an animal lover." She bent over to scratch Prince behind the ears.

There was a lull in the conversation as we both stared at the cat. I wondered if Grace wanted to bring up moving in but wasn't sure how. I was going to say something, but she beat me to it.

"I know Henry texting me last night was a foody call, and not a real offer for me to move in. I mean, I realize it's not his decision. But when you get around to thinking about a roommate, I hope you'll consider me. Your house is great," she said as she looked around. "I'm easy to get along with. I made French toast because it's quick, but I like to cook. I can't pay a lot in rent to start but as soon as I get a day job, not waiting tables, I can pay more."

Wiping my mouth with the paper towel I was using as a napkin, I dropped it on my empty plate and looked at Grace. "Henry and I had a very informal living arrangement. When he moved in, we were both in high school and he needed a place to stay. Any financial stuff sort of evolved the longer we lived together," I explained to Grace, letting her know that the situation with Henry was unique. "I was more than a little surprised when he told me he was moving out and it's been an adjustment for me, not having him here." I was rambling. As I was talking, I was still trying to figure out if this was a good idea, but I didn't let that stop me. "Can we start with rent plus half utilities?"

Grace sat up in her chair and stammered out, "Yeah, yes. Thank you."

We talked details for over an hour after cleaning up the kitchen, agreeing on an amount for rent and discussing expectations as roommates. She was so excited, she asked if she could move in tomorrow. I couldn't think of a reason why not.

The Tylenol and coffee must have kicked in because Henry was more himself after his nap. He even cleaned the litter box. Grace offered to give him a ride home, so he took the last of the boxes he still had here with him.

"Love ya," said Henry after he gave me a big hug.

"Love you too."

I stood on my porch and watched them leave. My heart felt heavy knowing that Henry wasn't moving back, especially now that Grace was moving in.

| FIVE |

Sunday was usually a quiet day, even with Henry. I felt a pinch of regret as I thought about having a near stranger move into my house. Grace had texted me last night and told me that she and her dad would be over around nine.

After getting ready for the day, I walked into the open kitchen, the sun shining from the sliding glass doors that led to the wooden deck that spanned the back of the house. I tidied the kitchen and emptied the dishwasher, something I hadn't done in a long time. I usually just rinsed the dishes in the sink after I microwaved something frozen.

Prince trotted over to me. I picked him up, holding him close. "It's no longer going to be just you and me," I whispered into his fur. I kissed him on the top of his head and put him down as I looked into the big room.

My mom bought this house before I was born. She worked as a real estate agent and fell in love with the house and yard as she was showing it to a client. It was a three-bedroom Craftsman she remodeled into an open floor plan. I walked down the short hallway right of the entry-way, with doors on either side that led to the other two bedrooms. The hallway ended in a full bathroom. I turned on the light to make sure it was clean. It hadn't been used in weeks and I checked to make sure there was toilet paper and tissue in the cabinets beneath the sinks.

I opened the door to the first bedroom with the window that looked over the front porch. It had revolving occupants throughout the years. Initially it was a guest room with a full-sized bed and a dresser, and when my aunt moved in to help take care of my mom, she slept there.

When my mom passed away, my aunt moved into her room, leaving the guest room empty until Henry moved in. Now it was a room to store stuff that we didn't want to get rid of but didn't know what to do with. There was a small desk with a color printer that I rarely used, my old twin bed and dresser, along with some of my aunt's stuff and the bar stools we put away when we couldn't keep Prince from jumping up on them to get onto the island counter. Sometimes we called it the Room of Requirement. The door was usually closed to hide the mess.

I opened the door to Henry's old bedroom. This had been my room growing up with pink walls and pink curtains. When my mom's cancer returned, I wanted to paint my room black, but my mom would only agree to black curtains, which still hung in the room.

When Henry moved from across the hall into this room after I moved into the main bedroom, he painted the walls a soft gray. He had found a job at American Eagle in high school and saved his first few paychecks to buy a queen-sized bed with a nightstand and dresser. He insisted on taking the furniture when he moved in with Daniel, even though that meant Daniel had to move his treadmill out of his spare bedroom.

As I gazed around the empty room, a sigh escaped my lips. My mind wandered to a few weeks before Henry left for good.

Standing in this same spot, I watched him pack a large duffle bag to take to Daniel's for another three-day sleepover. I had confessed that I missed him when he was gone.

"It's just a few days," he said as he grabbed his AirPods from the dresser. He wasn't looking at me as he stowed them in the zippered pouch inside the bag. But then he stopped what he was doing and met my gaze. "Actually, there's something I need to tell you."

I found myself holding my breath. I didn't want to hear what he was going to say.

"Daniel and I have been talking about moving in together. Me moving in with him, I mean."

"Oh." I hesitated, not knowing what else to say. My shoulders slumped and my body felt heavy. I walked over to his perfectly made bed and sat on the corner, not trusting myself to remain upright. "I didn't know you guys were that serious."

"Jane, we spend most of our time together when we're not working. How could we not be serious?"

"Well, you guys haven't been dating that long. It just seems like a big step."

"It is." He went back to packing, folding T-shirts and sliding them into the corners of the wide opening. "I know you never wanted me to have people stay the night here and so I'm always over there most of the time anyway."

I frowned. "I didn't know you wanted to have people stay over here. And would Daniel, who has his own place, really want to spend the night here?"

"When I was dating Seth, you said he couldn't stay over. I assumed it was a blanket policy."

"Seth? From high school? The guy who stole sixty dollars from your dresser? And when my aunt still lived here?" My mind jumped back nine years. Could Henry seriously be harboring some perceived slight from years ago? Honestly, I didn't remember that conversation. Henry never had any long-term relationships. They seemed to fizzle after only a few months. It was one of the reasons I wasn't excited when I found out that he and Daniel were dating. If they broke up and I had to pick sides, I would of course choose Henry, but then I assumed I would have to find somewhere else to go on Friday nights. Losing Daniel as a friend would be hard. I didn't say any of this to Henry.

"I've never felt like I could bring anyone home is all I'm saying. But this is beside the point. We're talking about me and Daniel moving in together. Look, I've got to go, but we can talk about this later." With that, he left, while I sat on the bed feeling like I was just punched in the stomach.

We never did talk about it again. Two weeks later, he told me he was moving out. Then he did.

I jumped at the sound of the doorbell. Before leaving the room, I walked to the window, opening the blinds and watched as the light bounced off the hardwood floors as the shadows fell on the soft gray walls.

For some reason, I was nervous when I opened the door for Grace and her dad. They were both holding boxes.

"Welcome." I stepped back to let them in.

"This is my dad, Charles. Dad, this is Jane." Charles and I exchanged hellos.

"It's nice to meet you. I can help too. I just need to find some shoes." Walking past the kitchen into the laundry room, I grabbed my tennis shoes. I heard Charles murmuring his approval as Grace showed him around. As I sat to put my shoes on, they disappeared into Grace's room. I fell in behind them as they walked out of the house to grab more boxes. Grace's car, an older Honda, was parked next to a rental truck in the driveway. The sun was out, although there was still a brisk morning chill as we walked to the back of the vehicles.

Grace and Charles pulled a piece of a bed frame from the rental truck and carried it together, navigating through the front door. I followed them with two of the smaller boxes from Grace's open trunk.

"Jane, do you know your neighbors?" Charles glanced at me as he navigated through the door of the bedroom.

Grace interjected before I could answer. "Dad, we talked about this. No questions, remember?"

"You said no questions, but I didn't agree to that, and you knew I never would." He looked at his daughter as she rolled her eyes. They set the bed frame down against the wall. In the opposite corner, I piled the boxes on the floor.

"I know most of my neighbors, some better than others. But we haven't had new neighbors in four or five years," I said answering his question. I wanted Charles to like me.

"I see you have an alarm system. Do you use it?" Charles glanced at the corner above the front door while we made another trip to the car.

"Yes, Dad, she uses the alarm. Please." Grace looked at me and shook her head. She grabbed a big box from the truck and walked into the house leaving Charles and me alone outside.

"I don't know if Grace told you, Jane, but I'm a detective with the Seattle Police Department. This is a safe neighborhood, but you still have to be careful. I try and instill that in my daughter, but she doesn't always listen."

Grace was not happy with her nosy police detective dad and expressed her displeasure by keeping her comments to a minimum. We made quick work of the boxes and then moved in the box frame and mattress, which was more cumbersome followed by a dresser and a chair. The rest of the boxes we left in the big room rather than piling them up in Grace's new room. After the bed was set up and everything was unpacked from the cars, I looked at the time and realized it was later than I thought.

"I have to be somewhere at noon, so I need to leave in a few minutes." For some reason, I was pulling up my sleeves now as I looked around.

"Thanks for all the help," said Grace as she opened boxes, looking at the contents and then moving on to the next one. "I didn't think I had this much stuff."

"Yes, thank you," said Charles. "One step toward independence. Now she just needs to find a real job." Grace ignored the jab, and instead she picked up a box and carried it into her room.

"Nice meeting you," I said to Charles.

Grace peeked her head out from around the corner. "Pizza for dinner tonight? On me."

"Sounds great." I grabbed my keys and my purse and headed to the garage through the laundry room.

After church, I ran errands which took longer than I thought. I forced myself to go to the mall and look for a bathing suit. It wasn't easy. I almost gave up when I found a flattering turquoise one-piece that was simple but not old-lady-looking. And then as I was walking over to the sales counter, I found a cute orange two-piece that I decided to get too, along with a white cover up. Now I had options. I envisioned spending our days lounging by the pool or strolling on a white-sand beach with umbrella drinks in our hands.

As I was paying, I found a folded napkin in my purse. I glanced at it as I pulled out my credit card. It was Todd's phone number. A bit old school but maybe he wasn't sure after the car thing. I folded it up and put it back in my purse.

We ended up eating early after I came home. All the boxes we had left in the big room were now in Grace's room and she was as hungry as I was.

We grabbed a few slices of pizza and a couple of Cokes and sat on the couch. "Maybe there's something on TV worth watching," I suggested as I looked through the guide. I found *Legally Blonde*.

Henry thought only old people watched TV and would make fun of me when I scrolled through the channels hoping to find some old rom-com. He'd usually sit down next to me though and watch. At first, I knew he just indulged me, but then I think he actually liked to watch them. He wouldn't admit it, but he was a romantic at heart.

Grace tucked her legs underneath as she looked at the TV. "I used to watch a lot of investigative true crime shows when I was in high school, but now I listen to true crime podcasts. You know the ones where the wife goes missing. Spoiler alert—the husband did it. So, are you going to see Todd again?"

The conversational whiplash threw me for a second. I thought we were going to talk TV or podcasts, but I guess we were going to talk boys. Grace took a big bite of her pizza followed by a long drink of Coke as I finished chewing to answer her question.

"I told him that I was going to Hawaii and then Henry interrupted us, so we didn't make any plans. Honestly, I want to relax for a few weeks in the sun and not think about anything—not even Todd. I did go swimsuit shopping today, and actually bought two," I said like I had just solved world hunger.

"Have you been to Hawaii before?" Grace asked between bites.

"I haven't done much traveling at all. Henry and I got our passports and went to Vancouver a few years ago. Oh, and I went to Arizona when I was in grade school. I barely remember the trip. I think I'll like tropical over dry desert." I took a drink of Coke. "Thanks again for taking care of Prince while we're gone. We weren't sure who to ask."

"It worked out for the best then. So, how long have you worked at the law firm?"

"Since I was sixteen. After my mom died, I needed a job. Maxine hired me as a file clerk. Eventually I became her legal assistant." I wiped the corners of my mouth with my napkin.

"I haven't seen Maxine in the bar lately. She used to come in all the time, especially for lunch. What has she been up to?"

"She's been busy. She's going to Europe for two months. She leaves in a week."

"So do you have two months off too?"

"Well, there's my trip and then I'll go in to work occasionally to check the mail and take care of anything that can't wait, but the plan is to study for the LSAT while Maxine is gone."

Grace glanced at the TV as Reese Witherspoon was doing the bend and snap. "So, you want to go to law school?"

My hand with the can of Coke froze near my face as I thought about how I wanted to answer the question. I should know by now because it was a question I was asked a lot. "I'm exploring the option," I hedged. "Maxine is really encouraging me to go. She thinks I would be a good lawyer. She pushed me to go to college when that seemed out of reach, and she was right about that, so I figure I should at least consider it. I'll probably take the test in October."

"How did you meet Maxine? Am I asking too many questions? I get it from my dad. You can tell me to mind my own business."

"It's fine. Maybe you should be a police detective," I suggested.

Grace laughed. "Thought about it but there's no way my dad would approve. Or my mom."

"Maxine was my mom's attorney. She set up a trust so that when my mom died, I would be able to stay in this house and go to college." It didn't quite work out that way, but I still have the house and I did go to college. I decided not to tell Grace about my aunt. At least not yet.

"How do you know Daniel? Just from Friday nights at the bar?" asked Grace.

"Yeah. One Friday when I was nineteen, a paralegal in the litigation department invited me to join everyone at the Straight & Narrow after work. She didn't think they would card me if I was with the group, and they didn't. Of course, Daniel knew everyone at McMahon & Wright. They had been going there for years, and for the longest time he called me 'New Girl.'

If he was surprised when we all celebrated my twenty-first birthday there two years later, he didn't show it. He bought me a drink like everyone else. Because it was my birthday, I invited Henry. After that he would join us most Friday nights. That's how Daniel met Henry."

I remembered when I found out they were dating. I was one of the last people to know.

"They seem like a good couple," observed Grace.

I took a bite of pizza and didn't say anything.

| SIX |

The Fernwell Building was a stump in a forest of steel and glass. Only twenty-five floors, the squat, brick building was located a few blocks from the water, with a jewelry repair shop on the first floor next to a Thai restaurant. The offices of McMahon & Wright filled the entire fifteenth floor.

I stepped into the empty elevator and watched the doors close. I was glad to be back in the office. The weekend was a lot and now that it was over, Maxine and I had until Friday to wrap everything up before she left on her trip. And in less than a week and a half Henry and I would be hopping on a plane.

I was planning a bon voyage party for Maxine at the Straight & Narrow on Friday afternoon. Technically, I was the impetus for Maxine's trip. I gave her and Henry one of those DNA ancestry kits for Christmas last year. Her results included German, British, Irish, and some Danish ancestry. She decided she wanted to travel to her ancestral homeland to see where her people came from. She connected with some distant relatives in Ireland and Germany and made plans to meet them on her travels. I can't remember the last time Maxine even took a week off. She deserved this extended vacation.

It was quiet and dark when the elevator opened to the firm's lobby. Over the empty receptionist's desk hung the firm's name in big metal letters. Maxine was the Wright. Jeanne usually greeted me when I stepped off the elevator, but I beat her in this morning. As I walked back to my office, the lights automatically turned on, filling the open area and the hall with light.

I had a small internal office on the far side of the floor. It was oddly shaped, and the size of a walk-in closet. There was a built-in desk that wrapped around two-thirds of the room. When I was sitting in my chair, my back faced the door. To the left of my desk, instead of a wall, there was an interior window that looked out into a large room.

After turning on my computer, I grabbed my mug and walked to the kitchen for some tea. Usually the smell of dark roast greeted me, but the kitchen was void of smells and sounds as I entered and switched on the light. More often than not, when I came to get my tea on a Monday morning, Steve Baxter, one of the partners, would be on his second donut and regaling people with stories of his weekend and his amazing granddaughter.

Returning to my office, holding my steaming cup of Earl Grey in one hand, I pulled up the calendar to see what we had scheduled for today. As I sipped my tea, I heard a tap on my door. I swiveled in my chair, and Maxine walked in with a couple of files in her hand. She was in early too, probably for the same reason as me. I set my cup down.

"Hey, Jane. How was your weekend?" She put the files on the edge of my desk and sat in one of the two chairs next to mine.

"It was…interesting." I didn't want to get into the details. "Are you ready for your trip?"

"Getting there. I'm hoping this week will be relatively easy, although we have a new probate." She put her hand on the files. "Let's try to get the petition and order filed by Wednesday. Then you can get the oath out and file the notice to creditors before you leave." She picked up the top file off the corner of my desk and opened it. She handed me two documents. "Here's the will and the death certificate."

I took the documents and glanced at the first few pages. "Did we do this will?" The name didn't sound familiar. I flipped through until I found the list of the heirs and the distribution of assets. It looked like a straightforward will.

"No. But I know the brother of the widower. He must have given him my name."

I scanned the death certificate. "She died after she fell down the stairs. That's awful." I glanced at Maxine before I continued looking at the form. "An accident," I said. "She was only fifty-three. And she died a year ago. Why did they wait to open the probate?"

From the look on Maxine's face, this information was new to her. She reached for the death certificate, and I handed it back. "I didn't catch the date of death." She stared at the paper. "I'll look into it. As of now, the husband will be here on Wednesday morning to sign the documents. I also received an email from Hilary Smith. She wants to change her will again."

This wasn't a surprise to me or Maxine. "Who is she disinheriting now? One of her daughters?"

"Her son. Now she wants to leave him a dollar. I'll forward the email to you, but let's try and get her in on Wednesday to sign her new will. I'll look over Henry and Daniel's documents today." She paused, her features softening. "Are you getting excited for Hawaii?" The tone of her voice changed, sounding less business and more motherly.

"I am. I need to get a few more things but I figure whatever I don't get now I can get there. Thanks again for letting us use your condo and car. Henry is really excited." Henry and I wouldn't be going without Maxine's generosity. Maxine knew Henry; after all he was with me when I showed up at her office so many years ago, trying to figure out if the only home I had ever known was going to be sold in a foreclosure auction, leaving me homeless. Maxine wasn't just my boss, she was my guardian up until I turned eighteen. She hadn't changed much over the years. Her hair was still short, but now it was speckled with gray. She was wearing her usual dark slacks and button-down blouse.

"Well, you deserve a tropical vacation." She stood. "I'll forward you the email from Hilary." She walked out, but before I could turn back to my computer, Sarah popped her head into my office.

"Got a minute?" she asked, plopping down in the chair Maxine just vacated.

"Sure, I can spare a minute." I put the documents back down.

"Derrick is such a dick. We had a huge fight this weekend," Sarah complained. Derrick was her live-in boyfriend and she threatened to break up with him at least once a month. Usually, I just listened, but this morning I thought I would change things up.

"Sarah, you don't have to stay with him," I countered, tasting my lukewarm tea.

"Well, he's not always a dick," she said, now defending him.

"Okay. Well…" I watched Sarah's eyes get big as the look on her face changed.

"Oh, shit. How was your date? I totally forgot."

"It's quite the story, but Maxine just gave me a new probate. Can you do lunch today?"

"Yes, can't wait." Sarah, with her endless enthusiasm, stood and bounced out the door. Sarah and Jeanne, the receptionist, were the closest in age to me of all the firm's employees. Sarah was the paralegal for several family law attorneys, so I thought she would know that she was dating a dope. Their huge fight was probably about getting married. In Derrick's defense, he had told her multiple times that he didn't see himself getting married. I don't know why she didn't believe him.

/ / /

Sarah and I went down to Starbucks on Tuesday afternoon to get a drink and to chat for a few minutes. When I returned to my office, there was a beautiful pink orchid on my desk. The card read *Aloha, Todd.* I felt my smile grow as I held the plant in my hand. After setting it on my desk, I reached for my purse and found the napkin. I stared at the number for a second wondering if this was a good idea. I decided to text him to thank him, at least. He officially had my number now. He quickly responded with, "Have a good trip."

I spent the rest of the afternoon preparing for client meetings scheduled for tomorrow. As I reviewed the documents for the new probate, I remembered Grace's comment regarding her true crime shows—the husband did it. Was it possible this man murdered his wife by pushing her down the stairs? I quickly dismissed the thought from my mind and finished my work, leaving the office early rather than starting something new. Usually, I commuted by bus except on Fridays, when I either drove, sucking up the thirty bucks to park, or I caught a ride home with someone. Riding the bus wasn't terrible. It was full of other commuters like me. Maxine offered me her parking pass to the building garage to use while she was traveling, which I gladly accepted.

It was nice coming home to another person and not just the cat. Grace and I had dinner together and she had asked me to look over her resume and cover letter. She was applying for another job. I suggested a few edits.

I had a craving for something cold before bed since Seattle was still experiencing warmer than normal temperatures. As I pulled two half-gallon containers from the freezer, I called out to Grace, who was sitting in the big room, giving her the choice between French vanilla and cookies and cream.

"Cookies and cream, please."

I placed a bowl in front of her and settled into a nearby chair. As we sat in silence enjoying the cold treat, my mind wandered.

"Do you think you would still be in Colorado if you didn't walk out that night?" I asked.

Grace looked up from her bowl. "That's a good question. Actually, I had thought about coming back home. Losing my job and having an extra five hundred bucks made it easier. Why?"

"I don't know. I was just wondering." Leaving behind a life that she had lived for eight years must not have been easy. It occurred to me that the reason Grace was sitting in my house eating ice cream was because of some jerk waiting for a table in a bar. I picked up the remote and turned on the TV. I lucked out when I saw *Notting Hill* was on.

"So, what's with all the old rom-coms?" asked Grace as she nodded toward the TV.

"When my mom was sick, or I guess *sicker*, we would sit in her bed and watch old romantic comedies. She grew up in the eighties. I guess watching these movies makes me think of her. That, and I'm a sucker for a formulaic story of two people destined to be together."

/ / /

Hilary Smith was in rare form when she came to the office to sign her new will. I wondered what she was like as a mother.

Does she tell her kids when she cuts them out of her will? Or does she want it to be a surprise? She must have been close to eighty and seemed in perfect health, though maybe a little hard of hearing. I doubted she was going anywhere any time soon. I was sure she would be back in the office within six months to change her will again.

I briefly saw the husband of the woman who fell down the stairs when I brought in a revised oath for his signature. I was surprised to see a much older man. He seemed almost frail. Maybe it was the grief from losing his wife so tragically. I regretted that I had entertained the idea that he might have had something to do with his wife's death. A younger man was with him, who I assumed was one of his sons.

The afternoon was spent printing and organizing the documents for Daniel and Henry's will signing the next day. Henry decided he wanted a will after we made our plans to go to Hawaii. Flying across the Pacific Ocean—his first time flying—had him excited and a little nervous. If he died without a will, his mother would be entitled to his assets, which Henry didn't want to happen. He left everything to Daniel and Daniel updated his will to include Henry.

As I shut down my computer for the day, I looked at the orchid that Todd gave me. It made me think about my tropical vacation. Next week I would be sitting on a beach with a flower in my hair and a drink in my hand.

/ / /

After Henry and Daniel signed their wills, I made copies and then we all went to lunch at Thai Time, the restaurant on the first floor of the Fernwell Building. After we ordered, we found a table next to the front window. While we waited for our food, Maxine pulled something out of her purse. "Since you're both here." She handed me two sets of keys and then gave Henry and me some instructions for her car and her two-bedroom ocean front condo, including the Wi-Fi password. "There's a nice community pool and it's just a ten-minute drive to shopping and a few good restaurants."

"This is so cool of you, Maxine, to let us use your place. I can't wait to get on the plane," Henry said.

"I've offered it to Daniel, but he won't leave his bar." Maxine nudged Daniel. "I'm glad you guys will get to enjoy it." I listened while Maxine and Daniel exchanged some light-hearted banter about Daniel's inability to take a vacation once in a while. It made me smile. Like I was a part of something.

After we finished with lunch, Maxine looked at her watch. "I should get back to the office. I have a conference call at one-thirty. Jane, stay as long as you want." She disappeared after saying her goodbyes.

"Thanks for coordinating the wills, Jane," Daniel said as the three of us sat around the table.

"Happy to do it. It's never a bad thing to plan for the future."

"You mean our future deaths," said Henry.

"To be prepared for the inevitable. And now you don't have to get married. Instead of one piece of paper, you have ten," I said as I checked the time on my phone and saw that it was later than I thought. "Crap, I need to go pick up Maxine's gift." I collected my plate and fork, depositing them in the nearly full bin of dirty dishes. I returned to the table to grab my purse. "Thanks for lunch, Daniel. I'll see you guys later."

| SEVEN |

Home from work, I threw my bag in my room and walked into the kitchen to get a glass of water. I didn't accomplish much once I returned to the office after picking up Maxine's gift. Mentally, I fast forwarded to tomorrow thinking it should be a relatively easy day because we had nothing on the calendar except Maxine's party at three o'clock. Daniel helped me organize it and most of the office planned to attend.

With Maxine gone for two months, I was concerned about what I was going to do with myself after Henry and I came back from Hawaii. The plan was to study for the LSAT, but I wasn't looking forward to it. I wasn't sure I would make a good lawyer, even if Maxine thought differently.

With my back to the sink, I finished my water when I heard someone at the door. I wasn't expecting anyone, and I assumed Grace was at work—her car wasn't out front—so I thought it was a solicitor. I pondered whether to ignore it when I heard another knock. Putting my glass in the sink, I walked to the door and stuck my eye up to the peephole. I was surprised to see Henry's face, or the side of his face, because he was looking toward the neighbor's house. I opened the door wide and stepped back so he could come in.

"Since when do you knock? Did you lose your key?" I noticed his collar was askew as he slowly turned his head to look at me.

"I need to talk to you." He hesitated, and then stepped into the house stopping in the entryway. I was barely able to shut the door behind him. After looking down for a second, he said, "I don't think I can go to Hawaii with you." His voice sounded flat.

I blinked and frowned as I processed what he was saying. "What? Why?"

"Why did you say, 'Now you two don't have to get married?'" His stare was cold, and I pushed down a feeling of uneasiness.

"What?" I asked, confused by the question and his demeanor.

"At lunch today, after we signed our wills, you said to me and Daniel that now we don't have to get married."

I thought for a second trying to recall what I had said. "I guess I did say that." I slowly stumbled out an answer. "But I didn't mean anything by it. Henry, you've told me forever that you never want to get married. The first time was when we watched *Four Weddings and a Funeral*."

"This isn't one of your stupid movies. This is my life."

"I guess I said it because you're in a relationship, you live together, and you guys are committed to each other, even if there's no marriage certificate. There was no big meaning behind it." I walked toward the big room. When I realized that Henry wasn't following me, I turned around. As I looked at his face, I realized Henry wasn't upset. He was angry. At me.

"Let's sit down," I said, attempting to diffuse the tension.

"I don't want to sit down. Are you trying to sabotage my relationship with Daniel? Are you jealous?"

"What are you talking about?" I struggled to keep my voice calm.

"I'm trying to figure out why you said that. I know your religion doesn't believe in gay marriage. Is that why you said it?"

"My religion? Look, Henry, you've told me on numerous occasions that you never want to get married. That's why I said it. And honestly, I didn't mean anything by it. I think you and Daniel are great together." I heard the pitch of my voice getting higher. "Hell, I introduced you." I gestured with my arms and hands for effect.

"Have you talked to Daniel about me? Did you tell him I never wanted to get married? Before today, I mean."

I wondered if he had heard anything I just said and I found myself getting angry. Henry's behavior was way off base, and I realized he had been drinking. I took a deep breath.

"Is everything all right, Henry? Did you and Daniel have a fight?"

"Just answer the question."

"I may have mentioned to Daniel that you didn't want to get married. I didn't know it was a secret."

"I can't believe you would talk about me behind my back. I would never do that to you." He stood directly in front of me. "Your fake piety is just a cover for your homophobic beliefs and your church-going bullshit. You spend your Saturday nights sitting at home and you want to ruin what Daniel and I have because you're jealous. You need to get a life. You're about as spontaneous as a fart." He ran his hand through his hair. "Well, not a fart because they can be spontaneous, but you know what I mean." Flustered by his weak analogy, he stopped talking.

I let his words sink in and I felt a rise in my chest and my voice matched the feeling. "I can't believe you called me homophobic. I have always been supportive of your relationship with Daniel. I'm sorry if you thought I didn't want you to bring guys home to spend the night, but it would be the same if you wanted girls to spend the night. I might be a prude, but I'm not homophobic. I was upset when you moved out. And it seemed as if you didn't care about my feelings when you left. But never in a million years would I knowingly do something to hurt you." I took a deep breath. "Daniel is a good friend," I said as I tried to control my emotions but feeling over-whelmed. "You know what Henry? You're not. You come here accusing me of sabotaging your relationship, you call me names and blame my beliefs because you've been drinking and you're insecure in your relationship with a grown-up." I stepped to the door, opening it as I kept my eyes on him. "You need to leave." I felt my heart pounding in my ears. He stood still, not saying anything.

"And don't worry, I don't want to go to Hawaii with you either," I said.

He didn't move.

"You need to leave now."

He hesitated, but then walked past me and out the door. I slammed it shut. When I turned around, Grace was standing in the hallway next to her room.

"Wow," she said as she held a sandwich in her hand.

I guess she was home.

"Looks like you got dinner and a show." I fled to my room slamming the door.

| EIGHT |

The fog from little sleep hindered my ability to process what had occurred the evening before. The accusations that Henry hurled at me left me shaken and sad. After he left, I ended up giving Grace a ride to pick up her car at the dealer's service department, which is why she was home.

We probably spoke twenty words between us and not one of them was about Henry. She grabbed poké for dinner on her way home and we sat on the couch and watched *Working Girl.*

The thing is, I couldn't figure out if Henry truly believed everything he said yesterday or, if between the alcohol and his insecurity about his relationship with Daniel, he created a narrative that made me the bad guy. Either way, he crossed the line.

I rubbed my face and tried to convince myself to get out of bed. Yesterday afternoon, before Henry came over, I was looking forward to today. Now I found myself dreading Maxine's party and having to face Daniel. I was almost positive that Henry wouldn't be there though, which was good because the thought of seeing him again left me with a pit in my stomach. I finally crawled out of bed and started my day. Grace was still asleep when I left.

I wasn't sure what to do about the trip and what I would tell Maxine, since she was letting us stay at her place. I had no desire to go by myself. Maybe Henry and Daniel could go, but I didn't see Daniel leaving the bar in someone else's hands for two weeks. Grace would ordinarily jump at the chance, but she had a couple of interviews next week. I didn't want her to choose between a trip and a potential job. I decided to stop thinking about it and focused on work and Maxine's party. I'd figure it out later.

Not feeling anything, "fake it until you make it" was the theme of the day. I put on a happy face and pretended all was right with the world for Maxine's sake. For the most part, I pulled it off. I didn't want her to think about anything except her trip. Maxine, unlike a lot of the attorneys at the firm, was organized. There were no last-minute fires to put out—just a few minor odds and ends to take care of.

The corner clock on my computer hit two and I shut everything down. As I walked to the bar, the knot in my stomach grew, knowing that Daniel and I would have to acknowledge what happened between Henry and me. A conversation I was dreading.

Daniel had insisted on closing the bar to the public, at least until five. When I arrived at the Straight & Narrow, there was a sign stating that the bar was closed for a private event. I hesitated, wondering if it would be locked, but when I tugged on the door, it opened easily. No one was at the front, so I cruised by and walked to Daniel's office.

I knocked on the slightly open door and stuck my head inside the room. He wasn't alone. Daniel's office was only slightly bigger than mine, but it was a perfect square. He motioned for me to come in. There was a woman standing next to a seated Daniel. As I walked in, he stood and introduced me to Nancy.

"It's nice to meet you."

"It's nice to meet you, too," I responded. Was this awkward? I wondered as I faced the petite, blond woman. Does she know everything that happened on my date with her son? I decided it didn't matter. What would I do about it anyway?

"Well, I was just on my way out." Nancy picked up her bag. "I'll see you on Monday, Daniel. Goodbye, Jane," she said with a warm smile and walked out the door. Daniel gestured toward the other chair next to his desk.

As I sat, I asked, "How's Henry?" surprising myself by the question. Was he at home wondering how I was doing? Did he feel any remorse about what he said yesterday?

"He's still upset. But I'm not sure who he's mad at—me, you, himself?"

"What did he say to you about yesterday?" I concentrated on a piece of paper that was hanging over the edge of Daniel's desk, picking at it.

"Not much. Honestly, I'm not sure why he's so upset. He said you said something at lunch, and he thought it was out of line. He didn't want to talk about it. I'm sorry about the plans for Hawaii though. Are you still going?"

"I don't think so. I would just sit in the condo and read or watch movies and I can do that here." I didn't mention that what I was looking forward to most was having my best friend to myself for two weeks with no distractions. The tropical location was just a bonus.

"I tried to convince him that you guys should still go, that you could work all this out."

Daniel. Always the optimist.

Less than twenty-four hours had passed since Henry came to my house. A part of me kept thinking I would get a text from him apologizing for his behavior.

"The thing is, Henry knows all the stuff I went through with my aunt after my mom died and my breakup with Mitchell. It has taken me years to trust people again. Yesterday he said some things that might be hard for me to forget. Maybe he won't be able to forgive me for whatever he thinks I did and, while that makes me sad, I know that I will be okay if ultimately Henry and I are unable to find a way back to where we were."

"When God closes a door…"

"What's that supposed to mean?" I didn't hide the irritation I felt by Daniel's words.

"It means, Jane, that unlike a lot of people, you have your faith to get you through. You're lucky to have that."

I didn't say anything for a second as I contemplated his observation. "Thanks. It does feel that way, a door closing when Henry moved out. I guess I need to look for a window." I thought about Maria leaving the Abbey in *The Sound of Music*, her future uncertain and then finding herself in the arms of the Captain.

"Well, I'm always here for you, Jane."

"Thanks, Daniel. That means a lot."

I hesitated, not sure if I should bring up the other thing that was bothering me. "Hey, maybe it's nothing, but I'm worried that Henry might be drinking too much. I'm sure he was drinking yesterday before he came over to my house."

His voice lowered. "I've noticed it too. It seems like it started after school ended. I chalked it up to letting off some steam after teaching all year, but I think he's still adjusting to us living together. Maybe he's worried that he'll have no place to go if things don't work out. He told me that his stepfather basically kicked him out of the house after his mom moved to Arizona and if it weren't for you, he would probably have been homeless."

"I think Henry saved me as much as he thinks I saved him. There's no debt. I don't know what would have happened to me when my aunt left. I would have been all alone if Henry wasn't there." I felt tears form in my eyes, but I didn't want to cry, and it felt like we were going down a rabbit hole that I didn't want to explore. "Would it be callous to say that Henry's your problem now, so I'll let you bring up the drinking to him? Plus, the whole we're not speaking thing. And really, I hope he still goes to Hawaii even if he goes by himself. I know he had already looked into snorkeling trips and found restaurants he wanted to try. I was just going along for the ride. You should go too. I think the bar will still be standing if you're gone for a few days."

"I'll ask Henry. It does sound nice." He leaned closer to me. "I feel lucky to know you, Jane, and I know Henry feels the same way, despite what he said yesterday." With a laugh, he said, "I think Nancy likes you too and she's only said five words to you."

"What? I was wondering if she knew about the car thing."

"Todd told her everything—that you got out of the car and then later accepted his apology. Nancy said he had a good time despite the rough start. Sounds like he's smitten. Can you blame him?"

"Ugh, Daniel, I don't know. I mean Todd is a nice guy and we did have a good time, but I need to figure out what I'm going to do for the next two months. I thought I could figure it out sitting on some beach." I didn't mention the orchid.

"I thought you were going to study for the LSAT."

"Maybe, but I don't even know if I want to take the test. Do I really want to be a lawyer? Don't tell Maxine I said that. Anyway, I can't think about any of that right now." I glanced at the clock on the wall. "People will be here in less than an hour and I need to wrap Maxine's gift and make sure the bakery delivers her cake. What else do we need to do?"

"I've got it covered. You know I've known Maxine longer than you have. I'll also tell you something you don't know. Maxine loaned me the money to buy this bar. She took a huge chance on me when no one else would. I have no idea where I would be without her, but I'm sure it wouldn't be here. So, I know why Henry feels like you saved him from a harder life." Daniel had a smile on his face as he stood and walked out of his office, leaving me alone to digest what he just said.

Leaning back in the chair, I mulled over our conversation. I thought that Henry was put in my life for a reason, but Maxine was too. I no longer had to fake it—I was genuinely excited to celebrate my boss, my mentor, and my friend.

Over the next hour, people filtered into the bar. Daniel had the kitchen make a variety of small bites and appetizers. Maxine's favorite drink was gin fizz, so that was the drink of choice for most people. After everyone had a glass in their hand, we gathered around the table topped with a cake decorated with a detailed map of the UK.

Steve cleared his throat and clinked his glass to get everyone's attention. Known for his stories, he probably wanted to say something before we cut the cake. We all settled in, knowing that at the end, we'd get some cake.

I had heard this particular story many times, as had most of the room. Steve was the first attorney hired at McMahon & Wright after the law firm was established. It was in a small space on the fifth floor of a building down on Third Avenue. He had interviewed for the job with just Maxine. She had said that Mr. McMahon was out of town and couldn't join them. A few days later, Maxine called and offered Steve the position, which he accepted. He was eager to meet Mr. McMahon, especially after seeing his office with the massive mahogany desk and the worn leather chair along with the matching bookcases that covered the back wall of the room. Steve was puzzled when he asked the receptionist about the mysterious Mr.

McMahon. She had never met him or talked to him. A few weeks later, Maxine took him to lunch and confessed that there was no Mr. McMahon—she had made him up. A ruse because she worried clients wouldn't take a young woman, a few years out of law school with her own practice, seriously.

I don't know if Steve or any of the other attorneys actually knew the real reason why Maxine started her own law firm with a fictitious man for a partner. Maxine was originally from Chicago and was hired at a large law firm right out of law school. She was excited to be a new associate and a partner in the firm took an interest in her, stepping in as a mentor. But after a huge real estate deal went south, costing the firm millions, the partner blamed Maxine for the screw-up.

After finding it impossible to find a new job, she moved to Seattle, taking the bar exam and starting her own firm. Initially it was just her and Steve, but as the client list and reputation grew, she hired more attorneys, running out of room and eventually moving to our current building. Somewhere along the way, Maxine had decided it was time for Mr. McMahon to retire. They even had a retirement party for him at the Straight & Narrow, except back then it was Scott's Sports Bar and Billiards.

Steve, finished with his story, raised his glass. "Maxine has been a mentor and a friend. She's made me a better attorney and a better person. We wish you the best as you go off and explore the world and find your people." Everyone in the room held up their glass. "To Maxine, we love you." There were a few hoots and hollers as we all drank in her honor.

She made a little speech, thanking everyone for coming and gave a shout out to me and Daniel for organizing the party. She eventually cut the cake. I had two pieces. Everyone laughed a lot, ate a lot, drank a lot, and had a good time, especially Maxine. She loved the lightweight Fjällräven backpack I gave her embroidered with *M. Wright*.

Grace was working during the celebration and grabbed a piece of cake, taking a quick break. A little before five, we moved the tables back and everyone sat in the same section to continue the festivities, even though the bar was now open to everyone.

Maxine left around seven-thirty and people slowly straggled home. Part of me didn't want to leave because I had the next two months off with no plan, but even worse, I no longer had my trip to look forward to. I feared that I would sit at home doing nothing. I could probably fill my days, but the nights would be hard, and Grace wouldn't be around much because she usually worked.

Toward the end of the evening after most of the office had left, we moved to our usual back booth, and I sat with Sarah and Jeanne. I nursed my third drink of the night and half-listened to Sarah as she complained again about her boyfriend. She gestured emphatically as she told Jeanne a story I had already heard but, honestly, I would only be half-listening if it were a new story about whatever lame thing Derrick was doing now. Sarah's phone buzzed. As she turned her phone over to see who was calling, Derrick's face filled the screen.

Sarah sighed. "I wonder what he wants." She scooted out of the booth to take the call somewhere less noisy. We heard her answer her phone. "Whatever it is, I'll be home in an hour." Jeanne stared at me with her eyebrows halfway up her forehead. I gave her a shake of my head and shrugged my shoulders, but neither one of us said what we were thinking. There was no need. Jeanne changed the subject. "Are you excited for Hawaii? I can't believe you've never been."

"Yeah, me either," I responded. I hadn't told anyone that I wasn't going, and I wasn't sure if I should. It was a lot to explain, and I was trying to keep Maxine from finding out. If Henry did decide to go alone or with Daniel, I would have Daniel bring it up to Maxine to make sure she was fine with the new plan. He could also explain why I wasn't going. She might be disappointed, but I was sure she'd understand.

"What island are you going to again?" asked Jeanne.

"The Big Island. Any suggestions?" I couldn't think of a way to change the subject.

"There's the national park to see the volcanos. That's always cool. And the beaches. You should go snorkeling too. Oh, and shaved ice. It's nice that you guys are there for a couple of weeks."

I watched Sarah walking down the aisle toward us. She rolled her eyes. "Apparently, he didn't remember that it was Maxine's party and that I would be out later than usual," she said. "He's been sitting at home waiting for me. I'd better go." She gulped down the rest of her drink. "Have fun, Jane. I'm so jealous. Send pictures." She leaned over and gave me a half hug. "See you Monday, Jeanne." Then she was gone.

"Is it wrong that her relationship makes me glad I'm single?" asked Jeanne.

I laughed. "Not at all. There are a lot of things worse than being single. Everyone just makes you feel like there's not."

"On that depressing note, I'm going to head home to my cats." She grabbed her jacket, dragging it as she slid out of the booth. "I was wrong; that's more depressing," she said with a tone of despair.

"Tell Whiskers and Pumpkin that Prince says hi."

"Oh, that's even more depressing. Thanks for that, Jane. Have a good trip anyway." She gave me a little smile, turned, and headed down the aisle, stopping at the end of the bar to say something to Daniel. Alone in the booth, I was still unable to make myself go home. Grace popped by and picked up the empty glasses. "Can I get you something else?"

"Nah, I guess I should go home. When do you get off tonight? Any big plans?"

"I think ten. I plan on heading home."

"I'll probably be up, so maybe I'll see you then." I gathered my stuff and looked for Daniel to say goodbye and to thank him for all of his help. He was behind the bar searching the cabinets underneath the back counter.

"Hey, Daniel, I know you're busy. I just wanted to thank you for everything tonight." I put my hand on his shoulder. "I think Maxine really enjoyed it."

Daniel stopped what he was doing and turned to face me. "Yeah, it was definitely a success. You're leaving?"

"It's been a long week," I explained.

"Okay. I'll let you know if Henry changes his mind." He gave me a brief hug.

| NINE |

Prince jumped on my bed, walked toward my feet, then turned and walked toward my face, where he sniffed my mouth. He made himself comfortable in the middle of the bed, making it impossible for me to move without disturbing him. With my right hand, I brushed his fur and listened to the house.

When Grace came home last night, she finished watching *Joe Versus the Volcano* with me. With Jeanne's talk of volcanos and my current situation, it seemed like a logical choice. And also, it's an awesome movie. Tom Hanks—"Joe"—suffering from a brain cloud, falls in love with Meg Ryan and marries her before he is about to leap into a volcano to appease an angry island god. Grace had never seen it.

The moral of the story is to not live your life in fear, especially if it means leaving behind something that doesn't feed your soul, and instead embrace the journey, choosing a path that allows for self-discovery, including the divine.

What I needed to do was find my path. Maybe I needed to go on a journey—do the opposite of what I had been doing. Maybe I should go to Hawaii by myself. My phone jolted me back to reality. I grabbed it from my nightstand.

"Hey, Daniel."

"I only have a minute." His voice was low, and he was talking fast. "Henry is in the next room. I convinced him to go to Hawaii and I'm going for a few days too. We would still leave on Tuesday. I just want to know if you're still okay with it?"

"Uh, yeah, sure," I said, thinking that the odds of me actually going by myself were slim to none and Henry needed the vacation more than me. He spent the last ten months educating fourteen- and fifteen-year-olds. Not an easy job. "Did you mention the drinking?"

"Not yet. I thought maybe when we're sitting on the beach, I would bring it up."

"Good plan. Will he be holding a drink?"

"What?" He sounded distracted.

"Never mind. Will you let Maxine know that you're going?"

"I will. I'll explain everything. Thanks, Jane." He hung up. Okay, new plan. I rolled over to put my phone back on my nightstand and spied the LSAT book. I picked it up and flipped through it.

My brain balked at the higher level of cognitive reasoning required to comprehend what I was reading, and Prince was much more persuasive in his argument for being fed. I threw the book on my chair and wearily walked into the laundry room to feed the cat. I jumped in the shower, hoping the hot water would wash away the disappointment. When I walked into the kitchen, Grace was sitting at the table in front of the window. She was staring at her phone.

"Hey." She didn't look up.

"Hey." I walked to the stove to turn on the burner. I grabbed my mug and opened a tea bag.

She put down her phone. "What do you think I should wear to my interview on Monday?"

"Slacks and a blazer?" I must be channeling Tess McGill after watching *Working Girl* the other night.

"Well, I don't own either one of those things." She stood up from the table. "Come look in my closet. You have to dress better for work."

I followed her to her room. Her closet was full of clothes, but mostly of flannels and T-shirts.

"Are you sure this isn't Paul Rudd's closet?" I pulled on one of the shirts to make my point.

"Ha ha," she fake-laughed. "I like to be comfortable. What's with the judgment?"

"No judgment." I turned to face her. "I love Paul Rudd. Ever since I saw him in *Clueless.* I just think you need to channel more Cher and less Josh. Let's look in my closet."

We walked across the house to my room.

"What have you worn to other interviews?" I asked as I walked to my closet, turning on the light.

"I borrowed something from my mom. She helped me pick it out. I left it there, which reminds me. They invited us to dinner tomorrow night. You should come. My mom likes to cook, and you can be a buffer when they ask about the whole looking for a job thing. I haven't told them I have an interview on Monday."

"I'll have to check my schedule. I might have to move some things around."

"You mean watch a movie or clean the cat box? Well, it will also keep your mind off Henry and the LSAT. A brain break. You can play some video games with my brothers."

"I didn't know you had brothers." I wondered why she hadn't mentioned them. I mindlessly pulled a long-sleeved sweater down and stared at it trying to figure out if it would work for an interview situation.

"Jack and Zac." Grace sat on the corner of my unmade bed. "They're twins. They just turned sixteen. Huge nerds but damn funny as hell."

"That's quite the age difference between you and your brothers." I put the sweater back and started sliding hangers across the top pole looking for something else.

"My parents married young, and I was born a year later. They divorced when I was eight and remarried when I was eleven. I begged for a little sister, and I guess they tried to make that happen, but my mom suffered from secondary infertility. I know, my parents can sometimes overshare. But then she got pregnant when I was fourteen and no longer wanted a sibling. And definitely not two. Being a teenager with a pregnant mom? It was the worst."

"Two babies and a teenager. I can't imagine what that would be like."

"Well, as soon as I turned eighteen, I got this." Grace pulled up her sleeve to show me her tattoo. "I also got a navel piercing and two cartilage piercings. My parents weren't thrilled and after two quarters of subpar grades, they said they wouldn't pay my tuition or room and board, so that's when I dropped out and moved to Denver."

I pulled a cream-colored blouse from my closet. I heard the tea kettle, so I handed her the hanger.

"Here put this on. I'll be back in a minute."

When I returned with my tea, Grace had the blouse on. It was hard to tell if it looked flattering because it was paired with tie-dye pajama bottoms. Grace had a few inches on me, so I doubt she'd find any pants to wear in my closet.

She did a little twirl. "Well, what do you think of this ensemble?"

"It's hard to say with the pajama bottoms." I held the hot cup between my hands waiting for it to cool enough for a sip.

"You have a lot of clothes," she observed, turning around to face the back of the closet.

"Actually, this whole wall is full of my mom's clothes and those in the back are my aunt's." I pointed to the back wall. "I just haven't done anything with them."

Grace ventured into the narrow, long closet. The bulb in the second light fixture was burned out so the back of the closet was cave-like. "Some of these clothes still have their tags on. Did you know that?"

"My aunt liked to shop. She's close to your height. If you see something you like, you can try it on." I put my cup down and moved hangers as I continued to look through my clothes.

"When did your aunt move out? And why do you still have her stuff?" Grace pulled off the top she was wearing and put on a new one. Then she shimmied out of her pajama bottoms and put on a pair of navy slacks.

"She left not long after Henry moved in and then she had a stroke. She lives in a nursing home in Kirkland.

"Oh, God, that's terrible."

"It is. I try to visit her every few weeks. At least she's in a nice place."

I changed the subject, and we spent the next hour looking through both of our closets trying to come up with the perfect outfit and accessories for her interview.

Eventually, we settled on a pair of light gray slacks and a crisp white shirt with a simple necklace and silver hoop earrings.

/ / /

When I came into the kitchen Sunday morning, Grace was in her same tie-dyed pajamas sitting at the table with a cup of coffee in front of her as she stared at her phone.

"You're up early," I said as I got a glass of water.

She put down her phone. "It's hard to sleep when the sun is so bright. It makes me feel like a bum if I'm lying in bed. You're all dressed and ready to go."

"I'm headed to church," I explained.

"Do you go to church every Sunday?"

"Yep, every Sunday. Sometimes they make us go on random days too. It's a cult thing."

Her brow furrowed. "Just asking a question. I didn't say anything about a cult."

"Sorry." I guess Henry's jabs bothered me more than I thought. I finished my water. "Is your family not religious?"

"I think my grandma was Lutheran. I can remember when I was little, we would go to church with her. But when she died, that ended. Did you go to church with your mom growing up?"

"We didn't go every Sunday. My religious upbringing was spotty. I was the oldest kid at my first communion. Like a head taller than everyone else. It took my mom awhile to get around to signing me up."

"I don't know. It's hard to believe in God when so many bad things happen in the world."

"As someone who has had some bad things happen, I can understand that. It's also probably easier not to believe in God." I didn't want to preach to Grace. No one wants to feel judged about their beliefs, religious or not. Then I remembered Joe.

"The movie I was watching Friday night, *Joe Versus the Volcano*. There's the part where they're on the boat before it sinks and Joe asks Patricia if she believes in God, and she says she believes in herself. But Joe wondered, after being all alone for so long and facing imminent death, that maybe there was a higher power." I turned and put my empty glass in the dishwasher while finishing my thought. "I was kind of like Joe after my mom died. My aunt wasn't around much, and I had broken up with my boyfriend and I felt lost and alone. One day, after school, I went for a run, and I ended up at our church. The last time I had been there was for my mom's funeral. I went in and I sat down, and I asked God for help. The next day, as I was leaving school, I found Henry by the football field. He was suddenly alone too. He came back to my house and he stayed for almost ten years."

Grace stared at me with a funny look on her face. "You know I just saw the end of that movie, right?"

I straightened up and grabbed my purse from the counter. "It's still in the blue-ray player. It's a deep movie disguised as something else if you don't want to think. There's a lot of philosophical stuff in there. And Tom Hanks." I looked at the clock on the microwave. I didn't want to be late again. "I need to leave now if I'm going to get my usual spot. Let me know if you ever want to join me at Mass."

"Thanks, I will. Hey, don't forget you're going to my parents with me tonight. You're my buffer."

"I haven't forgotten. Looking forward to it." I walked through the laundry room and into the garage. Before I closed the door I said, "I know he can get the job, but can he do the job?"

Grace called out, "What does that mean?"

"Watch the movie," I yelled back.

After church, I went grocery shopping and ended up with a bunch of random stuff as I wandered the aisles of my neighborhood Safeway. It was nice that I didn't have to worry about dinner tonight. A home-cooked meal sounded better than eating out and much better than something frozen.

It's been a while since I've had a real sit-down family dinner and I was looking forward to meeting the rest of Grace's family too. Family was something I was always short of. I often wondered what it would be like to have brothers or sisters.

My mother had prepared me for life after she was gone from this earth. She assured me that ultimately, I would be okay. She knew that I would always remember her in the everyday, ordinary collective of living each day as her daughter. I just wasn't prepared for the loneliness.

As I stood in the bustling bakery section of the store looking at the assorted cakes, I thought about Henry. He was my family for so long. It had been a long time since I thought about the day I asked him if he wanted to come home with me.

I had accidentally walked down the hallway where Mitchell's locker was, probably out of habit after meeting him there after the last bell for most of my junior year. It wasn't a good breakup. Once I realized where I was, I quickly went out the side entrance to the football field, a way I had never gone before to get to the parking lot.

As I passed through the doors, I watched Henry pitch his phone across the field and then ignored him when he called my name while I kept my head down, focused on my own problems. I turned around the third time he yelled my name. It took us a good twenty minutes to find his phone as I called his number repeatedly while we stomped around the field.

I asked Henry if he needed a ride, but he admitted he had nowhere to go. His mom had moved to Arizona after she divorced Henry's stepdad, and Henry didn't want to move to another state during his junior year of high school. His stepdad agreed that he could live with him if Henry's mom paid part of the mortgage and chipped in for utilities and groceries, which she did initially, but then she stopped sending checks. His stepdad had just told him he needed to find another place to live and to get his stuff out of his house, the reason he chucked his phone. I invited him to stay with me. I have no idea where I would be without Henry. He was the answer to a prayer.

As I stared at the six perfectly frosted cakes behind the glass, I decided against buying one. It seemed overindulgent even though I thought I could justify it. I should have been packing for Hawaii, but instead I was hanging out in a Safeway stocking up on frozen meals.

/ / /

We left for Grace's parents' house at five. It was a fifteen-minute drive up I-5 with light traffic. Their neighborhood was a mix of older homes with a fair number of remodeled ones, most with a new facade to eliminate the look of the early seventies. Some were more successful than others, especially the homes that had a second floor plopped on top of the first, like a second scoop of ice cream. Middle-aged trees lined the street with their long, saggy boughs stretching over the sidewalk.

We pulled up in front of a neat split-level home. A big oak tree consumed the front yard. Flower beds lined the front of the house, and an American flag hung by the garage. As we walked to the front door, it occurred to me that I should have brought something. I mentioned it to Grace.

"Why, it's just my parents." She opened the front door and we walked into an open entry hall. I followed Grace around the corner into the kitchen. A woman was standing at the stove with her back to us. Whatever she was making, it smelled delicious.

"Hi, Mom." Grace's mom turned around.

"Hi, sweetie." She wiped her hands on her apron and gave her daughter a hug.

"This is Jane," Grace said.

"Hi, Jane, it's nice to meet you." She turned back to the stove, tending to one of the pots. Looking over her shoulder, she said, "Dinner will be ready in a little bit. Why don't you go find your dad and brothers? They're downstairs somewhere."

"Do you need any help?" I asked. I was spiraling about not bringing something. I felt like I was not making a very good impression.

"You're sweet to offer, but I think everything is under control." A timer went off and she turned her attention to whatever was in the oven.

Grace's mom was an older version of Grace, except she had short, mostly whitish hair that was probably once blonde, like her daughter's. It occurred to me as we walked out of the kitchen that I didn't know her first name. I could always call her Mrs. Miller.

I followed Grace down the stairs into a large open family room with a big picture window that overlooked a small, perfectly manicured backyard. Grace's dad, Charles, was in a recliner facing the TV. His head tilted downward, and his chest rose and fell evenly. Grace pointed down the hall and with soft steps we headed in the opposite direction and into a room where her two brothers sat playing a video game. They were fixated on the screen.

Without looking up, one of them said, "What are you doing here? You moved out."

I looked at the two boys and determined that they must be identical twins. I knew Grace and her parents could tell them apart, but it would have been hard for me, except that one of them was wearing glasses. Grace ignored the question. "Hey, can you guys stop for a minute. I want to introduce you to my friend Jane."

"Hi, Jane," they said in unison.

"Now be quiet. We need to concentrate," said a twin.

Grace looked at me and rolled her eyes.

"Hey, it's Gracie," said a voice from behind us. We turned and saw Grace's dad in the doorway. "And Jane. Nice to see you again."

"Hi, Mr. M—" I couldn't get anything else out of my mouth before Grace's dad interrupted me.

"Charles. Please." He looked at me like I should know better than to try and call him anything other than by his first name.

"Hi, Dad," said Grace. I moved aside so she could hug her dad.

"Come and sit down." He turned and walked back toward the other room. "That's all those knuckleheads do. Play those damn video games."

We followed Charles back to the comfortable family room. On the wall opposite the picture window were various portraits of the family preserved in time, framed in dark wood. I wanted to take a closer look at each one. I was sure there would be another opportunity to view the photographs. It looked like Grace sported bangs in high school. That was definitely worth a second look.

Grace sat in the other recliner, and I chose the wide, green couch that faced the oversized window with the photos above my head. The wooden coffee table that sat in front of the couch was full of magazines, mostly home and garden with a few fishing ones.

"How goes the job search?" said Charles.

Wow, I thought, no small talk first. Straight to the question Grace was dreading. I felt bad that I didn't offer any sort of buffer. I needed to come up with some interesting topics to steer the conversation away from Grace's job prospects, but my mind was blank. I haven't spent much time around parents lately. Or in the last ten years.

"I sent out some resumes on Friday, so hopefully I'll hear something next week."

"Did you ask the university for any help? Don't they have a resource center or something?"

"Yeah, I've talked to them. They helped with my resume and some other stuff. It's hard to get a job if you don't have experience."

"All your experience is waiting tables," said Charles. He sounded a little judgmental.

Grace looked at me. I couldn't tell if the look said, "You're useless" or "Can you believe this guy?" I tried to think of something to say. The only thing that came to mind was lawn care.

I piped up with, "Your yard is beautiful, Charles." From where I sat, I could see the lush green lawn that looked like it had been freshly mowed. "You must spend a lot of time working on it."

He glanced at Grace. I could tell that he didn't really want to change the subject and obviously had more to say to his daughter but he decided to humor me and talk about his lawn. I should have prepped better. I racked my brain to think of dinner topics. My hands felt sweaty.

"Dinner's ready," Grace's mom called out. Grace and I both jumped up from our seats. She was evidently also relieved that there would be no more talk of jobs or lawns.

Charles moved a little slower as he pulled himself up from his recliner. Grace and I followed him up the stairs to the dining room. Grace glanced at me, and I mouthed "Sorry" as I hunched my shoulders while flipping my palms up. She gave me a reassuring smile.

I pulled out the chair and sat next to Grace. It was just a minute later when the boys sat facing us. There were several dishes in the center of the table. Grace's mom plopped down two more before she sat in a chair opposite Charles. Without further instruction, everyone who had a dish in front of them picked it up and started loading up their plate. I followed along. I decided to speak up, hoping that I wouldn't break everyone's concentration but wanting to ward off any job talk.

"Who's Jack and who's Zac?" I asked. With both of them in front of me, I had a better view to see if I could tell them apart. The one on the left was wearing glasses. I was almost positive they weren't prescription and were more for looks than function. I put some mashed potatoes on my plate and handed the dish to Grace's mom and took the pot roast from Grace's hands.

"I'm Zac," said the Glasses. In addition to the frames, Zac's dirty blond hair was longer than his brother's. They were both tall and skinny, which I noticed before they sat down for dinner.

"And you guys just finished tenth grade?" I sounded like I was cross-examining them on the witness stand.

"Yeah," said Jack, "but more like crushed tenth grade." They high-fived each other. I understood why Grace called them nerds.

My thoughts veered toward Henry. "My friend," I hesitated for a second, "teaches ninth and tenth grade math at Clark High School."

"We're taking AP Calc next year, along with four other APs," shared Jack. By now all the dishes had circulated the table and were back in the middle, ready if anyone wanted another helping.

"Sounds like a heavy load." I looked down at my plate. Some pot roast, green beans, mashed potatoes with gravy, and a salad. I wondered if they ate like this every day. I took a bite of the pot roast and turned to Grace's mom. "This is delicious. Thank you for inviting me."

"Of course. We're happy you could join us," Grace's mom said, smiling.

"Judy, did you get rolls?" asked Charles.

Judy. Now I knew everybody's name. Judy put down her fork. "Oh, I forgot. They're warming in the oven." She started to get up.

"Sit down. I'll get them," he said getting up from the table and disappearing into the kitchen.

"Gracie," said Judy, "do you remember Ryan Edwards? He had an older brother. I think his name was Nick."

"Yeah, I remember Ryan. We used to hang out all the time in high school. He went to college in Florida, I think. Why?"

"I heard he was killed in some sort of accident." Judy took a bite of green beans, still looking at Grace.

"Oh my God, really? When did that happen?" She put down her fork and took a drink of water.

"I'm not sure, but his funeral is on Tuesday. I didn't get a lot of details," explained Judy.

"I went to homecoming with him freshman year. He was a year ahead of me. He dated Emma for a while."

"Emma Carson? Do you still talk to her?" asked Judy, interested in her daughter's social life and changing the subject at the same time. They had a brief conversation about Grace's other high school classmates.

Judy turned to me. "Where did you go to high school, Jane?"

"I went to Clark."

"When did you graduate?"

"I left high school after the eleventh grade. I took the GED and then enrolled in college courses," I said, explaining my unusual path out of high school.

"I didn't know that," Grace said, looking at me as she took a bite of pot roast.

"Did you get your degree?" asked Charles as he placed the rolls on the table. I was beginning to understand Grace's reluctance to share information with her parents.

"Yes, I have a BA in English and a minor in business. I'm studying for the LSAT." I had no idea why I shared that. Grace's parents made me nervous. It must be the judgment of their own daughter's career path.

"An attorney." Charles sounded impressed. "I tried to get Gracie to go to law school."

I sensed that the conversation was headed in the wrong direction, so I tried to think how to navigate to a different topic. I looked across the table and I found my answer.

"What do you guys want to study in college?" I asked Jack and Zac. I assumed they were college bound after they told me they were both taking five AP classes next year.

"Computer science," said Jack.

"Biology," said Zac.

We managed to stay clear of any more talk of jobs for the rest of the dinner. Charles and the boys went back downstairs after they helped clear the table, I assumed to watch TV and play video games, respectively. I insisted on helping with the dishes. I washed since I had no idea where things went. Judy took care of the leftovers and Grace dried and put everything away. We chatted with Judy as we cleaned up.

After we were done in the kitchen, Grace and I wandered back downstairs. The boys let us play video games with them. I sucked at it, but I was starting to get the hang of it when Grace decided it was time to head home. There were more hugs, a bag of Tupperware full of leftovers, and a promise to come back for dinner again soon.

Once we were in the car, Grace visibly relaxed as she exhaled. "Thanks for running interference tonight. Usually there are multiple lectures on how I'm messing up my life and what I need to be doing instead of what I'm doing."

"I had a good time. Your brothers are hilarious. I can see why you didn't tell your parents that you have an interview though."

"I know they just want the best for me, but I'm thirty-one and I've figured out a few things on my own. I know when I get a job they'll back off and it'll be easier to spend time with them. It's been good for all of us that I no longer live with them, so thanks for that." She backed out of the driveway. "I'm getting nervous about tomorrow. I hate interviews."

"You'll be great," I said, trying to reassure her.

"I watched that movie, Joe Jumps in a Volcano."

I didn't correct her about the name. "And?" I was curious to hear what she thought.

"It got terrible reviews."

"I guess they didn't understand it." I couldn't lead Grace somewhere she didn't want to go. We all have to figure things out on our own and she had a mom and a dad who liked to share their opinions about her life.

"I can do the job, but I can't get the job," she said in a loud voice imitating Joe's old boss and butchering the line from the movie.

I laughed.

| TEN |

Lying on my couch with a book, I realized I had read the same paragraph three times and I still wasn't sure what was going on. A key in the front door startled me and I lost my place. I watched Grace walk in, looking around the big room. She put her bag on the small table by the front door and called my name before she spotted me.

"There you are. I need to be somewhere in thirty minutes, and I need you to come with me."

"I don't want to go anywhere. I'm pretending I'm lying on a beach. I just need a drink with an umbrella. Fetch me one, will you?" My voice was filled with melancholy because I was very aware that I was nowhere near a beach. I set my book down on the floor and put my arm over my eyes. The next thing I knew, Grace was grabbing both of my hands and pulling me up.

"No, no, no. You need to get out of this house. But you need to change first. Let's go look in your closet." She led me to my room. She picked out a pair of black slacks and a dark-colored blouse. "Put these on while I go change." I did as I was told. I didn't know why. Maybe because I was actually doing something instead of lying on the couch.

Ten minutes later we were in my car with Grace behind the wheel. I should have asked questions, but my brain was in low-power mode. As Grace drove, the surroundings had a familiar feel. Modest but well-kept homes lined the wide residential street.

"Hey, I had my first communion in a church near this neighborhood. It was too late at my church, so I went to Saint Mark's."

Grace made a left and turned into the back parking lot of Saint Mark's Catholic Church.

"What a coincidence. That's where we're going," she said, seeming genuinely surprised that I had been here before. People were congregating near the entrance and a black hearse was parked in front.

"You brought me to a funeral? How is this going to cheer me up?"

"I never said anything about cheering you up. I said you needed to get out of the house. Plus, you don't know the guy."

"Grace, no. I'm not going to a funeral. This is the complete opposite of sitting on a beach."

"They're sad, you're sad. No one will notice. You'll fit right in. Come on. I can't go by myself. Please."

The last funeral I went to was my mother's, ten years ago. Before the service had started, people who clearly hadn't seen each other in a long time chatted like old friends who had run into each other at Starbucks. I was angry that they didn't realize this was the saddest day of my life. Shouldn't my worst day at least be acknowledged with a somber tone and attitude, and not like the social hour at a country club? At least wait until after the service was over.

Grace stared at me as we sat in the parking lot with people walking by the car heading into the church.

"Whose funeral is it?" I asked.

"Ryan Edwards, the guy I went to high school with."

"Your homecoming date in ninth grade?"

"My mom couldn't make it and I didn't want to go alone. We better hurry or we won't get good seats."

With her hand on the car door handle, she turned to look at me. "That came out wrong. I'm terrible in situations like this. That's why I need you here, so I don't say or do anything stupid."

"Too late." As I exhaled a deep breath, I opened the door and stepped out and Grace followed. I met her gaze over the hood of the car. "Let's go." I was resigned to the fact that I would have to go to this funeral.

We approached the front doors of the church and waded into a sea of people, most wearing black and standing in clumps, chatting quietly. As we made our way into the worship space, two young men on either side of the entrance handed out printed memorials. Grace and I both took one. A handsome man's face stared up at me from the paper.

My heart beat faster as the memories of my mom's funeral came flooding back. I took a deep breath and then another. I wanted to sit down, hopefully somewhere in the back. I followed Grace to the left. As I glanced around, I was comforted by the fact that everything looked the same as I last remembered it. An usher was setting up chairs, obviously anticipating more mourners than the existing pews could hold.

I followed Grace along the back, where we chose two chairs against the wall. I opened the folded paper in my hand. It was a funeral Mass. The left side had another picture of Ryan from when he was a child. He was thirty-two when he passed away. The readings ran down the right side of the program: Proverbs, Psalm, Revelation, and Matthew. Printed on the back of the program was Psalm 23:

The LORD is my shepherd; I shall not want.

He maketh me to lie down in green pastures; He leadeth me beside the still waters.

He restoreth my soul: He leadeth me in the paths of righteousness for his name's sake.

Yea, though I walk through the valley of the shadow of death, I will fear no evil; for thou art with me; thy rod and thy staff, they comfort me.

Thou preparest a table before me in the presence of mine enemies: thou anointest my head with oil; my cup runneth over.

Surely goodness and mercy shall follow me all the days of my life: and I will dwell in the house of the LORD forever.

Someone Grace knew sat down next to her and they attempted to whisper, but their voices carried to the seats around them. It sounded like an old high school classmate.

We stood as the organist started playing "Amazing Grace." I looked over to where Ryan's family must be standing in one of the front pews. There was a man close to Ryan's age. Judy had mentioned an older brother at dinner. He was standing next to an older woman. My guess was their mother. She leaned against a tall, stoic-looking older gentleman. Their grief was undeniable.

Father O'Brien's homily was comforting and succinct. After communion, he invited Ryan's brother, Nick, to say a few words. Anticipating the introduction, he had moved over to our side of church. He approached the ambo and pulled a piece of paper from his pocket. My view was unobstructed, and my gaze relaxed on his rather ordinary face. His black suit fit his broad shoulders and tall frame well and matched his dark eyes. He cleared his throat and began speaking.

"Ryan was twelve months and fourteen days younger than me. My mother used to say it would have been easier if we were twins. My dad called Ryan my 'shadow' when we were children. But Ryan was definitely his own person, even though we had similar interests like basketball and football. In high school, Ryan's drive to compete and excel on and off the court or field stopped the comparisons. His smile and charm were no match for me. As children, the only time we didn't go to school together was between grade school and high school. I was a freshman, and he was finishing his last year here at Saint Mark's. I had made the varsity basketball team, which for a freshman was a big deal. At least I thought it was. Some of the seniors were throwing a party and invited me. Another big deal. I didn't plan very well though and instead of a clever cover story, like sleeping over at a friend's, I snuck out of the house after my parents went to bed. I consumed a few beers and was a little unsteady on my feet when I crawled back in through the window, making too much noise. Ryan found me first and then my dad. I was busted and knew that not only would I be grounded for eternity, I would also most likely be kicked off the team. But Ryan spoke before I could confess and told my dad that he was the one sneaking back in after meeting some friends at the park. He told Dad that I had heard him coming in and went to investigate. I'm not sure my dad bought it, but he didn't question it. Ryan was always a step ahead. No wonder he always beat me at chess.

"The summer before my senior year, we convinced our parents to let us go to the family lake cabin in Eastern Washington for a long weekend with some high school friends. When we stopped at a rest stop outside of Moses Lake, Ryan met a couple of girls who were stranded with a flat tire. He put a spare on their car and persuaded them to follow us up to the cabin. He was always meeting new people and cultivating friendships wherever he went. He was up for anything and lived his best life.

"Ryan always remembered our mom's birthday with flowers, and after he moved to Florida, he would often fly in to surprise our parents. He was a loving and devoted son."

He finished his remarks by thanking everyone who reached out and shared their favorite memories with the family.

We followed the large crowd out of the worship space and made our way downstairs to the reception in the church hall. The wide, low-ceilinged room with a linoleum floor was filled with tables. The church ladies had a spread of salads, including a rainbow of gelatin along with sandwich meats, bread, and an abundance of desserts. There were a couple of stainless-steel coffee dispensers, punch, and cups of water on another table. The older ladies were working hard in the kitchen to provide the comfort of food for the bereaved and those of us who were just crashing.

Grace had found a group of high school classmates while we were standing in the food line. They followed us to a table in the back by the large windows that overlooked the parking lot. I made a small sandwich with a dinner roll, but only because I thought it would look bad if the only thing on my plate was a piece of cherry chip cake.

Sitting around the large, round table, Grace introduced me to everyone. I should have paid closer attention to their names, which would have been the polite thing to do but I figured I would never see these people again. I ate quietly and listened to what everyone had been doing since high school. Now in their thirties, most had careers, and some had families.

I took a page from my date with Todd and took refuge in the women's restroom for a few minutes. When I walked out of the bathroom, I ran directly into Nick, stepping on his foot. He reached out and held onto both my arms to steady me as I lost my balance. As I stared into his face, I saw his eyes were a deep brown. He winced, most likely from the pain of his smashed foot.

"I'm so sorry. I didn't see you," I stammered. I could feel my cheeks getting warm.

"Are you okay?"

"Yes, thank you. Sorry. I'm just a little embarrassed." I didn't know what else to say. He let go of my arms and I quickly walked back to the table, still feeling the flush in my face.

I slid into my seat next to Grace, my mind on my literal run-in with Nick. The conversation at the table had moved on to Ryan and the last time everyone had seen him. Before I could get Grace's attention, I saw Nick heading toward us.

Grace saw him too and was the first to speak as he approached the table. "I'm so sorry about Ryan. I was shocked when my mom told me that he had passed away."

He nodded at Grace. "Thank you. And thank you all for coming today." He looked around the table. His gaze lingered on my face. I was sure he was wondering who I was, besides the girl who stepped on his foot. "I know Ryan had so many friends and it's a great comfort to my family that so many people showed up today to remember him." He found my face again after a glance around the table.

Maybe he thought I was a classmate.

"Brook mentioned that a group is going up to the cabin next weekend like we did in high school with Ryan," said a blonde girl sitting next to Grace. "Sort of a celebration of his life. Doing some of the things we know he loved to do." Grace stared at the girl as she spoke.

"Brook suggested it and it sounds like a great idea," said Nick. "She said she would coordinate it so you should find her. Everyone is welcome, even if they just want to come up for the day."

"Wow, that sounds like a great weekend and something that Ryan would have loved," Grace said. "I'll have to see if I can get time off from work."

Only half-listening to this exchange, I was still feeling self-conscious and wishing we would leave. Trying to look everywhere except at Nick, I noticed a woman standing by herself next to the doorway of the hall. Her eyes fixated on Nick, but his back was to her. I wondered if they were related. Her mouth was tight, and her body tense. She looked older than Nick and Grace, but not by much. He must have sensed someone watching him, or perhaps he wondered what I was staring at, and he glanced behind him looking in the direction of the woman and then turned back to the table.

"I'll make sure Brook lets everyone know the details for next weekend. It was nice to see all of you and thank you again for coming." He excused himself and walked over to the woman by the doorway.

I watched them as he pointed to the hallway. She didn't want to leave and as Nick moved his arm toward her, she jerked her body back. Her voice was loud, but they were too far from me to hear what she was saying. Nick must have said something to convince her to move from the doorway and they walked out of the hall. It struck me as an odd exchange.

Some of the women working the reception came over to pick up the empty plates. The group collectively decided that it was time to go, and Grace and some of her old classmates added numbers to their phones as they readied to leave. They said their goodbyes, then Grace and I were alone.

"Let's go," she said as she looked at her phone. As we walked out, I saw Nick and the mystery woman talking in the corner. It seemed like Nick was still trying to calm her down.

My eyes adjusted to the sunshine. "I'm driving home." Grace didn't object and handed me my keys. "Why did we take my car anyway?"

"I'm out of gas and we needed to hurry. Thanks for coming with me. It wasn't as bad as I thought. A lot of people I haven't seen since high school showed up. I missed my ten-year reunion. Actually, I didn't miss it; I just didn't go. But I think I might go to the cabin with everyone." More to herself than to me, she added, "I think I have Thursday and Saturday off so I would just need to find someone to cover my Friday shift." She pulled out her phone and started texting. "Sam owes me a favor. She owes me a lot of favors."

I let her type for a minute and then I asked, "Do you know how Ryan died?"

"It was a car accident. But he didn't have any identification on him, and he was driving a rental car. He hit a tree. It took a while to figure out that it was Ryan. Celeste said they think he came back to surprise his parents but since he didn't tell anyone, no one was looking for him."

"What about the brother, Nick? Did you hang out with him in high school?" I tried to sound casual as I remembered his hands on me.

"He was usually with us, but he also kept to himself. Celeste told me that his wife died a few years after they were married. But she didn't know the details."

I could see Grace's fingers flying over her phone out of the corner of my eye. I guess Sam couldn't work for her on Friday and she moved onto plan B.

///

After Grace left for her shift at the Straight & Narrow, I made something to eat. My mind wandered to the funeral and to Nick. He lost his wife and now his brother. I could imagine what he must be feeling. Losing my mom was excruciating and even though I didn't have a lot of memories of my dad, I missed him. I lost my aunt too. Not exactly a death but a loss.

I conjured a picture of Nick. Tall and lean, he had a seriousness about him. But he had just buried his brother, so that might not be an accurate assessment, and Grace couldn't fill in any blanks.

I grabbed my computer from my bedroom and typed his name into Google. He had a LinkedIn profile, but that was all I could find. He was an analyst at an investment firm in

Seattle. Since I wasn't on LinkedIn, I couldn't see his actual profile. I thought briefly about joining but decided against it. It all seemed a little stalkerish. What were the odds I would ever see him again anyway?

| ELEVEN |

The days melted together, and I found myself lacking all motivation. Daniel had sent me a text saying he was home, along with a photo of a Hawaiian sunset over the water. A figure on the beach had his back to the camera. It was Henry. For some reason, I didn't text him back.

I thought about going into the office, but I wasn't expected back for another week or so and I didn't want to answer questions. I've had minimal contact with Maxine. She sent a few photos of architecture and food, but since I wasn't on social media, my window into her adventures was narrow. She joined Facebook just to be able to post pictures and update everyone on her travels. It looked like she was having a fabulous time from the few photos she sent me.

As I lay on the couch with my arm draped across my eyes, I could hear Grace in the kitchen opening the fridge and cupboards. She was making something, but I couldn't see from my horizontal position. Her phone started pinging, breaking the silence. And then the mixer started whirling.

A push on my shoulder made me move my arm and when I opened my eyes, Grace was standing over me, hand outstretched with a spoon full of cookie dough.

"Here. It's sort of like cake," she said, holding the giant beater from the mixer in her other hand. That must be for her.

Cookie dough was nothing like cake, but who didn't like raw cookie dough? Sitting up, I grabbed the spoon, setting the opened LSAT book that I was using as a blanket on the couch beside me. Grace sat on the corner of the coffee table and followed the bend in the beater with her finger, scooping up a big chunk of dough.

"Did I tell you that Sam is going to work for me on Friday so I'm going to go to the cabin with everyone? I've been texting Celeste and Stacy."

"That's cool. Where is this cabin again?" I asked as I bit off some of the dough at the end of the spoon.

"It's about three or four hours east. I don't exactly remember. Celeste is driving."

"Why are you leaving on a Thursday?"

"So we have two full days—Friday and Saturday. We'll pack up and head home early on Sunday."

Before I could say anything, Grace's phone rang and she stood, pulling it from the pocket of her jeans while handing me her beater. Her brow furrowed as she stared at the screen. She hesitated for a second, then swiped across her phone.

"Hello, this is Grace." She flashed a confused look at me as she listened. "Hello? Oh, hi, Cami." She gave me a thumbs-up as a smile filled her face. It didn't last long. She turned slightly and sat on the corner of the coffee table. I could tell it wasn't great news.

"Yes. Okay, thank you." She hung up the call and stood up again. "I didn't get it. She said they were really impressed, but they went with someone else who had more experience. They would keep me in mind if something else opened up. I've never had someone call to tell me I didn't get the job. Is that a thing, now?"

"You must have made an impression, because, yeah, it does seem weird that they called to let you know they hired someone else. You must have made it hard for them to choose. I'm sorry it didn't go your way." I knew they weren't comforting words.

"I'm so glad I didn't tell my parents about any of the interviews. I almost did because I really did think one of them would offer me a job."

I stuck out my hand with her beater, and she grabbed it like a consolation prize. The oven timer went off and she slowly walked back to the kitchen, where I heard a loud and forlorn "Fuck."

Grace spent the rest of the evening in her room, and there was nothing I could say or do to make her feel better. She had her trip with her friends and that would take her mind off the job search.

The thought of having a few days to myself while Grace was gone inspired me to spend less time on the couch and more time figuring out what I was going to do for the next two months. If I was going to study for the LSAT, I needed to actually study.

Thursday morning, I went for a run down by the small neighborhood park near my house and then around the deserted elementary school. The last time I ran was right before Henry moved out. Moving my body and breathing the outside air made me feel like I could figure out a plan for at least the next few days to get back on track. I didn't think about Henry or work or anything really.

By the time I finished showering, it was close to twelve-thirty and my stomach was rumbling. When I came into the kitchen, I was surprised to find Grace slumped at the table with a can of soda. She was scrolling on her phone with one hand and the other was propping up her head.

"What time do you guys leave?" I asked, turning on the tap to fill the tea kettle with water.

"I don't think I'm gonna go," she said, her voice subdued.

"Why? I thought you were looking forward to it." I turned on a burner, then opened the refrigerator to look for something to eat.

"I don't know. I'm just really bummed about not getting that job. I wouldn't be good company." She was still staring at her phone.

Not finding anything in the fridge, I grabbed a banana from the counter. "But going will take your mind off the job situation. You should take some time for yourself and then on Monday you can start fresh," I reasoned.

She took a sip from the can. She was still in her pajamas, one leg tucked under her. Her chair was pulled too far from the table and her messy bun was more mess than bun.

"Would you go with me?" She looked up at me, her eyebrows optimistic.

Her question caught me by surprise. "Why do you want me to go? I don't know any of these people or Ryan. It would be weird."

"It wouldn't be weird. Brook's husband is going, and he didn't know Ryan. It will be more fun if you're there. I would have a buddy. Otherwise, I'm the odd one out."

"Grace…" I was frantically trying to think of a way out of this. "I don't think so." And then my brain rallied. "I'm not a partier. It sounds like Ryan was, and that's the point of the weekend. To honor your friend's memory by celebrating his life." I pulled out a chair and sat across the table from her while I waited for the tea kettle to do its thing.

"But we're old now. Brook and Jason have a kid. They aren't going to do anything crazy. They probably just want a weekend away. I promise you can bow out of any of the activities. You can bring a book. I think it will be a mellow weekend. Please. You're right that it will take my mind off the job situation. It will be nice to just get away and get out of my head. I would think you would want the same thing."

I sighed. The buzz from my run had worn off and my resolve was slowly fading. I felt like I had to go for Grace's sake. If I didn't have two months of mostly unstructured time, I would have said no. This pushed back my plans for figuring out my life.

"Please," she begged.

"Okay, okay, I'll go." I sighed again. Grace didn't notice—or didn't care.

"Yay! Thank you, Jane." She jumped up from her chair. "Let's go throw some things in a bag. You get to wear your swimsuit. See, you were meant to go." She picked up her phone and walked toward her room. "I'll text Celeste to let her know."

My head fell into my hands as my elbows rested on the table. After a few deep breaths, I pushed myself up to go to my room. Then I thought of a problem. I called out to Grace, "What about Prince? I don't want to leave him alone for a long weekend."

After a minute, she had a solution. "Jack and Zac just got their licenses. I'll have them come over and feed him. They'll be excited to drive somewhere," she yelled from her bathroom.

"Well, make sure they can do it before I start packing," I shouted across the house as the kettle whistled. Shutting off the gas, I pulled the kettle off the burner, but instead of pouring a cup of tea, I dragged myself to my bedroom to throw some stuff in a bag. This was such a bad idea.

A little more than an hour later, still not sure what was happening, I was sitting in the front seat of Grace's car and heading to meet a group of people from the funeral. I knew I couldn't put a name to a face, except for Nick. I briefly thought about him holding me up as I tripped at the reception. I felt a blush move across my cheeks. I doubted he would remember the encounter and I chased the thought from my mind, focusing instead on the weekend.

"Why can't we just get the address and drive there ourselves? Why do we have to caravan?" I asked Grace as she informed me that we were meeting everyone at Saint Mark's.

"Because that's how we did it in high school. We would meet at a McDonald's and then all drive up together. It was fun."

"Was it? Sometimes we think something we did was fun, but it really wasn't," I countered. "I mean, it was high school. How fun could it have been?" My high school experience and Grace's high school experience were probably vastly different. I didn't even graduate. Grace wasn't listening to anything I said.

"Okay, here's some intel on the group. Brook and Jason were married a couple of years after high school. Their kid is like four or five. I don't know Jason very well even though I went to their wedding, but I haven't hung out with them in a long time. Brook was a cheerleader and dated Sean, a friend of Ryan's in high school. I wonder why Sean wasn't at the funeral. Anyway, I think Brook cuts hair now at a high-end salon. She always looks good.

"Celeste and I were friends in high school but after I moved to Colorado, we lost touch. She dated a lot and by 'dated,' I mean slept with a lot of guys. There was always some drama surrounding her. But she's smart. She works in HR at a hospital. I think she's a big deal." The debriefing continued until we arrived at our destination, but I wasn't listening. I was still trying to figure out why I was here.

We pulled into the church parking lot, where several cars were parked off to the side in a lower lot. "Why are we parking here?" I asked.

"The priest guy said we could leave cars here if we needed to."

As we approached the group, a dark-haired woman called out. "Hey, Grace. We're just waiting for Nick. He's running late." From Grace's notes, I figured this was Brook. Her hair did look amazing. A short, thick guy stood next to her. There were five other people standing around the parking lot.

"Cool," said Grace. She pointed at me, "Everyone, remember Jane? She's my support friend this weekend." It was as good an explanation as any. Several of the faces looked familiar. People nodded and said hi. I did the same.

As they discussed logistics, a sudden feeling of uncertainty and anxiety spread throughout my body. I looked at the church and decided to go inside. I leaned over Grace's shoulder. "Hey, I'm going to find a bathroom. I'll be back in a minute."

The doors were unlocked, and I walked through the entryway and into the worship space, sneaking into the back pew with a slight bow. Sitting down while making the sign of the cross, I soaked in the silence for a minute, feeling my neck and shoulders relax, and said a quick prayer for the weekend.

While I was gone, Grace decided we would ride with Celeste and Stacy because it would be more fun if we're traveling in a bigger group. I knew there was no point in objecting. If I were in Hawaii right now, I would just be following Henry—he was the one with the plans—and I decided to do the same here. I'd follow Grace's lead and hope for the best. I was going to be mad, though, if at some point this weekend I didn't get to sit in front of a body of water with a fruity drink.

Nick showed up an hour later and we finally left the parking lot, much later than planned. Grace and I were in the backseat of Celeste's Jeep with Stacy in the front. She hooked her phone up to the car and suddenly Taylor Swift was singing.

Grace leaned over and nudged me. "Hey, this is good. Trust me. Sitting around your house all weekend thinking about Henry and Hawaii would make you crazy."

"Well, I can't guarantee that I still won't be thinking about Henry." Really, I was mostly wondering if he missed me.

"This will be fun. You'll have fun. The cabin is beautiful. And even though it's not Hawaii, there's water and I'll mix you a tropical drink. We can paddleboard and you can sit on the dock or the deck and read."

She looked at me, trying to make sure I was convinced.

We hit the freeway and after forty minutes, we headed up toward the pass. It had been years since I had crossed the mountains to the other side of the state. As the road ascended, a sheer, crevassed cliff topped with trees bordered the right side of the road. As we came down from the summit, there was a serene reservoir filled with the melted snow of the mountains and the spring rainstorms. Its glass-like surface reflected the surrounding trees.

We followed the lake as the terrain flattened, and towering deciduous and coniferous trees flanked both sides of the wide concrete path. Eventually I directed my attention to the bag at my feet, pulling out a book. I settled myself in my seat and sunk into the story held in my hands.

I looked up from my page when I noticed we were slowing down, eventually moving well below the speed limit as the cars lined up in front of us, bumper to bumper.

"Do you think there's an accident?" asked Celeste.

"The GPS shows red for four or five miles but nothing about an accident," said Stacy. From the back seat, I could see her staring at her phone. Everyone was silent, listening to the music as the car crept along the freeway. Celeste had turned down the volume now that it was no longer competing with the road noise.

"It looks like something is going on at the Gorge," said Stacy as she scrolled through her phone. "This must be everyone going over to camp out." She looked up at Celeste. Her phone pinged. "Mike just texted me and said he thinks it's because of a concert and there's also some road construction going on. It will most likely break up in a few miles."

As the three others chatted about their favorite bands to see in person, I stifled a yawn and set my book down, tuning out the conversation. I leaned my head against the window and closed my eyes.

When I opened them again, the sun was sinking behind us, and we were traveling at the speed limit. I was surprised I had dozed off. I sat up, looking around at my carmates. Everyone was quiet, and the music was playing in the background. Celeste, focused on driving, had her hands on the steering wheel at ten and two. Stacy was on her phone and Grace was staring out the window.

I leaned my head against the glass again. My mind wandered and I thought about Ryan. Thirty-two is too young to die. And it wasn't clear what happened. Nick gave a nice speech about his brother at the funeral. They seemed close. I didn't know what Grace told Nick about me crashing the memorial road trip, but he didn't seem surprised to see me in the parking lot when he finally showed up. He seemed distracted, like he would rather be anywhere else.

Celeste's phone rang and I lifted my head from the window, arching my back and stretching my neck. She pushed a button on her steering wheel to answer the call. It was Brook.

"What's up?" Celeste asked in a cheery voice.

"Since we got such a late start and then hit the slow traffic, we're going to stop at the next motel. Nick said he will pay for a few rooms. We're going to that bar that Ryan liked nearby."

"Got it. We'll follow you guys," said Celeste. The phone went silent, and the music started playing again. I looked at Grace.

"Change in plans. I'm almost positive this bar has karaoke. It will be fun," she said.

"You sure say 'fun' a lot. We might have different definitions of fun."

"Yeah, probably."

| TWELVE |

It was close to nine-thirty when we pulled into the parking lot of the Motel 6, the sun fading behind us. Reluctantly, I un-buckled my seatbelt and opened the door. I was the last one out of the car. It was decided that Grace and I would crash with Celeste and Stacy. Brook and Jason were getting their own room and Mike, other Mike, and Drew would share a room. Nick must be on his own.

"I hope you don't snore," said Grace as we grabbed our bags from the back of Celeste's car. "Let's go put our stuff in the room and then we'll grab something to eat. And drink." She threw her bag over her shoulder.

Food sounded good, especially since I had only eaten a banana. After Nick handed out card keys to the rooms, we climbed the outside stairs to the second floor. Grace opened the door and turned on the light. Standing in the doorway, I glanced around the typical motel room. The orange and brown camouflage comforters covered the two queen beds on the big wall facing a small flat-screen TV. We stashed our stuff, and while the other girls primped in the bathroom, I sat on one of the beds and pulled my hair back into a ponytail in front of the reflection of the TV. I tried to convince myself that this would be fun and that I needed to embrace whatever this was. Celeste and Stacy managed to reapply makeup and change their clothes in a matter of minutes. Grace brushed her hair and put on a new shirt.

We drove to the bar—a bar that hopefully served decent food. My stomach was grumbling. From the outside, the flat-roofed, single-story building in the middle of a parking lot appeared to be in need of some cosmetic repairs. A fresh coat of paint would be a good place to start. I was a few steps behind the group as we walked by several people vaping outside. My expectations were set to low. Celeste opened the door, and we walked through single file.

The bar was noisy, but I'd be concerned if it wasn't. I caught a whiff of Pine-Sol or some other cleaning product and wasn't sure if that should be a comfort or a concern. The lights were dimmed, and more than half the tables were occupied. Most of the bar stools were in use and the only bartender looked like he was struggling to keep up with demand.

There was a live band playing on a makeshift stage near the back and they weren't half bad. The song wasn't familiar, but it leaned toward country. The lead vocalist, with dark denim jeans and a white shirt, was attractive and probably in his twenties. The other band members seemed to be older, like in their forties or fifties. Grateful there was no karaoke, I followed Grace to the back of the bar.

The guys were already seated at a couple of tables that they had pushed together near the stage. As I sat next to Grace, I noticed it was even louder at the table, which would work in my favor. I figured you couldn't mess up a burger and fries, so instead of raising my voice, when the young woman with a bar apron approached my side, I pointed to the menu. The seat next to me was empty until Nick sat down with a bottle in his hand. He must have gone to the bar instead of waiting for the server. Apparently, he was in a hurry to honor his brother's memory with a beer. He acknowledged my presence with a glance and a nod, but he focused on the music coming from the stage and the thought of yelling over the band as we engaged in small talk was less than appealing.

After the first round of drinks arrived, Grace and a few others headed to the dance floor. She tried a few times to get me to join, but I waved her off and she eventually stopped asking. Dancing in a group, everyone looked like they were having a good time, especially Grace, and I was glad that I could help make that happen by coming along. Lead Singer Guy would pull girls up to dance with him on stage, and Celeste, Stacy, and Grace all took a turn.

Content with my crispy fries and Coke, I took this opportunity to observe all the players in this little ensemble. There was the married couple, Brook and Jason. Brook seemed nice. The weekend was her idea, and she seemed to be the one in charge rather than Nick. She and her husband sat out more songs than most of the group but joined in the dancing and drinking.

Then there were the two Mikes. One of them looked familiar. I was sure he was at the funeral, but I wasn't sure about the other one; at least I didn't remember seeing him before. The first Mike was taller than the second Mike and had short dark hair. The second Mike had glasses and was wearing Dockers and a button-down shirt.

There was also Drew, and he was definitely at the funeral. He was short and stocky, with dark, receding hair. Good on the dance floor, he seemed to pay a lot of attention to Stacy, but she didn't seem interested in him, despite his dance moves. Grace told me on the drive over to meet everyone that Celeste had liked one of the Mikes while in high school—I couldn't remember which one—but he'd had a serious girlfriend. None of the guys, except Jason, wore a wedding ring. As far as I knew they were all single.

The screen on my phone let me know it was close to midnight and I wondered how much longer we were going to stay. The band finished a song and announced a short break, cutting the noise level in half. This seemed like the perfect end to a mildly pleasant evening.

As everyone came back to the table, it occurred to me that this is what single people do—dancing, eating, and drinking—and maybe I had missed an opportunity tonight. If I truly wanted to get out of my rut after relying on Henry as my social circle, I would have to engage. Participation is a part of life. I thought about Joe and his willingness to jump into the volcano. Was I afraid to live my life differently? Could I take a leap into the unknown? I was too tired to try and figure it out tonight, but it was something to think about for the rest of the weekend.

Grace sat down hard in her chair after dancing with one of the Mikes. Grabbing her arm to steady her, I noticed her eyes weren't fully opened, and it looked like she'd had a lot of drinks. Many, many drinks. Before I could suggest we call it a night, the server approached, and Grace requested another. Surprised, I leaned back in my chair, realizing we would be here a while longer.

Grace struck up a conversation with Drew, who was sitting across from her. I stifled a yawn and looked around the table as I sipped my Coke. Celeste was hanging all over the other Mike, who didn't seem interested but played along. She caught me watching them, and I averted my eyes to my mostly-empty glass. Nick, who had left his seat when the band took a break, returned with a beer in his hand. I thought about saying something to him now, but nothing came to mind. Staring at my glass, I was tempted to close my eyes but instead looked up again and found Celeste staring at me.

"Who are you again?" she asked. Mike had disappeared.

Offended that she didn't remember who I was after spending several hours in the car with me, I said, "I'm Jane. I'm here with Grace. I was at the funeral." I sounded like an idiot.

"You didn't know Ryan?" Celeste didn't blink and her stare was intense.

I shifted in my seat, sitting up straighter. "I'm afraid not. He was lucky to have such good friends." I glanced at Nick. "And brother."

Celeste, who also appeared to be very drunk, wasn't satisfied with my answer.

"I just think it's bizarre that you're here. And you're not even like celebrating Ryan's life by having a good time. You're just sitting there staring at people. I don't think Ryan would want you here. He wanted people to have a good time."

Hearing this last bit, Grace leaned close to me, threw her arm around my shoulder, and put her face next to my cheek while looking at Celeste. "She's an introvert," said Grace, defending me.

Well, that should explain everything, and I hoped for my sake it did. Grace liked to share, and alcohol probably didn't stifle her need to do so. Unfortunately, Grace had more to say.

"And she's here because she had a big fight with her gay best friend who she was supposed to go to Hawaii with, but he went without her," said Grace. "He said she was a homophobic Jesus freak and a prude."

Stunned silent, I blinked my eyes, hoping I would disappear. No longer tired and my body tense, I looked around at the group to see who was listening. Nick sat up straighter and looked at me and Grace. He was probably the most sober one here, along with Brook and Jason.

Before I could say or do anything, Celeste had more to say.

"You do look like a Bible-thumping, Jesus-freak virgin who hates gay people. You've been sitting there all night drinking your Diet Coke and judging us."

"Excuse me?" I said, offended by her characterization. The same feeling rose in my chest as when Henry and I last spoke, and I could feel heat rising to my face. Before I could defend myself, Grace decided to chime in again.

"Oh, she's not a virgin," Grace said. She was still sitting remarkably close to me, her hot breath on my cheek. I leaned away and swung my head around to look at her while she elaborated.

"After her mom died, her high school boyfriend moved in with her. But she dumped him and then Henry, the gay guy moved in."

I regained the ability to speak and move. My heart pounding, I stood up, bumping the table and almost knocking my chair over as I grabbed Grace's elbow and pulled her up. "Okay, that's enough of this. We're going back to the motel." My voice brusque, I tightened my grip on her arm. "Let's go, Grace." My eyes found Nick, who had the slightest smile on his face, and I said, "This has been fun. Thanks." I didn't wait for him to say anything. From his lack of participation in the evening's activities, he must have found all of this entertaining.

Turning away, I maneuvered Grace from the table and then realized that we didn't have a car. There was no way I would ride with Celeste back to the motel. I let out a deep breath. "I guess we can try and get an Uber, or we can walk back," I said to myself as much as to her. Her confused look at our abrupt departure made me realize she had no idea what she had done. "Come on, big mouth, before you share anymore." I pulled her toward the front door while taking my phone from my pocket.

From the corner of my eye, I saw Brook and Jason stand up from the table. They were sitting next to Celeste and had front-row seats to Grace's one-woman show. They caught up to us and Brook tapped my arm. "Hey, we're going back to the motel. We can give you guys a ride."

| THIRTEEN |

Jason kept looking at us in the rearview mirror as we sat in the back of the crew cab of his Ford F-150. "Grace, you better not barf in my truck." That was the refrain for the entire ride back to the motel. I assured him I had it covered if she got sick. He explained it wasn't just the barf, but the smell that would send him over the edge. Brook must have told Jason to give us a ride. I was sure he was doing it under duress.

I managed to get Grace out of the truck, although she seemed to be getting drunker by the minute. With Brook and Jason's help, it took a good ten minutes to get her up the stairs of the motel. As we reached the top, I told them I could manage the rest of the way, and they headed in the opposite direction to their room.

As I opened the door, I turned to Grace. "How did you know my high school boyfriend lived with me?" I was half-carrying and half-dragging her into the room. I wasn't sure she could comprehend the question and give a coherent answer, but I was interested in any explanation she could offer.

"Henry told me at the bar the night you had the date with Tom. Was that his name? Tom? Tim? No, that doesn't seem right either. I don't feel good. I think I'm going to barf." We made it into the bathroom in time for her to throw up all over the bathtub, which was better than the floor. Moving to the toilet, I sat her down in front of the bowl, fairly certain there was more to come. I washed my hands and sat with her for what seemed like forever while she threw up a few more times. I cleaned out the tub the best I could—I planned to take a shower at some point.

I heard the door to the room open and two voices, one female and one male, filled the space between Grace retching into the toilet. I poked my head out from the bathroom. Celeste and the singer from the band were laughing and stumbling over to the bed farthest from the bathroom. Knowing where this was going, I figured when they realized that Grace and I were here, they would find somewhere else to go.

Making sure Grace stayed put, I stepped out of the bathroom. Lead Singer Guy's shirt was stuck on his head, and it took him a second to pull it off.

"Hey, you guys need to go somewhere else. Grace doesn't feel well," I said in a clear, firm voice. They ignored me. Celeste struggled with her clothes but managed to get her jeans off without falling down and was now down to her pink panties and matching bra. She was working on getting Lead Singer's pants off when they fell on the bed.

"Hey," I shouted at them, "I'm not watching the stage production of 'Celeste Gets Laid.' Get another room." But it was like I wasn't even there. I had no idea what to do. I went back to get Grace so we could leave, but she was passed out on the bathroom floor.

"Grace, get up. We need to go." Her arms noodled as I tried to pull her up. Dragging her out of the bathroom and to the empty bed, I ignored the noises from the next one. I faced the opposite wall as I managed to get the top half of Grace's body on top of the covers. Quickly grabbing her feet, I pulled them up and positioned her on her side in the middle of the bed. I grabbed my bag, putting it behind her so she couldn't roll over onto her back. I heard a low shriek and a thump. It sounded like the lovers had fallen off the bed. Shaking, I grabbed the key to the room and my phone and made it to the door, barely in control of my emotions. As I left, I spit out, "I hope you both get a drug-resistant STD." Then I flicked off the light. Not my finest work.

Angry at so many people, I could barely see straight as I ran down the stairs. The pool was to the left and even though the sign said closed, the chain between the gate and the fence was stretched, leaving a gap.

Pushing the gate wider, I slipped under the barrier. Along with several white round tables and chairs, there were nine or ten white lounge chairs randomly placed on the cement patio. I walked toward the kidney shaped pool with my back to the gate. Pacing, I tried to figure out if I was a bad person for leaving Grace alone. I pulled out my phone. I was only in this situation because of Henry. I texted him, narrating at the same time.

Me: I hope you're enjoying Hawaii

Me: I spent the evening holding Grace's hair as she puked all over a cheap motel bathroom floor after she told a group of strangers that I wasn't a virgin because I lived with my high school boyfriend which she said you told her

Me: I think that's the definition of going behind someone's back

Me: I'm changing my locks

Me: Lose my number

Me: We're done

I wanted to kick something.

"Are you all right?"

I jumped, startled by his voice. Turning around with my hand on my chest, I saw Nick sitting on the side of a white plastic lounge chair with a six-pack of beer at his feet.

"You scared me. I thought I was alone." My heart was pounding.

"Obviously, but you walked right past me." He reached for one of the beers. "I didn't want to interrupt you. I wouldn't want to be on the other end of those texts."

Dismissing his comment, I focused on the situation upstairs rather than my internal outrage at Henry. "Celeste and the singer from the bar are up in our room having sex with Grace passed out on the other bed. Who does that? Grace said Celeste got around in high school. I guess she hasn't changed." I sounded judgmental, exactly what Celeste accused me of. "I made sure Grace was lying on her side, but she had so much to drink. I'm worried she'll roll on her back and choke if she gets sick, but I had to get out of there."

"Celeste had a lot to drink too." He held out his hand. "Give me your card. I'll go check on Grace." Under his breath but loud enough for me to hear, he said, "I haven't lost anyone on one of these weekends yet and I'm not going to start now."

As I walked over to where he was sitting, I pulled out the plastic key card and held it in front of him.

Nick stood and grabbed the key from my outstretched hand. "Have a beer. I'll be back in a sec."

I watched him walk toward the stairs until he was no longer in my line of sight. Turning toward the pool while taking a few deep breaths, I sat down and removed my sandals. I rolled up the bottom of my jeans while I surveyed my surroundings.

Looking past my reflection, I saw the gray-green bottom of the pool. I stuck my hand in and then swung my legs around and submerged them into the cool water. As I moved my feet, creating ripples across the surface of the water, I assessed the last few hours with the benefit of the quiet and I came to the same conclusion as before. This was all Henry's fault. He told Grace something that I told him in confidence—and he accused me of talking behind his back.

I glanced at my phone to see if Henry had responded to my texts. I did tell him to delete my number, so it was no surprise that he hadn't. The adrenaline that had been fueling me had evaporated and now fatigue seeped into my limbs. It was close to two in the morning, which was way past my bedtime. I pulled my feet from the water and moved to a nearby lounge chair. I leaned back and briefly closed my eyes. Sensing someone approaching, I looked up and saw Nick standing over me. He was holding out his hand with the key card.

"She was snoring, so she's still alive. I didn't see anyone else, but I heard the shower running."

"Thank you for doing that." I took the key. Nick sat back down on the edge of the lounge chair and picked up his beer. I sat up and moved my feet to one side, facing him.

"I want to apologize for coming along this weekend. I should have stayed home. I don't know why I let Grace talk me into coming."

"No need to apologize. Ryan attracted attention everywhere he went. Grace should have warned you. I called it the 'Ryan effect.' There always seemed to be drama when he was at the center. It's not a surprise, at least to me, that it's the same when we're doing something in his memory."

"Why are you here then?"

"My mother. She loved it when in high school all the kids would hang out at our house. Or go up to the cabin." He looked down at his beer. "She got to know some of the kids—Brook, in particular. When she said something to my mother about a weekend trip to honor Ryan, my mom insisted I go. So, here I am." He held his arms out wide and then took a drink of his beer. "Checking on drunk people just like in high school."

"I guess that was the point of the weekend—to relive some of those high school memories, memories of Ryan. I'll admit, drinking and parties weren't part of my high school experience, but I know Grace wanted to be here. She was upset about Ryan's death." I stared at my feet as I thought about why we were here. "You gave a nice speech at the funeral. It sounds like Ryan had your back too. The story you told. Sometimes I wish I had a sibling."

Nick didn't respond, and I realized that was the wrong thing to say. "I'm sorry, that was insensitive. I'm sure you miss your brother."

He cleared his throat. "Let's not talk about Ryan anymore." There was a brief, uncomfortable silence. "So how do you know Grace? Do you work together?"

"Roommates. She's a server at a bar that my friend owns. She was looking for a new living arrangement and Henry had moved out so…" I trailed off. "She moved in a few weeks ago."

"And Henry is the best friend you had a fight with and who was on the other end of those texts you just sent?"

I nodded.

"And he's in Hawaii right now?" He continued his questioning. He had paid attention to Grace's performance at the bar.

"Yes." I hesitated and wondered why I should tell him anything. I did anyway. "We were supposed to go together, but he accused me of trying to sabotage his relationship and talking behind his back. He also said some mean things about me and my beliefs."

"That you're a Jesus freak."

I searched his plain face with his dark eyes. "So, you don't believe in God?"

"I believe in God, just not organized religion," he said, opening another beer.

"Oh, sort of like people who believe in democracy but don't vote?"

His hand stopped midair as he pulled the can to his face. "It's not anything like that. My parents made us go to Mass every Sunday. The rules seemed arbitrary and didn't apply to everyone. The Catholic church is very black and white."

"I don't agree. And that's just an excuse. Participating in something you believe in is what makes it worthwhile, which is probably true of most things, not just religion. Being a casual observer gets you nothing."

"You seem to judge Celeste. Why do you care what she does or who she sleeps with? And what about the guy? Why aren't you judging him? You aren't a friend to your sex." His tone didn't match the accusation. I was surprised at the turn in the conversation and wondered if he believed what he was saying. It was true that the singer was equally guilty. He could have left when he found out they weren't alone in the room.

"She made it my business when she decided to have sex with a stranger in front of me." I emphasized the last four words. "If she hooked up with him in his room or, heck, her car, I wouldn't know and wouldn't care." My voice was getting louder. "You're right, she can do whatever she wants. And for the record, I think I have been equally judged this evening by Celeste and now by you. You don't know me, and I'm only here because a friend had a rough week and I thought this trip would take her mind off it."

"But you have a problem with Celeste's choices."

"People aren't animals. We should be able to control ourselves. Using someone for sex is wrong."

"Sounds like they were using each other. Do you always think in terms of right and wrong or black and white maybe?"

"It sounds like you don't believe in rules. I don't think of right and wrong as an abstract. I find the one thing people are exceptionally good at is rationalizing their behavior, especially when it serves as a reason for doing something they want to do, despite the consequences."

Leaning forward in the chair, he slumped his shoulders, holding his beer loosely with both hands. "How old are you? Don't you ever have fun?"

A small laugh escaped my mouth. The word was beginning to lose all meaning. "Fun is how Grace described this weekend. That exact word repeated over and over. Is this how you define fun?" I looked around the deserted pool area of a motel that had seen better days. "Has this evening been fun for you?"

He didn't say anything, and I decided there was no point in continuing to engage with him.

"Let's just agree to disagree," I said, exhausted and tired of this conversation. He stared at me with a crooked smile and shiny eyes as he took another sip of beer. I couldn't make out his expression, but it almost did look like he was having fun.

| FOURTEEN |

A hand on my shoulder, gently shaking me, caused me to sit up. Disoriented, I tried to figure out where I was. The sun was bright, but sitting in the shade of the motel, I couldn't feel its warmth. As I looked down, I appreciated the scratchy white towels that covered my torso and legs. I looked up at the figure standing over me. It was Nick.

"What time is it?" My voice cracked.

"Almost seven. I thought you'd want to go check on Grace. Do you want me to go with you?"

I slowly swung my legs over the side of the lounge chair and sat for a second. It wasn't the most comfortable place to sleep. I must have been really tired. I wondered if Nick spent the night in a lounge chair too. After arching my back, I grabbed my sandals next to my chair and put them on.

Our conversation from last night, or actually early this morning, floated to the surface of my consciousness. Unsettled by the recollection, I decided it might be best to avoid Nick as much as possible for the rest of the weekend.

"No, I think it will be fine. Thanks, though."

As I climbed the stairs to the room, I thought of Grace and then Celeste, and each step was harder to take. The idea of spending the weekend with Celeste made my stomach turn and then the queasy feeling gave way to something else. I felt my jaw tighten and the anger I felt last night began to rise in my chest. Maybe Grace would feel so remorseful that she would agree to bail on the weekend and head back to Seattle if we could somehow find a ride.

As I was about to put the card key in the door, I heard loud talking from inside the room. Two female voices, but neither sounded like Grace. It felt weird to eavesdrop, but I didn't want any more surprises. The voices were getting louder. A fight? One voice in particular was clearer, and that was because it was right on the other side of the door.

Fearing I would be caught listening, I quickly backed up, turned, and stepped lightly toward the top of the stairs. The door to our room opened and Stacy walked out. She saw me but didn't say anything as she quickly passed me with her bag in her hand.

Walking back to the room, I slowly opened the door, afraid of what I might find. Grace was still asleep, snoring. The other bed was empty, the sheets and comforter heaped on the floor. Someone was in the bathroom. I looked around and then sat on the end of the bed and stared at the door to the room.

My heart rate had ticked up while I was trying to avoid being caught listening at the door and the anger I had felt melted into mild despair once my breathing became more even. I looked back at Grace, and then Celeste stepped out of the bathroom. Our eyes briefly locked, and she stopped for a second when she saw me but then walked past not acknowledging my presence. I must be invisible today. That was probably a good thing. I had no idea what she remembered about last night. It looked like she had showered, and her hair and makeup were done, so she was in much better shape than Grace. I grabbed my bag from behind her and decided to shower, leaving Grace to sleep a while longer.

After stepping out of the tub, I dressed, dried my hair, and applied some mascara and lip gloss. I stretched my neck from side to side trying to work out some of the soreness from sleeping on a lounge chair, when I heard a phone ring. I opened the door and saw Grace's phone face up on the nightstand. "Take This Job and Shove It" was displayed on the screen as it continued to make noise. I shook her.

"Grace, I think someone is calling about an interview." I grabbed her shoulder and shook her again.

A groan escaped her mouth.

"Grace, I think it's about a job."

She mumbled and tried to roll over to the other side. I sighed and answered her phone.

"Hello?" I listened to the cheery voice confirm that it was Cami calling back. "Yes, I'm still interested in the position." I stared at Grace wishing she could articulate her interest herself. I scanned the motel room, while concentrating on the words coming from the other end. "That's great. Thank you so much." With my other hand I pushed Grace's arm, but she didn't respond. Cami was still talking.

"Oh, um, yes, I can meet today." I glanced at the clock beside the bed and did the math. "Sure. Okay, great. See you then."

I ended the call. "Grace. Grace, wake up. They offered you the job. They want you to come to the office this afternoon. I said you would be there." She wasn't moving. "You need to get up so we can head back." Crap. How are we going to get back without a car? "Okay, Grace, come on. We need to figure this out." I was moving back and forth between the side of the bed and the bathroom, stopping intermittently to shake her. She wasn't responding.

This called for something drastic. Grabbing a cup from the counter next to the coffee maker, I filled it with water. I started to pour it over her head and then decided that was too drastic, even though I really wanted to do it. Instead, I stuck my fingers in the glass and flicked water at her.

She swatted her face. "What? Ohhh," she moaned, grabbing the side of her head with her hand. "My head hurts."

"Grace. You got the job. They want you to come in today. You have to get up so we can get back."

"What?"

"They decided to hire two people, so they are offering you the other spot. Cami just called. She wants you to come in this afternoon for a quick orientation and to fill out some paperwork."

"I got the job?" She still sounded a little drunk and definitely hungover.

"You did. So get up and get in the shower. We need to find a way to get back home." I helped her into the bathroom so she could take care of the aroma of the dried vomit stuck in her hair and the mascara smudged around her eyes. I continued to answer her questions about the phone call.

After sitting her bag next to the tub, I pulled out some Tylenol from my purse and filled a glass with water. I set it on the sink and barked out some instructions that hopefully she could follow and then shut the door. With my hand still on the handle, I thought about how we could get back. Who could I call for a ride?

Celeste, who had been listening to Grace and me, looked up from her phone. "I'm heading back. Grace can ride with me."

"Great," I said. "Thank you." I was surprised by Celeste's offer after our interaction at the bar and in the hotel room last night.

"Just Grace. You'll have to find another ride."

"What?" I blinked my eyes more than normal, my brow furrowed as I processed what she was saying.

"You'll have to find your own way back." She picked up her bag. "I'm going to find some coffee. Tell Grace to hurry." She left.

Stunned but now comprehending what this meant, I sat on the edge of the bed leaning forward. First Henry left me behind and now Grace. I was beginning to think there was something wrong with me. Why did I always end up alone? I felt my eyes fill, but that wasn't going to help. I wiped away a few fallen tears and sat up.

Celeste would get Grace back to the city in time for her to meet Cami and I would figure something else out. It would have been an uncomfortable car ride anyway. I'm used to things falling apart—that was my entire teenage years. Getting a ride back to Seattle shouldn't be that difficult, but it might be expensive.

As I straightened up the room, making sure we weren't leaving anything behind, I thought about grabbing something to drink across the street, but I didn't want to leave Grace. I wasn't entirely sure what kind of shape she was in. I searched on my phone for a bus schedule but didn't have much luck. Then I checked some car ride apps, but it was hard to focus.

Twenty minutes later, Grace emerged from the bathroom, with her hair wet but vomit-free. She was dressed in shorts and a T-shirt, with no makeup. She said the shower helped and the Tylenol was kicking in. Celeste returned to the room, and I wondered if she had been waiting outside the door until she heard Grace's voice.

"I'm going back to Seattle if you want a ride, Grace. I'm leaving in ten minutes, so you need to be ready then," she said as she zipped up her bag.

"We'll be ready. I'm sure Jane can't wait to get home." She looked at me, with a crooked smile.

"The offer is just for you, Grace. See you downstairs." Celeste picked up her bag and left the room again, not acknowledging me. Grace had a confused look on her face.

"What's up with Celeste? Why can't you come back with us?" She sat on the side of the bed.

"What do you remember from last night?"

"I said some things at the bar." She trailed off, I assume trying to remember the evening. "And you and Brook and Jason dragging me up the stairs, then throwing up. The rest is a blank."

"You said some things, Celeste said some things, and I said some things. Celeste brought a guy back to the room. They wouldn't leave so after you passed out, I left. Maybe you should ask her about it." There are two sides to every story, and I would be interested in hearing Celeste's side.

"Well, how will you get back if I go with her?"

"I'll figure something out. You don't need to worry about it. I'm sure Daniel would come and get me if I needed him to. We're just wasting time talking about this."

The events of the last twenty-four hours and the little sleep I had were taking their toll. My shoulders tensed and I felt irritated by this conversation and by Grace's presence. I never should have agreed to go on this trip. I just wanted to get home and the way to do that was to get Grace home first.

"I can call Cami back and ask if I can come in on Monday."

"Grace don't screw this up. Go with Celeste. I'll be fine." I could hear the edge in my voice but I needed Grace to find a job so I could lie on my couch in peace.

She didn't say anything else. We grabbed our stuff and opened the door. As we stepped out, the bright sun blinded me, and my eyes had to adjust after leaving the darkened room. Now I felt the sun's warmth. I closed the door behind us.

| FIFTEEN |

Everyone was waiting as we walked across the parking lot of the motel. Both Mikes and Drew were standing next to a gray Audi. Stacy was sitting in the front passenger seat of the car with the door open and Celeste was standing next to her Jeep. Scanning the motel grounds and parking lot, I realized I was looking for Nick. He must still be in his room.

Jason and Brook were walking across the parking lot with food from McDonald's. Brook was carrying a tray of drinks in each hand and Jason had two large paper bags. I heard footsteps on the stairs, and I turned to see Nick walking toward the group. By then, Brook and Jason were handing out drinks and food to anyone who was hungry. I grabbed an orange juice and pulled some sort of breakfast sandwich from the opened bag that Jason held in front of me.

"Hey, Nick," Celeste called out. "Grace and I are heading back to the city. Grace has to be at work, and I don't feel well. Sorry." She waved off Jason's offer of something to eat as Grace grabbed a coffee from Brook. Probably a wise choice not to eat anything just yet.

Nick nodded toward Celeste and then turned to me. "You're staying." I couldn't tell if it was a question.

"I'm going to go too. I just need to find a way home." Grace looked at Celeste but didn't say anything.

"Let's go, Grace." Celeste opened her car door.

Grace gave me a big hug, whispering in my ear, "I'm so sorry."

I managed to bring my left arm up in an attempt to return her hug but quickly pulled back from her embrace. "You better get going." Even with the shower, she needed a few more hours to pull herself together.

"Thanks. Text me later so I know what's going on."

I watched them leave the parking lot. There goes my ride, I thought. Stacy's too, but it looked like she had made other arrangements.

My stomach rumbled and I looked down at the sandwich in my hand. First things first. Making decisions on an empty stomach was never a good idea. Some of the others had opened their car doors and were sitting down, eating. I spotted a bench against the side of the motel. I tried not to snarf down the food, but it tasted really good. I hadn't eaten McDonald's in a while. Nick wandered over with his duffle bag, standing next to the bench where I sat. I had taken a big bite of the sandwich.

"Why did Grace leave?"

I chewed fast and swallowed. "She was offered a job. They called this morning to see if she could come in this afternoon."

"Ah. And Celeste left because…"

"I don't know. She didn't tell me, and I didn't ask. She said she would only take Grace with her." He raised his eyebrows. "It's fine," I added. "I can call someone or an Uber or I have two working thumbs. I'll figure it out." I took another big bite. I didn't care if Nick thought I was a pig. I was hungry.

"You can ride with me. We can go to the lake and hang out for a few hours and then we can drive back tonight. These are Ryan's friends." He gestured to the others while still looking at me. "I don't have a lot in common with them."

His offer surprised me but not the comment about Ryan's friends. I remembered that his mom wanted him to go on this trip and maybe I could be his excuse to leave early. I didn't respond because I was still chewing. And I needed to think about it.

"Anyway, I can't leave you here until I know you have a plan," he said. "This seems like the easiest solution."

I pondered his proposal and took another bite of the sandwich, trying to figure out if this was a good idea.

"Think about it. I'm going to go throw my stuff in my car. I promise I have no ill intentions."

"Good to know," I said. Maybe I shouldn't be a jerk to someone who's offering me a ride, but I was still reeling from the situation. I watched him walk to his car wondering what we had in common. The only thing I could think of was loss. He lost his wife and brother, and I lost my mom and dad. He seemed harmless. A bit of a dick, if I was being honest, but he did help me out yesterday with the whole Grace situation. And he did offer to give me a ride home. My phone buzzed. I pulled it out of my pocket. It was a text from Grace.

Grace: How are you getting home? I feel bad that I left

I shoved the rest of the sandwich in my mouth and typed,

Me: Nick offered to drive me home. We'd go to the lake for a few hours and then head back tonight. What do you think? Would you go with him?

The three dots appeared and then:

Grace: Yeah, Nick is solid

Well, I don't know much about some random Uber driver, which is probably my only other option. Daniel would come and get me, but I didn't want to bother him. It seemed like the easiest thing to do was to go with Nick. I texted Grace and told her she could track me on my phone. That way they'd know where to find my body. I stood up and threw the food wrapper and cup in the garbage and walked to the parking lot. It looked like everyone was getting ready to leave, and they were discussing directions and timing.

I hadn't paid attention to what kind of car Nick drove. It was a Subaru Forrester, like my car, only newer. I approached Nick. "A ride sounds great if the offer still stands."

"Hop in." After putting my bag in the back, I slid into the front passenger seat. It was a much better view than the back of Stacy's head. I looked at him as he pulled out of the parking lot. I was tempted to tell him that my last car ride with a man I barely knew didn't turn out well, but instead I buckled up and tested my imaginary brake.

After a few minutes of nothing but road noise, I decided to break the silence.

"So, this is your parents' cabin?" The joys of small talk.

"It's my dad's and my uncle's. My uncle lives in California, as do most of my cousins, so they don't use it much. It's been in the family for close to sixty years."

"Did they come to the funeral?" I didn't know why I asked that, and it probably veered from the definition of small talk.

"A couple of my cousins did and my uncle. They left the next day."

The silence settled in again, and I decided to let him steer any future conversation. He turned on the radio instead. I turned my attention to outside of the car, where there was a fair amount of traffic. The highway was surrounded mostly by open spaces with the occasional farm or other random building. I thought about closing my eyes, and then found it impossible not to.

I jolted awake, lifting my head from my shoulder where it was resting. The car was slowing down and moving toward an off-ramp. For a second, I was confused about where I was and then looked over and saw Nick. He offered a one-word explanation. "Gas."

Not saying anything, I looked at the clock. I had only been asleep for twenty minutes, but I felt better. An Egg McMuffin and a power nap—who knew? He turned right at the top of the exit ramp after waiting for the light to turn green. I saw the blue road sign that offered up all the available options. Food, gas, and lodging. The gas station was immediately on the left and he pulled in front of one of the vacant pumps. As he stepped out of the car, he asked if I wanted anything. I shook my head.

His phone, sitting in the cup holder, buzzed. I picked it up and opened my car door. Holding out his phone, I asked if he wanted to answer it. He looked at the initials displayed and took it from my hand. Even with my door shut, I could still hear part of the conversation.

After listening for a few seconds, he said, "Let me talk to her. She can still listen." There was a pause. "Olivia, I'm sorry, but don't do this. It just makes it hard on Grammy and Pop Pop and I know you don't want to hurt them. Olivia? Olivia?" I heard him sigh. "Give the phone back to Grammy." He sounded defeated.

He listened for another few seconds. "Of course. Yes. Okay, thanks." I wondered if Olivia was his daughter. I didn't see that coming, but it wasn't surprising. He had been married. I tried to recollect if there were any kids at the funeral, but I didn't remember any. After filling the tank, he slid into the driver's seat and started the car.

"Everything okay?" I asked, hoping for an explanation.

"My daughter is staying at her grandparents'. Her mom's parents," he clarified as he looked straight ahead. "She's mad that she couldn't go to the funeral and then she somehow found out about the cabin trip. My mom must have told her.

She stopped talking two days ago in protest, but she stopped eating yesterday and her grandmother is concerned. I need to pick her up."

"Uh, okay." I could start asking questions, but I waited to see what he would say. My first thought was that a child who manipulates people by not eating or talking is probably a brat. But I couldn't say that. At this point, I had no choice but to go along for the ride.

He started the car. "We'll have to turn around. It's over two hours back in the other direction," he explained. Using the controls on his steering wheel, he called Jason and Brook.

"We're going to be later than expected," he said without giving an explanation. "There's a key to the cabin in the eaves of the shed out back. Call me if you have any problems getting in. I'm not sure when we'll get there."

Brook asked if everything was okay. Nick confirmed that he just needed to make a quick detour and hung up the phone. Silence descended again. He needed to do the talking and so I waited.

It took longer than I expected, but finally he said, "Olivia is nine."

I didn't say anything hoping he would say more. I was beginning to think that was the end of the explanation when he continued.

"Maybe you can imagine a little girl who has only grown up with a father. Me as her father," he added, like that would mean something to me. "She acts older than her age, and she's smart and gifted."

Again, it sounded like everything should make perfect sense to me now, but it didn't. And "gifted"—what does that even mean? Doesn't every parent think their child is gifted?

I decided that my silent treatment wasn't necessary and truthfully, I could relate. It was just me and my mom.

"I can imagine that," I said. "She probably struggles with a friend group because she doesn't have a traditional family and then throw in smart and gifted… and she probably spends a lot of time in the company of adults." I might be projecting. But no one would ever describe me as smart and gifted.

"Well, she's not talking or eating because she's mad. For nine, she really knows how to wield what little power and control she has. She's stubborn as hell. The thing is, she usually only does this when I've done something wrong. I didn't want her at the funeral."

"Why?" My resolve to only listen didn't last long. "I'm sorry. I shouldn't have asked that. You're her dad and I'm sure you had your reasons."

"But were they good reasons?" he asked as he glanced at me. I didn't say anything. But I wanted to. I had so many questions.

I left Nick to his thoughts for the remainder of the ride. I assumed he was worried about his daughter. He seemed to question his decision to exclude her from the funeral. Olivia, having lost her mom, must understand death. But I could understand if Nick was trying to shield her from further loss.

| SIXTEEN |

We exited the freeway and a few turns later, we were on a two-lane road with dense trees on both sides. Single mailboxes next to nearly hidden driveways lined the narrow road, the dense vegetation shielding the houses from view. We slowed down and made a right turn onto one of the gravel driveways. There was a canopy of trees and undergrowth on either side of the worn dirt road that was blocked by a metal gate.

Nick punched a code into the keypad and we drove a little further through the surrounding brush. Suddenly the tall trees and shrubs were behind us, and the road curved into a large clearing with several small buildings. A farmhouse with a metal roof and wide front porch sat in the middle of the clearing surrounded by verdant pastures.

Not far from the main house was a large pond with still water, framed with cattails and clumps of tall grass. Big hydrangea bushes waiting to bloom hugged the perimeter of the house along with variegated shrubs and budding flowers. It reminded me of a photograph in a home and garden magazine—a centerfold taking up both pages with the crease between the pond and green pastures. We pulled up in front of the detached garage and parked next to another Subaru. Nick turned to me with his hand on the handle of the car door.

"You're not afraid of dogs, are you?"

"No," I said, assuming a dog or two would greet us.

"Good. Because they have ten."

What if I had said yes? I thought. As I looked at the front of the house, I could see several additions—the house had at some point been much smaller. There was a door on the side by a large cement patio and a door in the middle of the big front porch. An empty swing hung at the far end.

A middle-aged woman opened the wooden screen door and walked out to greet us. Her floral apron covered her white T-shirt and the top of her dark-colored jeans. Her light brown hair was pulled back. She had a plate in her hand with what looked like a sandwich on it. Behind her, several large dogs of various breeds and colors trotted out to see what was going on. Nick exited the car to meet the woman. I hesitated, wondering how this was going to play out, but I quickly joined him as he faced the woman while standing at the bottom of the stairs.

"Where's Olivia?" With a quick backward nod of his head, he introduced me. "This is Jane." He sounded rude and abrupt, but the woman didn't seem fazed by Nick's unpleasant greeting.

She walked to the edge of the porch steps and handed Nick the plate. She acknowledged me, and in a sweet tone said, "Hi Jane. It is nice to meet you. I'm Sylvie." She turned to Nick and said in the same voice, "She's in the studio." Nick turned and walked toward a small building near a fenced pasture, the pack of dogs following him. I stood there, not sure what to do.

"Come on in," Sylvie said, reading my mind. "Are you thirsty? I just made some iced tea."

"Iced tea sounds great. Thank you."

She held open the screen door as I walked up the steps and I was immediately greeted by another group of dogs, a few smaller than the first group.

"I assume Nick told you about the dogs." She maneuvered herself toward the refrigerator.

"He just mentioned that you have a lot of them."

"They're old dogs that have been abandoned or rescued by a local shelter called Old Dogs Go to Heaven. When they have trouble placing a dog, they tend to wind up here," she explained.

The dogs were now surrounding me like sharks, bumping and circling both me and each other. They sniffed at my clothes and I held out my hand, patting them as they moved by me. They seemed excited to see me, but after they realized I didn't have much to offer in the way of smells or food, they wandered off to other parts of the house.

I glanced around as Sylvie poured the iced tea. The house was long and narrow. To the left, it looked like a patio had been enclosed. The two stairs led down into the sunlit room, with big windows that faced out to the yard beyond. The kitchen was almost in the center of the house. The cupboards and sink were on the same wall as the front porch and to my right was an eating area. The far wall caught my attention. Fifteen or twenty paintings of dogs, mostly of their faces and upper bodies, and most with their tongues hanging out filled the space. My gaze lingered as I absorbed the bright, detailed canine artwork.

I turned my attention to Sylvie when she handed me a tall glass of iced tea with a napkin underneath, water beads outside the glass racing to the bottom. It tasted so refreshing. I tried not to drink it all at once.

"I love your farm," I said as I swallowed, trying not to cough from the cold drink.

"Thank you. When Richard retired from Boeing about six years ago, we decided we needed something to keep us busy, which it does and then some. But we love it here and it's a wonderful place for Olivia. Let's go sit on the porch."

We walked back outside with our drinks. As we sat down in the Adirondack chairs next to several pots overflowing with vines and flowering plants, we could see Nick heading back from the small outbuilding. He was empty-handed and alone.

"Maybe Olivia finally ate something," said Sylvie in a hopeful tone. "I don't remember her mother being so stubborn." I tried to think of something comforting to say as we watched Nick, but nothing came to mind.

He stood in front of us with a frustrated look on his face. "She wants to meet you, Jane."

"She said something?" asked Sylvie. She held a napkin tight in her hand.

"No, she wrote it down on a piece of paper. I told her she had to eat the sandwich while I came to ask Jane to come and say hi."

"Okay," I said as I stood, putting my drink on the little table between the chairs and followed Nick. As we made our way to the little house, my mind and legs were trying to keep up. A few seconds ago, I was enjoying a cold drink and now I'm going to talk to a little girl I've never met before. Can't I just go home?

"Why does she want to meet me?" I struggled to keep up with his long strides without breaking into a jog.

"She must have seen you get out of the car, and she wants to know who you are," he explained in a matter-of-fact tone, like I didn't understand the concept of meeting someone.

"What did you tell her?" I realized I should have stayed in the car.

"I didn't tell her anything. I'm just trying to get her to eat a sandwich and to stop with the silent treatment."

"Well, what am I going to tell her? I've known you less than twenty-four hours and I didn't know your brother." It felt like there was a lot riding on the conversation I was about to have with Nick's daughter, and I didn't have the faintest idea of what to say.

"Just answer her questions. You can be as brief as you want." I felt panicked and then I remembered that she was only nine. Nick said she was smart but maybe she's a little manipulative. Oh, and stubborn.

As we approached, the French doors opened, and I could see a tall, skinny girl standing in the middle of the doorway. She had on faded jeans and a smock with a flower print. She was barefoot. Her long blonde hair was in a loose ponytail fastened at the nape of her neck, and some wisps of hair escaped, framing her narrow face. We reached the doorway and Nick said, "Jane, this is my daughter, Olivia. Olivia, this is my friend, Jane."

I threw a look in Nick's direction. We're friends now, huh? "Hi, Olivia. It's nice to meet you."

"Hello," she said in a sweet voice.

Maybe my work here was done. She turned around and walked into the studio, a rectangular room not much bigger than an extra-large bedroom. Light poured in from the wide windows that framed the room. There were six or seven easels with paintings on them situated near the windows. Most of the paintings were finished, but there seemed to be a few in progress. Many were landscapes of the farm, but there were also a few portraits of dogs and goats. On the easel closest to me was the face of a big yellow lab, his tongue hanging out.

The level of artistry depicted in the paintings was stunning, and I was no longer worried about what to say to Olivia. As my gaze wandered the room, I found it hard to believe that a nine-year-old created all of them.

"Did you eat your sandwich?" asked Nick as he looked around the room for the plate. She held up three fingers.

"Three bites? That's better than nothing," he said.

She was still playing her dad. Gifted, yes, but I hadn't ruled out brat. I spied the half-eaten sandwich sitting on a stool in the corner.

"What have you painted this week?" asked Nick. She didn't answer. He looked at me.

"Can you show me what you've painted?" I asked. She led me over to a landscape sitting on an easel. "It's beautiful, Olivia. You're an amazing artist."

"Did you know Ryan?" she asked me.

Usually, a person says thank you when someone pays a compliment. I was trying to figure this kid out. I looked at Nick and then back at Olivia.

"My friend went to high school with your Uncle Ryan and your dad, but no, I didn't know him."

"Me neither," she said as she looked at her dad.

Her comment surprised me. How could she not know her uncle? This was more than not letting her go to a funeral. I looked back at Nick, but his face was blank.

"Did you go to the funeral?" she asked.

"Yes, I did. I went with my friend." Finally an easy question to answer.

"My dad wouldn't let me go, even though Grandma Cookie and Grumpa wanted me to." She looked at her dad. I assume she was talking about Nick's parents.

"Is that so?" I didn't want to say the wrong thing here. I couldn't figure out whose side I was on—Nick's or Olivia's. "There were a lot of grownups. I didn't see anyone your age there," was all I could think of saying. Before Olivia could ask another question, three big dogs barged into the room, each heading in a different direction, their tails slapping against anything in their proximity. My mind flashed to the scene in *A Christmas Story* when the dogs knocked the turkey on the floor and wreaked havoc on Ralphie's house on Christmas day.

One of the dogs found the sandwich and scarfed it down before anyone could stop him. I watched, frozen, as Nick rounded up the dogs, yelling at them to get out and herding them toward the door.

"Does that happen very often?" I asked, still surprised.

"More than it should," said Nick. "Let's go find something to eat. I haven't had any breakfast or lunch." He started walking toward the door.

"I want to go to the lake cabin," said Olivia.

Nick stopped in his tracks and turned to face his daughter. "Olivia, it's just a bunch of Ryan's old high school friends. And no place for a child. You'll be bored."

"When have I been bored, Nick?" She had the same matter-of-fact tone her dad used. "I'll bring my sketchbook. I won't be in the way, and I'll go to bed early."

Nick sighed. "Fine. No more silent treatment and hunger strike?"

When she nodded, Nick hung his head and slumped his shoulders, looking for the answer he wanted to hear.

"Okay." There was a little sass in her reply. She was a formidable nine-year-old.

As Olivia negotiated with her dad, I looked around. Painted canvases, three or four deep, were propped up against the walls. There must have been close to a hundred spread around the room. I wondered if Olivia had painted all of them.

"Good, now put your shoes on. You know better than to run around without shoes." There was an edge to Nick's voice. Olivia headed to the corner of the room and pulled out a pair of mostly white tennis shoes from underneath a limp bag. She sat on the floor and put them on over her bare feet and then ran out the door in front of us. The three big dogs were waiting close by and ran behind Olivia as she sprinted toward the house.

"Thanks for talking to her. I think it was easier with you here." I nodded and offered a small smile. He must have known this was an odd exchange for me to be a part of. Why didn't Olivia know her uncle? I had other questions.

Nick's face softened. "Hey, would it be alright if we spent the night here? I know I said that we could go back tonight, but this way we can get an early start and reach the lake by mid-morning. We can then spend the day and head back to the city by early evening."

"Uh, sure." I wondered what Olivia would think. Would she be okay with this new plan? Another question I wasn't going to ask.

| SEVENTEEN |

Now that we weren't in a rush to leave, I mulled over the situation as we walked toward the main house. A soft breeze waged against the warm sun as we crossed the expansive green lawn at a leisurely pace. I no longer had to try and keep up with Nick's long strides. While I decided not to ask questions about Olivia, there was a question that did need an answer.

"Aren't your in-law's curious who I am? I also don't want to impose." I wondered if Nick often brought strange women to his in-laws' house.

"I'll explain it to them later. They won't mind if you stay." Nick's phone buzzed. He looked at the number but didn't answer, putting the phone back in his pocket.

When we reached the porch, Olivia and Sylvie were sitting in the Adirondack chairs and Olivia was scratching the belly of a capsized hound dog. As we all headed into the kitchen, Olivia asked Sylvie if she could have a cookie. Nick's phone buzzed again. This time he didn't look at the screen as he declined the call. The dogs greeted us, making sure we had nothing for them, and I gave some of them a pat as I watched Sylvie grab a bag of potatoes from the fridge.

Nick's phone buzzed for a third time. He shook his head and answered.

"Hello? Hold on, who is this?" He looked at me. "She's standing right next to me. Okay, just a second." He handed me his phone. My eyebrows furrowed as I put it up to my ear.

"Hello?"

Grace's voice was on the other end.

"Jane, is that you? Why aren't you answering your phone? I looked to see where you were, and you're nowhere near the cabin. Are you okay?" She was talking fast, her voice higher than normal.

I turned my back on Nick and Sylvie and walked out to the front porch and down the steps to the car. Opening the door, I saw my phone on my seat. I picked it up and looked at the screen. I had eighteen missed calls and even more texts. "We just made an unexpected stop. I'm fine. I accidentally left my phone in the car."

I could tell she was still upset. "When I called Brook to get Nick's number, she said that Nick had to make a detour. We should have a code word, so I know that you're not being held against your will."

"Grace, it's fine."

She ignored me. "I know. If you can't talk, say, 'Prince William.'"

I didn't respond. I had lost track of time, but I figured it was early afternoon. "Grace, shouldn't you be getting ready for your orientation?"

"I should be, but instead I've been calling you for the last half hour and worrying that Nick kidnapped you and you're chained up somewhere. It's not always the husband, you know."

"Now you don't have to worry about me anymore," I said. "How do you feel?"

"Better." She cleared her throat. "I'm really sorry about last night. I was so bummed about not getting the job that I literally drowned my sorrows. I know I said some stuff. I don't remember everything, but I promise it won't happen again."

"We do need to have a conversation about last night at some point. But just focus on this afternoon." I wandered from the house, into the front meadow. "I'll explain when I see you, but it looks like I won't be home until tomorrow. I'm at Nick's in-laws' house." I didn't want to say too much. Grace probably had questions but I didn't want to answer them.

I assured her that I was fine and agreed to tell her everything when I returned. I ended the call. The doubts about Grace resurfaced in my mind, but maybe that was an outlier, and she really did have my back. She did track me down when she saw I wasn't where I was supposed to be. I went back to the house, where Nick was making a sandwich.

"Grace was worried about you?" he asked, staring at me as he put a small slice of cheese in his mouth.

"I left my phone in the car and she couldn't get ahold of me." I handed his phone back. "She called Brook to get your number."

"I figured. Do you want something to eat?"

I could see a spread of sandwich fixings on the kitchen island behind him. "That sounds great." I understood that it was self-serve and I found an empty plate.

Olivia came down the stairs with her bags packed. "I'm ready to go." She had a big smile on her face.

"We're going to stay here tonight. We'll get up early tomorrow and head to the cabin," Nick said as he finished assembling his lunch.

She dropped her bags. "Why didn't you tell me that before?" She crossed her arms.

"You ran off before I could tell you. Jane and I are going to have something to eat." He looked at me, and Olivia's gaze followed.

"Jane, do you want to come out to the studio with me after you're done?"

"I would love to." But I wondered if there would be more questions.

Sylvie spoke up. "While you wait for Jane to finish eating, you can go feed the goats and the pigs."

"Can I have another cookie?" Olivia asked as she walked to the corner of the kitchen counter.

"Last one," Sylvie agreed. Olivia already had her hand in the jar. She took a bite and chewed while holding the cookie above her head as the dogs headed toward her. She skipped out the door, humming.

"I'm glad she's back to herself," said Sylvie as she continued to peel potatoes over the sink. Nick picked up his plate and headed to the front porch. I followed, sitting down in the chair where I sat less than an hour ago with Sylvie, drinking tea.

"Did Grace think you were in danger?"

"I let her track my phone and when she checked my location, she was concerned."

He raised his eyebrows, but didn't respond and we sat in silence while we ate. My eyes scanned the surrounding property, everything colored in varying hues of green. The air was fresh and smelled of cut grass. I watched as Olivia filled the water trough for the goats and started feeding them. After I finished my lunch, I sat back in my chair.

"Since you'll be hanging out with Olivia, I'm going to find Richard," said Nick. "Sylvie said a tree fell a few days ago, and all the wood needs to be brought back to the shed. I'm sure he could use some help."

"And they're okay with me staying here?"

"Sylvie offered before I even asked."

We both stood at the same time. Nick took my plate into the kitchen. Olivia had finished feeding the goats and was heading toward her studio. I took a deep breath of the crisp air and made my way across the green grass.

One of the glass doors was open and I stepped into the sunlit room. My eyes darted over the paintings that were in every corner. Olivia was standing in front of the easel by the door.

"Is this one of the dogs that lives on the farm?" I asked as I walked over to her.

"It's Buzzy. He died a few weeks ago."

I remembered the wall of dog paintings in the farmhouse. A photo of the yellow lab sat on the easel. It matched the painting, except Olivia had captured something that the photo didn't. It was the eyes. Buzzy looked like a happy dog, and I couldn't help but smile at his face, his long tongue hanging from his mouth of white teeth.

"It's amazing, Olivia. Did you paint all of these?" I glanced around the room again.

"Yes. I started painting when I was six." Her gaze followed mine. "I only like to paint here. I have a sketchbook too." She picked up a brush and casually said, "When you were talking on the phone, my dad said that I shouldn't ask you a lot of questions. He said it would be rude."

I moved around the room and now faced the far wall of windows as I continued my study of Olivia's work. I wanted to tell her that I had a lot of questions myself, but I couldn't ask Nick's daughter to fill in the details her dad wouldn't share. "I think it's normal to be curious about a person you've just met." I stopped and picked up a painting that was leaning up against the wall to expose another painting. Setting the first one down, I picked up the newly discovered one.

It was of a young woman wearing a print dress sitting on a wooden bench in a park. Unlike Olivia's other paintings, it was done in watercolor. It had a simple wood frame with a wide mat around the painting. The woman was looking down with her hands in her lap. It reminded me of my mother. Olivia noticed that I was staring at it.

"I painted that when I was seven."

"Do you mind if I take a picture of it with my phone?"

"You can have it if you like it."

Surprised at her offer, I asked, "Are you sure, Olivia?"

"I want you to have it."

"Thank you. I love it. I know just where to hang it in my house." I continued to stare at it in my hands. "Why do you think she's sad?"

Olivia's eyes narrowed, her eyebrows drawing closer together. "She's not sad. She's praying."

Now I saw the painting in a different way, and I felt tears well up as I thought of my mom. "Of course she is," I said to myself as much as to Olivia. I blinked my eyes so the tears wouldn't spill over.

"Sometimes my Grandma Cookie takes me to church, but my dad doesn't go. She said I can pray anywhere though."

Nick had mentioned by the pool that he went to church as a kid, and I remembered his eulogy where he mentioned that he and Ryan went to grade school at Saint Mark's.

"That's true. Sometimes I go to church when it's empty and pray, especially if something is bothering me."

I continued to wander the room, perusing the artwork and talking to Olivia about painting. She decided she wanted to finish her portrait of Buzzy before we left tomorrow. As she added more details to the painting, I watched.

"How did you learn to paint?"

"Grammy. She paints too. She showed me. She said that I paint better than her and that I have a gift."

She sounded matter-of-fact, not boastful.

"I think your Grammy is right."

"My Grandma Cookie said it's a gift from God," she said. I didn't say anything, but I thought her grandma was right too.

We spent a couple of hours in Olivia's studio before we walked back to the house. She finished her painting of Buzzy and then showed me some of her other favorite paintings. We talked about the other animals on the farm besides the dogs and she told me about catching frogs in the pond. Before we left, she wrapped the painting she gave me in brown paper and tied it with string.

As we walked across the field toward the farmhouse, I held her gift against my chest. I could see Nick on the porch, watching us.

| EIGHTEEN |

Olivia and I climbed the steps to Nick. He didn't acknowledge the wrapped package I was holding but his forehead wrinkled as he looked at me. I had to drop my gaze to my arms, unable to hold his. He turned his attention to Olivia.

"Pop-Pop is washing up. Supper will be ready in a little bit. You go wash up too." She opened the screen door and ran toward the bathroom.

"Is the car still open?" I asked. Nick pulled out a key fob from his pocket and pushed the button to confirm the door was unlocked. I put the painting in the back seat and then returned to the porch. "Make sure you lock it," I said as I walked past him to open the screen door.

I was introduced to Richard, a tall, thin man with graying hair at the temples and a firm handshake. After I offered to help, Sylvie put me to work cutting up watermelon and cantaloupe while she finished putting together the potato salad. Then we gathered around the faded wooden picnic table underneath the pergola on the opposite side of the house, with a view of the pond and enjoyed a delicious summer meal.

Afterward, Olivia suggested a walk. It was a picture-perfect evening. Or a painting-perfect evening, as I remembered several of Olivia's paintings of the pond, with the perimeter of trees framing the entire clearing. As we started down the well-worn path, the tall grass on either side swayed in the gentle breeze. We went from full sunshine to filtered sunlight as we entered the woods. It was noticeably cooler as we stepped over fallen branches and brush.

I heard thunder and turned to see the pack of dogs running down the path toward us. Most ran by, but a few caught a scent of an animal and stopped to sniff the trunks of trees or the surrounding undergrowth. Four or five dogs surrounded Olivia as she stretched out her open hands to pet them as they clung by her side. She talked to them in a low tone.

Once we circled the property and the sun had set but the stars were still hidden, Richard piled wood on top of the blackened embers of a previous fire and lit a match. The breeze had left with the sun, so the smoke rose straight into the air. We settled in the surrounding chairs, watching the dancing flames. Sylvie brought out some thick blankets that she deposited in an empty chair, anticipating the cooler evening air.

After Sylvie refused my offer to help, insisting that I stay put, she went back to the house to gather the ingredients for s'mores. As I sat back in the chair, I fought the urge to close my eyes. I didn't know if it was the fresh air or that I didn't get much sleep the night before but suddenly I felt my entire body sink into the cushioned seat and my eyes closed. Olivia's laughing made me open them and sit up. She was throwing a ball with her dad, but the dogs wanted to play too. I could feel the smile on my face grow as I watched the silhouetted figures. My mind wandered to earlier and my initial encounter with Olivia in her studio. As I wondered why Nick kept his brother from his daughter, my smile faded. There must have been opportunities for them to spend time together even though Ryan had moved away from his family. From my own past, I understood that family dynamics could be complicated. Any scenario I imagined explaining the lack of familial bond between Olivia and Ryan probably would be much more drama filled than the actual truth. Still…

They continued with their game of catch until there was no longer enough light to see and one of the dogs—Toby, I think—carried the ball away, officially ending the game. As they walked toward me, I sat up taller in my seat, confident that no one had seen me napping.

We gathered around the fire with sticks in hand, toasting marshmallows then assembling the s'mores. It tasted like summer. Marshmallow dripped on my chin and Olivia laughed at my messy face. I couldn't read Nick's expression, but he stared at me until I had to look away.

Richard opted not to put another log on the fire and Nick decided to call it a night.

"All right, Olivia. Go get ready for bed, and I'll be up in a minute to read a few pages." Nick stood poking the fire with a stick to get a few more flames to rise above the burnt log of the dying fire.

"Can Jane listen too?"

"If she wants to." His gaze was fixated on the glowing embers.

I hesitated, not knowing the proper protocol for this situation. I decided not to worry about it. "I would love to," I said. It would be nice to be read to instead of doing the reading.

Sylvie and Richard gathered the s'more fixings and blankets and walked back to the house with Olivia. Nick and I were alone in front of the fire.

"How long is it to the cabin from here?" I asked, thinking about tomorrow even though I was enjoying the evening.

"Around three hours, depending on traffic." Nick sat, leaning the stick next to his chair. "Sylvie will insist on making breakfast. We'll try and leave by nine or ten." Nick noticed my attempt to stifle a yawn. "You didn't get much sleep last night. You must be tired."

"I did have that nap in the car today." The blackened log snapped in half from the heat of the fire. Embers from the shifted wood rose up and quickly fell. "This has been a really nice day. It's so peaceful here, and what a beautiful night. You can see all the stars," I said as I looked at the sky. "The air just smells different here."

"It's Olivia's favorite place," said Nick. "She spends a lot of time here in the summer."

The light from the fire was enough for me to make out Olivia's studio and some of the larger trees that stood alone in the open clearing.

"Her paintings are incredible. She really is gifted. I hope you don't mind but she gave me one."

"They're her paintings. I was surprised though. She must like you." Before I could say anything, Nick stood again. "She's probably wondering where we are." I rose slowly from my chair, and we walked back to the house, stopping at the car to grab our bags. The frogs calling from the pond filled the night air.

We climbed the set of stairs beyond the kitchen and dining area, which led to a large loft. Olivia, sitting in the middle of the queen-sized bed, was reading a book with several stuffed animals surrounding her. Two dogs were lying on the hardwood floor. As I scanned the room, my eyes lingered on the white, wooden bookshelf crowded with books and knick-knacks but no framed photographs. I looked to the high ceiling, where a chandelier light fixture hung above the bed. An oversized chair sat in the corner with a blanket thrown over the back and a pillow propped to one side.

"Teeth brushed?" Nick asked.

She opened her mouth. "Yep."

"All right." Nick sat on the side of the bed and I sat in the comfy chair, even though I was concerned I might fall asleep again. He picked up the book, turned to the bookmarked page, and started to read. I immediately recognized the words from *Little Women.* One of my favorite books. Nick's voice, measured and calm, made it hard to keep my eyes open.

"Jane." I felt his hand on my shoulder.

I sat up a little embarrassed. "Sorry."

Olivia was trying not to laugh. "It's past her bedtime too, Dad."

"I guess so." He sat back on the corner of the bed. The book was now on Olivia's nightstand.

"It's true. I can't keep my eyes open." I stood. "Thank you for showing me your paintings today, Olivia. And I love the one you gave me. Thank you again."

"You're welcome." She turned to her dad. "You won't leave without me, will you?"

"I promise we won't." He leaned over and gave her a kiss on the forehead. "Good night. Love you."

"Good night. Love you. Good night, Jane."

I felt uncomfortable witnessing this exchange and maybe also a little jealous. I said good night to Olivia and headed down the stairs.

As I walked toward the kitchen, I saw Sylvie in the enclosed sunroom at the other end of the house. She was setting up a place for us to sleep.

"I'm sorry we don't have better accommodations. We just have the two bedrooms. Olivia has taken over the little house, which used to be for guests." She gestured to the two couches, one on each wall beneath large windows. I noticed two side tables crowded with plants and a framed photo of Olivia when she was much younger sitting on a stump holding a tulip. "There are fresh blankets and pillows. I hope the dogs won't jump up and try to sleep with you, but I can't guarantee it. You can push them off if they do."

"This is great, Sylvie, and thank you for everything today." I didn't mention that I slept on a lounge chair last night and anything would be an improvement. After Sylvie left, I headed to the bathroom to brush my teeth. I was glad I packed my light sweatpants, which I threw on with a T-shirt. I knew that Nick would occupy the other couch in the room.

He was in the kitchen when I emerged from the bathroom. I said good night and crawled into the makeshift bed, asleep when my head hit the pillow.

///

Richard was long gone when we sat down for pancakes, sausage, and eggs the next morning. Two home-cooked meals in a row were something I hadn't experienced in a while. Olivia was anxious to leave, so we didn't linger after we helped with the breakfast dishes. We packed up the car and were on our way a little after nine.

This ride was different than the previous one with Nick. There were no long stretches of silence. Olivia carried most of the conversation, and we played a few games as we drove. We bought some snacks at the gas station when Nick pulled in to top off his tank. I was still full from breakfast, but we picked up candy bars, chips, and some bottled water for later.

We eventually turned onto a concrete road with a faded yellow line down the middle. We traveled another few miles and then turned off onto a narrow road. Nick slowed down to avoid bringing up dust and gravel. After we made several more turns, we ended up in front of a large two-story house, parking next to a familiar car with the lake in the distance.

"This is the cabin, huh? It's bigger than my house." I said. There were more windows than walls and there was a dark wood-stained wraparound deck.

Nick ignored my comment. "We'll get our stuff later. Let's go see who's here and what everyone is doing."

Olivia was the first one out of the car. She ran to the house and tried the door but found it locked. She turned to watch us and then immediately turned back to the house, cupping her hands to look through the wide window to see if anyone was inside.

When we walked in, there was a large front room with a giant stone fireplace that cut through the center of the space. To the right was a galley kitchen with a sliding glass door out to the deck. As I walked behind the fireplace, I saw a hallway next to a set of stairs.

"Can I sleep upstairs?" Olivia asked.

Nick didn't answer her question. He still hadn't told her that we weren't staying. "I wonder where everyone is." He pulled out his phone and began texting.

As I walked around to examine the large room, I lost track of Olivia. Eventually, I made my way back to the fireplace and studied the framed photos on the wooden mantel. I recognized Nick and Ryan, although they must have been teenagers in most of them.

Nick's voice from behind me made me jump.

"Sorry. Brook and Jason went to the store to get stuff for dinner tonight. She said everyone else went over to Arrowhead Point, which is a little cove at the far end of the lake. They won't be back for a while." Olivia appeared at her father's side.

"Can we go down to the lake now?" She had a sketchbook in her hand.

Nick looked around. He walked down the hallway and opened several doors. He walked back to the front of the fireplace.

"Yeah, let's walk down to the lake."

Olivia ran ahead of us. The crunch of the gravel beneath our feet filled the air as we leisurely walked down toward the water.

"When was the last time you were here?" I asked.

"Olivia and I came up for a few days in March. Sometimes my mother will bring her up for a long weekend or when Olivia has a break from school.

"I pictured something a little more rustic," I said, looking around at the lake and the trees. In the distance you could see other so-called cabins, all on large lots.

"Most of the houses were built in the sixties. Ours, a little before that. I spent a lot of summers up here."

Summers full of memories, I imagined. Maybe that's why he was reluctant to go on this trip.

We finally caught up to Olivia at the end of the dock. She was sitting cross-legged with her head down sketching in her book, the water slapping against the wood structure. As I looked out across the lake, I noticed there were very few people around. Nick must have noticed the same thing.

"Twenty years ago, people only came up here on the weekends. Now, most people live here year-round, a lot of them retired." He glanced behind him. "There are paddleboards and a canoe. It looks like they took the boat to go to Arrowhead Point." He looked down at Olivia. "What do you want to do first?"

She didn't answer right away. She was busy shading in the neighbor's dock. "Let's go in the canoe first. We can paddle by the shore around the lake, and I can look for a bald eagle." She didn't look up from her drawing.

Nick looked at me. I shrugged my shoulders. "Jane and I will grab the canoe, so be ready when we bring it down to the dock."

Nick and I went back toward the house veering down a path to a small shed. The door was unlocked. We threw in three life preservers and the oars, and each grabbed an end of the sturdy canoe, heading back down toward Olivia.

As we turned on the main path to the dock, we heard the sound of an engine. I recognized Brook and Jason's truck pulling in next to Nick's car. We set everything down and walked toward them as they grabbed grocery bags from the back seat. They waved and waited when they saw us.

"We didn't know what to get, so we just bought one of everything," said Brook as we drew closer.

"Dibs on the lobster," said Nick.

His comment surprised me. I didn't think he had much of a sense of humor. When we reached the car, Jason was holding two bags and mentioned he had ice cream in one of them. He excused himself, walking toward the house.

"We're going to put everything away and then drive up to Arrowhead Point to meet up with everyone," Brook said. "We'll be back around five or six to start dinner, if you want to join us."

"My daughter is with us. We picked her up at her grandparents'. We're going to spend some time on the lake and then head back to Seattle tonight."

Brook shifted the bag in her arms. "Is it still okay if we stay for the weekend?" She seemed concerned that Nick was leaving and what that would mean for them.

"Sure, but will you make sure everything is cleaned up and put away when you leave? I'm not sure when I'll get back up here."

"Definitely. Thank you." Her face relaxed.

"My mom was touched that you all wanted to come up here and share stories of Ryan. I hope you can do that. It will make her happy," said Nick. He didn't seem upset missing out on commemorating his brother's life. Even before we picked up Olivia, he planned on leaving before the weekend was over. Celebrating a friend's life might be different than celebrating a brother's. I imagined it was more personal and the feelings ran deeper for Nick. I could see why he didn't want to stay.

"I bought his favorite beer," said Brook. Jason had returned from the cabin and was at Brook's side, taking the bag from her.

"Make a toast for me," said Nick. "And have a good time."

Back at the dock, we launched the canoe with Olivia perched on the middle seat. After a few minutes, Nick and I fell into a rhythm, and as Olivia suggested, we stuck close to the shore. Much of the ride was in silence, except for the slap of the oars as they pulled through the water. My eyes wandered to the surrounding beauty of the lake and to Olivia as she captured it on her sketch pad.

After a couple of hours, we headed back to the dock. My arms were tired, and we were all hungry. Nick and I put the canoe next to the shed and headed back to the cabin. We found the ice cream bars in the freezer and sat on the deck eating them fast before they melted down our hands. Nick gathered the wrappers, walking back inside to throw them away. He still hadn't told his daughter that we would be leaving soon.

Olivia, barefoot after her tennis shoes got wet, went to retrieve her sketchbook, which she had accidentally left by the boat shed. I watched her walk down the path, staying close to the edge to avoid the sharp gravel. I found myself alone for the first time in over twenty-four hours. I had been ignoring my phone for most of the day, but it vibrated, so I pulled it out. I had fourteen new texts—mostly from Grace, but Sarah and Jeanne were in the mix, along with others. I put my phone back in my pocket.

A high-pitched scream pierced the air. It was Olivia. Nick flew out of the sliding door, running past me. I ran after him, my heart pounding. Olivia was sitting on the ground a few feet from the shed, holding her leg with one hand and waving the other hand in the air. As I drew closer, I could see bees swarming near her. Nick picked her up as I reached them. He yelled at me, "She's allergic. There's an EpiPen in the glove box of the car."

As I ran, I could hear Nick's heavy footsteps and Olivia's soft sobs behind me. Nothing happened when I reached the car and pulled at the door. Praying under my breath, I desperately tried the back passenger side door, moving to the back driver's side door when it wouldn't open. I ran back to the front, passenger side. Then I heard the chirp from the car key fob as I tugged at the door again. Almost losing my balance as the door flew open, I steadied myself and tore open the glove box to search for the EpiPen. It wasn't there.

Turning around, I found Nick holding Olivia in his arms. He was breathing heavily, but he set her on the ground gently. Conscious, Olivia's face was tear-stained, and I could see the ugly red welts growing on her legs and arms from the stings.

"I can't find it." My voice was higher than normal. I moved out of the way so Nick could look.

"Dammit! Where is it?" He pulled everything out, throwing the contents on the floor, frantically searching for the pen.

"You gave it to Grandma Cookie." Olivia's voice was small as she tried to lift her head.

He closed his eyes for a second, hanging his head, and then he lightly picked up Olivia and moved toward the back seat of the car. I jumped over and opened the door.

"We need to get her to the hospital." His breathing had slowed.

Running around to the other side of the car, I slid into the back seat as Nick laid her down. I lifted her head so it was resting on my lap, and I grabbed the seat belt Nick was holding. After several attempts, my hands shaking, I was able to buckle it underneath her upper body.

Once we pulled out onto the concrete road, I looked up and I saw Nick looking at Olivia in the rearview mirror. Our eyes met.

"How is she?" He looked back at the road.

I could only imagine the worry he must be feeling even though he seemed in control. Looking down at her small frame, her eyes closed, I noticed the tempo of her breathing was uneven. Her skin felt clammy as I rubbed her arm. I was trying to control the panic rising in my chest. I couldn't answer Nick's question.

"Olivia, it's going to be fine. How are you doing?" I asked, pushing down the fear while I brushed her hair off her face. Feeling the sudden acceleration of the car, I glanced up at the road as we passed a large truck.

"I'm dizzy and it hurts." Her voice cracked and she winced in pain as she tried to shift her body. The redness around the stings was spreading and her pulse was racing.

"We'll be at the hospital soon, Olivia. You're so brave," I said, looking up to meet Nick's distraught gaze.

With one hand, I opened my phone and typed *bee stings*, thinking it was the easiest thing to spell with my thumb. Even though I spelled *sting* wrong, the sponsored content was about bee allergies. I scrolled past common and moderate bee sting symptoms to severe allergic reactions. Trouble breathing, hives or swelling, tightness of the throat, hoarse voice, dizziness, rapid heart rate, and cardiac arrest. As I scrolled further, it said not to lay your head on a pillow as it could obstruct the airway. I quickly put my phone down on the seat and lifted Olivia's head off my lap, knocking my phone to the floor.

"She should be lying flat." I could tell Nick was startled by my movements in the back of the car as I scooted directly behind his seat, still rubbing Olivia's arm.

Casting my eyes to the floor to see where my phone fell, I saw Olivia's painting wrapped in brown paper. The woman on the bench praying. As the Hail Mary rattled in my head, I turned my attention back to Olivia.

I watched as her arm swung toward the floor of the car, and suddenly her body went limp.

| NINETEEN |

The sun was setting as I pulled into a compact spot in the crowded emergency room parking lot. I grabbed my bag and phone and hurried toward the entrance. Nick had stopped in front of the emergency room doors, leaving the car running as he rushed Olivia into the hospital. As I passed through the sliding doors a few minutes later, I didn't see them in the waiting room and assumed they immediately took Olivia back to be treated. A weak nod was all I could muster when the woman behind the counter acknowledged my presence.

To the right was the waiting area and I fell hard into the cushioned seat of one of the metal chairs. I leaned forward, holding my head in my hands, and took a few deep breaths while I stared at the worn linoleum floor. She had to be okay. I felt like I was going to throw up. Following the sign on the wall, I found the restrooms. Once inside, I went into the first open stall. My stomach seemed to settle, and I leaned against the cold wall. I stayed like that for a few minutes and then walked to the sink to wash my hands.

When I returned to the waiting area, I saw it was full of people and must have been so when I first walked in.

Sitting next to the window, I stared out, my gaze unfixed. Was she okay? The panic I felt when she lost consciousness was unbearable and I didn't want to dwell on it, worried that it would overwhelm me. I was sure the first thing they did was administer an EpiPen, which should control her symptoms. If I just knew she was okay… I walked up to the woman at the desk.

"I know you can't give me any information about a patient, but can you just let me know if she's being treated? Her dad just brought her in a little bit ago. Her name is Olivia Edwards." I was on the verge of tears, and the woman looked sympathetic.

"You're right, I can't give out information about a patient. Are you a relative?"

I had known this child for a little more than a day.

"No, I'm not. Just a friend." My face fell knowing that she couldn't tell me anything. I understood client confidentiality.

"Just wait one minute," she said, and she went through the swinging doors to the left of her desk. It was longer than a minute, and the receding fear quickly ticked up a notch.

She smiled as she returned and sat at her desk. "It's okay. Why don't you take a seat, and I'm sure you'll hear something soon." I thanked her and walked back to the waiting area, knowing that Olivia was in the right place and receiving the treatment she needed. I let my shoulders relax as I sat in a chair for the third time. Opening my bag, I saw the water and chips I bought when Nick stopped for gas this morning. Realizing that my mouth was bone-dry, I opened the bottle of water. Then I pulled out my phone.

Nick needed to concentrate on Olivia and not worry about me getting home after being abandoned by a friend. I was in the way, no longer a diversion on a painful weekend to remember his late brother. Nick would probably take Olivia back to the farm rather than drive all the way back to Seattle.

I needed to find a way home. Maybe Grace would come and get me. Or I could call Daniel. Maybe I could find an Uber and I could meet him somewhere halfway. That might work.

I realized that I didn't have Nick's number to text him my plans once I figured out my way home. The woman at the reception desk could give him a message if it came to that. I pulled up my contacts and called Daniel.

He insisted on coming to get me at the hospital. It was close to seven when I reached him, and he said he would be there around ten. I didn't know how I was going to spend close to three hours in the waiting area of the emergency room without going a little crazy.

I rummaged through my bag and found my book. I tried to concentrate on the words but eventually gave up. There was still no update from Nick. I wasn't sure what was taking so long. Maybe I misunderstood the nurse's smile. My phone pinged and I glanced at the screen.

Todd: How's Hawaii? I hope you're sitting by the side of the pool.

I read the words, trying to process the question and juxtaposing sitting by the pool in Hawaii and sitting in an emergency room in the middle of nowhere. My date with Todd—that seemed like a million years ago.

I stared at my phone and then thought I could use the distraction.

Me: Long story but I didn't go. I'm sitting in an emergency room. A friend's daughter had an allergic reaction. Another long story

Todd: Not the response I was expecting. My mom said that Daniel went to Hawaii for a few days but I thought you were there too.

Me: Yeah, some sand, sun, and a drink sound good right about now. What are you doing?

We texted back and forth, mostly about him house-sitting for his boss, who lived near Bill Gates. It was a nice diversion from the present situation.

I started to type a response to Todd's question when out of the corner of my eye I saw someone walking toward me. It was Nick. I put my phone down.

As he faced me, I stood and the space between us narrowed. I saw the worry still lingered in his eyes. His hair was askew, as if he had been running his hands through it constantly. For some reason, the memory of him holding me up when I ran into him at the funeral flashed in my head.

"They want to keep her for the night to make sure she doesn't have another reaction. She was stung multiple times. She's also dehydrated, so they're giving her fluids. They put her in a room and she's sleeping."

We both started to talk at the same time. He stopped and I continued. "I'm glad they're keeping her overnight. I've called a friend, and he's coming to pick me up. He should be here soon. You should go be with Olivia."

He flashed a weak smile and his shoulders relaxed. "This weekend has been a disaster. I knew it would be. I just didn't think it would be this bad. You were a bright spot. Thanks for being so kind to Olivia. I don't know what I would have done without you tonight."

He hesitated, and I wondered if he wanted to hug me or something, but I just stood there. I realized I still had his car key. I pulled it from my pocket.

"Here. You'll need this." As he took it from me, his hand brushed mine. My phone started to ring, startling us both. It was Daniel. He must be here.

He stepped back from me. "I'll let you get that. Thanks again, Jane."

He turned and I watched him walk down the hallway. I answered the phone, my mind still on Nick, and I wondered if I would ever see him and Olivia again.

The emergency room doors opened into the dark night. Daniel was waiting by the curb. As I slumped into the seat, I tossed my bag in the back and felt his eyes on me. He drove through the parking lot and turned out onto the street.

"Do you want to talk about it?" He was looking forward, paying attention to the road.

"No." I leaned my head against the window and closed my eyes.

| TWENTY |

I had to remind myself what day it was as I slowly rolled out of bed and made my way to the bathroom.

The hot water eased some of the aches from sleeping on a lawn chair and a saggy couch the last two nights. After throwing on some jeans and a T-shirt, I wrapped a towel around my wet hair and walked into the kitchen. I glanced at the microwave clock and realized I missed twelve o'clock Mass. There was a late Mass at the Newman Center at UW. Opening the fridge, I grabbed a Coke and found a pizza box at eye level. There were three pieces left. I took a bite out of one and put another in the microwave.

My mind went back to the weekend. Olivia's cold skin and rapid pulse and Nick's worried eyes flashed through my mind. And then I thought about the firepit with s'mores and the bedtime story. I wished I had Nick's number, but then I realized I knew someone who did. I walked toward Grace's room while chewing on another bite of cold pizza. I listened at her closed door, but I didn't hear anything.

As I turned to head back to the kitchen, the front door opened, and Grace walked in with two bags from Trader Joe's.

"You're up." She walked into the kitchen, placed the bags on the island and started unpacking the contents. "How are you?" she said. Her back was to me.

I did a quick assessment before I answered. "I'm fine," I said and meant it. "How's the new job?" I asked before she could ask me another question.

"I think it will be good. Everyone seems cool." She opened the refrigerator to put a carton of oat milk away.

I pulled the warmed pizza out of the microwave and was going to take another bite but stopped. "Am I eating your pizza? There's still another slice in the box. I was just so hungry and it was the first thing I saw in the fridge."

"I picked it up on Friday after orientation. It's all yours."

Grace seemed to cast her eyes everywhere but on me. There was an odd silence. I took another bite of pizza as I watched her moving around the kitchen. When she was done putting everything away, she turned around to look at me. "Are we okay? I mean, after my performance at the bar, followed by barf-o-rama at the motel, and then leaving you with a complete stranger?"

So much had happened after Grace left with Celeste that I had pushed that day out of my mind. I knew she felt bad leaving me behind.

I swallowed the bite of pizza. "We're good. I mean, I hope it never happens again," I said putting my plate down. "The first part of your explanation to Celeste as to why I was there was a little crazy, but it was the second part, the part where you told everyone about Mitchell, that threw me. Just what did Henry tell you?"

"There wasn't a lot of detail. I remember asking him how much of a homebody you were. If you dated or had a relationship. He said you weren't on social media at all, which is strange for someone in their twenties. Then he told me that you had a serious boyfriend in high school and that he basically lived with you."

"You wanted to make sure I wasn't a Bible-thumping Jesus freak, and after hearing that I had a serious boyfriend, you figured that I must be okay?"

"I asked him about the slob thing too," Grace said with a smile.

It bothered me that Henry had shared my dating history with Grace. I wondered now though how much his drinking had played a part. And Grace probably wouldn't have shared that information with the table if she had been sober.

"I promise I will never share any details about your life with anyone ever again."

"Thanks. I appreciate that."

"So now that that's out of the way, when are you going to tell me what happened after I left on Friday? I couldn't get anything out of Daniel last night after he came back from picking you up," she added.

"I thought you had Saturday off?" I tried to delay the inevitable.

"I picked up a shift and then Daniel asked me to stay until he came back in case Marcus needed any help closing the bar. Now spill." She put her hands on her hips.

I guess I couldn't ask her for Nick's number without giving her some details. I sighed. "I'm still trying to process it." I put my plate in the sink before I faced her again. I gave her a SparkNotes version of the weekend. When I mentioned Olivia's studio full of her paintings, I suddenly remembered I had left the one she gave me in the back of Nick's car. I sped through the rest of my story.

"Huh, I never knew Nick had a daughter. But she's okay?"

"I assume she'll be discharged today, but I have no way of knowing because I don't have Nick's number. But you do."

"I just have one more question. Where did you sleep at Nick's in-laws' place?"

I frowned. "We each slept on a couch in their sunroom. I think a lab-mix tried to spoon me." I could tell Grace wanted to ask more questions about me and Nick, but I didn't want to answer.

"How was your ride home with Celeste? Did she mention anything about the singer? Is she going to see him again?" I sounded petty and regretted the questions but let them stand. Grace grabbed a glass of water.

"No, but she did sort of offer an apology. She said the weekend brought up a lot of memories, and in hindsight, she wished she would have stayed home. We basically talked about all the shit that happened in high school. A lot of it I had forgotten. She did tell me this disturbing story about Ryan."

Unsure that I wanted to hear the story, I didn't say anything.

"You can decide for yourself. On the ride home, she starts to spill about Ryan and stuff he did in high school that I don't remember. I guess he was almost suspended for shoving his junk in an athletic trainer's face while she was sitting down at her desk. He denied it happened when she reported it to the school. Nick was in the room, but he said he didn't see what happened. In the end, Ryan was benched for a few football games and the trainer ended up leaving the school."

"That sounds like a story the whole school would have heard if it was true, or even if it wasn't." I remembered how gossip ran rampant through my high school.

"Well, I don't remember hearing about it, and she didn't know if any of it was true. I guess it doesn't even matter now. It's not like Ryan can defend himself."

I thought about Nick and our conversation by the pool. He didn't want to talk about his brother, and it seemed like he didn't want to do anything that reminded him of Ryan. And Olivia didn't have a relationship with her uncle. Who was Ryan?

"I'll send you Nick's number," Grace offered, pulling out her phone to send me his contact information. As I looked at Grace's text with Nick's phone number, I saw Todd's last message and realized I owed him an explanation about why I stopped texting. I decided to leave that problem for later. I walked into the big room and sank into the couch. Of course, I wanted to know how Olivia was doing, so I started with that.

Me: Grace gave me your number. I hope you don't mind. How is Olivia?

I sent the text and then stared at my phone hoping to see him typing a response. I waited a little longer then distracted myself by straightening my room. I started some laundry and busied myself with other household chores. An hour later, there was still no response. I sat at the table and stared at the text I sent Nick.

I decided to text Todd.

Me: Sorry about last night

I couldn't figure out how to explain why I abruptly stopped responding. My thumbs hovered over my phone and I finally typed:

It was a crazy weekend

An understatement. I sent the text and waited a few minutes. Nothing.

I spent the rest of the day cleaning and running errands. As I was scooping out Prince's litter box, I thought of Henry. It was kind of fitting. With the distraction of the last few days, I hadn't had time to dwell on our fight. I looked at the calendar on my phone. He'll be back on Tuesday. Daniel and I didn't talk about Hawaii when he gave me a ride home. I should talk to him, but I looked at the clock and saw that I needed to get ready for church.

I had a late dinner of microwaved mac n' cheese. As I spooned the hot, cheesy goo into my mouth, I wondered why Nick hadn't texted me back. I tried not to overthink it, but it was hard not to. And I wondered if Todd was upset that I abruptly stopped texting him on Saturday night. Both were things I had no control over now. I decided to wait to reach out to Daniel. Maybe I'd have lunch at the bar tomorrow so we could catch up. I found the LSAT book and sat on my bed. If I was going to take the test, I should probably take it in August instead of October, which didn't give me much time.

After an hour, I put the book down and turned off my light. I had trouble falling asleep, and had weird dreams, so I wasn't surprised that I didn't wake up until nine-thirty the next morning. Grace had left for work. Her first official day at her new job. I should have been up earlier to wish her luck. I pulled out my phone and sent her a text. After a quick shower, I made some tea and began foraging for something to eat. My phone pinged. I thought it was Grace, so I was surprised when I saw a text from Nick.

Nick: Sorry I didn't respond earlier. Olivia wasn't discharged until late afternoon. She's doing fine. She wants to see you and give you your painting. I have the week off, so our schedule is wide open.

I could feel a smile spread across my face and without thinking about it, I typed out a reply.

Me: Do you and Olivia want to come over for dinner tonight?

I hope I didn't sound desperate. Nick didn't respond right away and then finally:

Nick: That would be nice. Olivia is still recovering so we won't stay long.

We texted a few more times to work out the details. And then I panicked. What should I make? I instantly regretted the dinner invitation. Henry and I would take turns cooking when it was only the two of us. He was the more adventurous cook. The forecast was projecting a warm day, close to eighty degrees. I briefly thought we could eat outside but decided against it. Bees.

If I couldn't come up with anything to make, we could always order out. I never said anything about me making dinner. Maybe I would make a good lawyer. I thought of Maxine. She texted me earlier and I never responded. I was too preoccupied with the events of the last few days.

I scrolled through my messages to find the one from her. And that's when I saw it. A text from Henry when we were at Olivia's grandparents. It was before one of Grace's twenty texts and was just four words long: "Jane, I'm so sorry." My heart sank because I had missed it. There was so much to say and I couldn't do it by text. He'll be home tomorrow.

Did Daniel know that Henry had apologized? Looking at the clock, I decided I had time to go to the Straight & Narrow to find out. This was a conversation I wanted to have in person. Grabbing my keys and purse, I headed out the door.

There was a back entrance into the bar. I parked a little haphazardly and snuck into the building behind two people who must work there but I didn't recognize. I had come in this way only a few times before. It was basically the kitchen, and I walked quickly toward Daniel's office.

I tapped lightly on the open door. He was alone and bent over his desk reading something. He swiveled around in his chair and his face brightened when he saw me.

"Jane." He stood and hugged me. He pulled back after the embrace and looked at me. "You look good," he said.

At least better than the last time he saw me. "I'm good. Thanks again for coming to get me," I said.

"You can call me anytime."

"You still have some color from Hawaii. It suits you."

"I could get used to island life. It's probably why I don't take vacations. But it was a nice getaway, even if it was short. Henry and I had a chance to talk and work some things out." He paused. "He misses you, Jane."

"He sent me a text on Friday and I just saw it today, like an hour ago. He apologized and now I don't know what to do. Actually, as I was driving over here, I thought maybe I should pick him up from the airport tomorrow. Surprise him. What do you think?" I stared at him to see if I could recognize any facial expression that would indicate that he didn't think it was a good idea. He took his time answering.

"You know, I can't think of a reason why not. He's expecting me though."

He gestured to the chair next to his desk and we both sat.

"I know he would be happy to see you. He feels bad about how he acted and I think guilty about going without you. He knows that he's been drinking too much too."

I suddenly wondered if this constituted talking about Henry behind his back and I shifted in my seat.

"Moving in with me was a bigger deal than he realized," said Daniel. "And what it might lead to down the road. He panicked."

"It's hard not having him around. Grace has filled some of the void."

"So, that's working out?"

"Yeah, I think so. I mean it's only been a few weeks," I said, reflecting. "She did drag me to a funeral and then emotionally blackmailed me to go with her on a bizarre weekend trip where she embarrassed and abandoned me, but other than that." When I said it out loud to someone else, it sounded terrible.

"She told me. About the embarrassing and abandoning. She was worried you were going to kick her out. I said she could sleep on my couch until she found another place. But she likes living with you."

There was a knock. A woman peeked her head through the semi-opened door. "Someone wants to bring twenty or so people in for lunch today."

"Yeah, that should work. Just move the tables on the far wall across from the bar."

"Got it," said the woman.

"It sounds like you're going to have a busy Monday. I'll let you get back to work. I assume Henry hasn't changed his flight or anything?" I asked.

"No, it's the same. I think he'll be happy to see you, Jane."

"It'll be good," I said, trying to convince myself this was the right thing to do.

"I almost forgot. I have something for you." He opened the middle drawer of his desk, grabbed an envelope and handed it to me.

"What's this?" I opened the flap of the unsealed envelope and pulled out a small stack of cash.

"It's to reimburse you for the plane ticket you didn't get to use."

"You don't need to do that. It was my fault that I didn't try to get a refund."

"Well, I know you had other things on your mind. Please take it."

I didn't have time to argue. I had guests coming over. "Thank you." I gave him a quick hug and left the way I came in.

| TWENTY-ONE |

I was back to overthinking the dinner invitation and I couldn't get out of my head. It felt like an interview. I wanted them to like me, which was so pathetic. All this angst about dinner made me admit to myself that I had feelings for Nick. There was always a little nervousness when he was around. My eyes couldn't help lingering on his face during the weekend. And Olivia. She was a force with a gift, and she was only nine. Her ability to capture life with a brush left me in awe. I couldn't wait to hang her painting. I knew right where it should go.

In the end, I decided on a simple dinner of salad, grilled chicken and salmon— because I couldn't decide—with berry cobbler for dessert. Cake would have been better, but I didn't have enough time to make it. Timing was a struggle when I cooked. Inevitably, something was done too early and went cold, or it took me longer than I thought to prep, and dinner was late.

When I texted Grace to let her know I was having Nick and Olivia over, she offered to give someone at the bar the night off. With a hint of guilt, I accepted her offer. After her first day at a new job, she probably wanted to come home and decompress. But most Monday nights weren't busy at the bar, and I couldn't imagine Nick and Olivia staying much past nine. I thanked her and told her I would text her when they left.

Prince rubbed up against my leg as I started on the salad. The chicken was marinating, and the cobbler was baking. I was less worried about dinner and things seemed under control. A little after six, the doorbell rang and I wished I had looked in the mirror one last time. I grabbed the metal spatula to look at my face, but the distorted reflection didn't make me feel any better.

When I opened the door, I worried the smile on my face would give it all away. Standing on the porch, Olivia held the painting, which was still wrapped in brown paper, and Nick had a bottle of wine.

"Come in." I stepped back to let them in. Nick held out the wine and I took it from him. "I'm so glad you're feeling better, Olivia, and thank you for bringing the painting. I know just where I want to hang it."

"Can we hang it now?" she asked. I could see the faint rash that covered her arms and face but was so relieved to see her smile.

"Sure. I have a hammer and some hooks."

"Why don't you show us where you want it hung, and Olivia and I can put it up," said Nick. I don't want to interrupt you. It smells great."

"Okay, it's just here." I led them to the far wall of the big room opposite my reading chair next to the fireplace. "I can sit in my chair and look at the painting whenever I want."

"It's a good spot," said Olivia.

I grabbed the hammer and a hook from the mantel of the fireplace and handed them to Nick as the timer went off.

"I'll be right back." I pulled the cobbler out of the oven, the cooked berries bubbling up beneath the lightly browned dough. It smelled delicious.

From the kitchen, I heard Olivia and Nick talking about the height at which to hang the painting as I ripped up the lettuce for the salad. It sounded like they were arguing. Then I heard light taps and more talking. I pulled the chicken and the salmon from the fridge and opened the sliding door to the back deck, setting the plates on the metal table that sat off to the side. I had turned the gas grill on earlier, so it had been heating up for a while. Probably too long. As I laid the chicken and fish down on the hot grates, sizzle from the heat and steam from the marinade rose from the grill. I closed the cover.

"Come look," said Olivia, standing by the sliding door. I followed her into the big room, but I could already see the hung artwork.

"It's perfect." I stared at the woman on the bench with her head bowed and her hands folded on her lap. "Thank you so much."

As my gaze stayed fixed on the painting, Nick asked, "What can we do to help?"

I turned toward the kitchen. "You can open the wine." He followed me while Olivia stayed behind to look at my collection of books.

"Have you read all of these?" she called to me.

"Most of them. Some of them more than once." I pulled out the wine opener from the drawer and handed it to Nick.

"I've read all of the Harry Potter books," she declared.

"Those are some of the ones I've read more than once."

"Why do you have so many of the same book?"

"I collect copies with different artwork on the cover," I explained. "It's another one of those books I've read more than once."

I accepted Nick's offer to take over the grill and I quickly set the table. Olivia saw the treehouse in the backyard and instantly wanted to climb the ladder to look inside. Nick promised she could explore after dinner. She then turned her attention to Prince, who had wandered out of Grace's bedroom. The loud noises from hanging the picture must have woken him from his nap. He allowed Olivia to pet him while he lay on the floor with his tail whipping back and forth.

Dinner turned out better than expected. After we finished, I cleaned up the kitchen, putting dishes in the dishwasher while Nick and Olivia sat on the deck. Once I joined them, Olivia brought up the treehouse again.

"Can I climb up now?" she asked, looking at her dad. Nick looked at me.

"It's fine with me if it's okay with you," I said. He saw the broom standing against the far railing of the deck.

"Can I use that?" He pointed to the broom with his head.

"Of course."

He grabbed the broom and climbed the ladder as Olivia and I watched. "Who built this treehouse?" asked Olivia.

"My dad. When I was little."

"Younger than me?"

"I was two or three. I don't remember when he built it. It's just always been here."

Nick stuck his head out of the window. "All ready, Olivia. You can climb up now."

"I forgot something," she called out and then ran back in the house. She appeared almost as soon as she left, a sketch pad and a pencil in her hands. Nick climbed down and waited by the ladder for Olivia. She swiftly climbed up and poked her head out. "I see you." Then she disappeared.

Nick sat beside me after he put the broom against the railing. "Are you okay that she's up there?" I asked. I had already searched the tree and treehouse for wasp nests before they arrived in case Olivia wanted to explore.

"It's hard not to worry, but I can't keep her locked up inside every day. It was hard trying to do it for only one day," he said while still looking for Olivia. "She's never had a reaction that bad. Thank you again for your help."

"I don't know if I was much help. I'm just glad she's okay."

Olivia's head peeked out the window as she briefly glanced at us sitting on the deck. Then she was gone again. We sat in silence. I wondered if Nick was holding his breath until she was out of the tree.

"It's nice watching someone else enjoy the treehouse. To be honest, it's been a while since I've spent any time up there," I said, hoping to distract Nick from his thoughts. "It's full of good memories—mostly of my dad. He built it. He died when I was four." I felt like Nick, with the loss of his wife and brother, would have some idea of the pain of losing people you love. It's not something I would have said to just anyone.

"You lost both your parents by fifteen? That's a lot to deal with at such a young age."

"It makes you grow up fast, that's for sure."

"Do you remember your dad?"

"I don't think they're actual memories of him. Just fragments cobbled together from the stories my mother told me. It's easy to conjure a dad when you don't really remember him. The treehouse is a wonderful reminder though. I look at it every day and think of him."

I took a sip of wine as I continued to stare at the tree looking for a sighting of Olivia. I wondered if she remembered her mother. I was too afraid to ask the question because there was a possibility that she was listening to our conversation.

From the corner of my eye, I could tell that Nick had turned his face toward me. His voice was low and there was a softness to it.

"I want to apologize for the night by the pool," he said. "You were having a rough time and I piled on. I didn't mean to be so confrontational. We were both in the same situation—only there because of someone else. You picked up on the fact that I really didn't want to be on that trip. But with everything my mother had been through, I couldn't say no when she asked if I would go along with Ryan's friends. You were in the same boat. Only there because you felt you couldn't say no to a friend."

I listened to his words while still staring at the tree. And even though I had pushed that evening to the back of my mind, I appreciated the fact that it must have been weighing on him and he wanted to let me know he felt badly about it. I think people underestimate the power of an apology.

I turned to look at him. "Thank you for saying that. I wasn't sure who to be mad at that night. Maybe Celeste should have been at the bottom of the list instead of the top." I looked back at the treehouse.

Olivia popped her head out. "I'm done and I'm coming down."

We both stood to greet her as she walked up the deck stairs with her sketchbook in hand.

"Can I see? I asked.

"Not yet."

"How about some cobbler, then?"

"Yummy," said Olivia, and we walked into the kitchen.

"So, you have the week off, Nick?" I grabbed bowls and spoons for dessert as I moved around the kitchen.

"I was supposed to fly to Florida this morning, but I postponed my trip until next week."

I assumed he wanted to spend time with Olivia.

"Do you have a job, Jane?" Olivia asked.

"I do. I work at a law firm as a legal assistant," I said as I found a serving spoon in another drawer.

"What's that?"

"I help lawyers with their work. They help people plan for when they get older. I write letters and file papers with the courts. A lot of different things." I felt I should inquire about Nick's employment, even though I had already looked him up on the internet.

"What do you do for a living, Nick?"

"I'm an investment analyst."

Olivia filled in the details. "He's a stock picker," she said, sounding like a proud mother of a successful child.

"Looking for the next Amazon or Microsoft?" I asked.

"That would be nice." Nick was leaning back in the hard kitchen chair, his eyes following Olivia. He had his arm bent at the elbow and hung over the back of the chair, his hand facing forward. I might have been staring at him longer than I should have.

"Do you want any coffee?" I asked, realizing I should have asked before I served the cobbler. I felt nervous again now that the evening was winding down.

"No, I'm fine."

"Well, who wants whipped cream, then?" I pulled a spray can from the fridge, squirting some on my cobbler.

"I do," Olivia said, and I handed her the can. She put some on her dessert and sprayed a little into her dad's bowl. After a few bites, Olivia reached for the can of whipped cream again as Nick watched.

"I don't think you need any more. It looks like you're almost done, and we should be leaving soon."

From the window, I saw the sun lower in the sky. I glanced at the kitchen clock. It was close to nine.

Olivia took one last bite and then rested her spoon in her bowl. "I'm going to look for Prince." She wandered into the big room.

"Do you miss all the dogs at Sylvie's house?" I asked her. I couldn't remember the names Olivia called her maternal grandparents. I was sure it would come to me later after I dissected the evening.

"I like dogs and cats. I like all animals."

Olivia found Prince on the couch and was petting him as she sat next to him. "Why did you name him Prince?"

"My friend Henry named him Prince William. He was a stray that started hanging around the house. I've always called him Prince. Prince William seems a bit pretentious, although you could make the case that cats in general think they're better than everything else."

"You could argue that in court and I'm sure you'd win," Nick said to me with a smile. He glanced at his watch. "We should be going. I don't want to keep Olivia out too late after…" He didn't finish his thought, but I understood. We both stood up from the table. "Okay, time to go," he called to his daughter.

Nervous energy flooded my body as they prepared to leave. I wasn't sure what this evening was. I knew they came to give me the painting, so was this the last time I would see them? Does Nick have any feelings for me? I had known this man for a little over a week.

We stood in the entryway. "Thank you again, Olivia, for the painting." I bent down and hugged her, surprising myself and maybe her.

"You're welcome," she said.

I straightened up and looked at Nick. "Thank you for the wine."

"Thank you for dinner. You can ask Olivia, but I'm not the greatest cook. She's lucky she has two grandmothers who excel at it. It was nice seeing you again."

"It was great to see you again too." I quickly added, "And you too, Olivia." Nick reached for the door and they stepped outside.

"I hope we see you soon," he said, turning to look back at me before they walked to their car. I watched them and waved as they drove off. Shutting the door, Prince sauntered over to me and I picked him up.

"I think that went well?" I wished that Grace was here. I sent her a text.

Me: All clear. I hope you had a great first day!

Feeling like I had drunk six cups of coffee, I wiped down the counters again, rearranged the dishwasher and took out the trash, a chore that Henry did when he lived here. My mind jumped to tomorrow. I hoped it wouldn't be awkward. I missed my friend.

The front door opened, and Grace walked in, dropping her bag in front of the door to her room. As she came into the kitchen, I noticed she looked tired and wired at the same time. She spied the wine, grabbed a mug from the dish drainer next to me and poured herself a glass.

"So how was the first day?" I asked. She sank into a kitchen chair.

"I met so many people. I don't remember half of their names. I hate being new at stuff. Can't I just jump ahead six months and know what I'm doing? Waiting tables after work felt good. I know how to do that and I'm good at it." She sipped her wine.

"I think everyone feels that way when they start a new job. Grace, you're smart and funny. I'm sure you'll be feeling like you belong there by the end of the week."

"God, I hope so." She left her wine and walked to the refrigerator. "Anything to eat? I'm so hungry."

"There's leftover chicken and salmon and there's cobbler on the counter," I said, using my head to point.

"Most definitely the cobbler." She grabbed a spoon and dished up a big bowlful. She looked at me with her cheeks filled with cooked berries. "How did it go? Are you and Nick a thing now?" she asked when her mouth was empty.

I pulled the can of whipped cream from the refrigerator, setting it in front of her. She swirled a mound on top of her dessert.

"I barely know him, so we're not a thing," I said. "But I wouldn't mind getting to know him. He's a bit of an enigma. He asks questions but doesn't share much. I don't know if it's because of Olivia."

"What does he do?"

"He's an investment analyst."

"Sounds lucrative. You should date him." She took another bite. "This is delicious. I thought you couldn't cook?"

"I manage. Henry and I would take turns cooking, although he was the better cook. Speaking of Henry, I'm picking him up at the airport tomorrow. Do you think that's a good idea?"

She scraped her spoon around the now empty bowl. "I think it will be fine. You've both had time to think about things. I mean, he does owe you an apology. He was an ass."

"I'm glad you said that. I can twist things in my mind to the point where I wonder if something is my fault, but he started it." I sounded like I was six. "I guess we'll find out tomorrow. Did you tell your parents that you got a job?"

"Not yet. But I will the next time I talk to them. I'm beat. I'm going to take a long shower and go to bed. I have to get used to these early mornings." She went to put her bowl and spoon in the sink. "Good luck tomorrow," she called as she walked out of the kitchen.

"Night, Grace. Thanks." My eyes fell on Olivia's painting, and I replayed the whole evening in my head.

| TWENTY-TWO |

Not wanting to be late, I left for the airport early and managed to park a few minutes before Henry's plane was scheduled to arrive. Nervous as I walked across the breezeway from the garage to the airport terminal, I found a screen with all the flight and gate information to see that his plane had landed. Daniel told me he was going to meet Henry at the top of the escalator to baggage claim. I had thought about bringing balloons or a sign to hold up, but in the end, I figured I should be enough.

There was always the possibility that Daniel had told him that I was coming to pick him up, but I thought I would be able to tell if he was genuinely surprised to see me. After what seemed like hours, I could see Henry walking toward me. He was looking around. I stood on my tiptoes and waved.

He was wearing shorts with an open button-down over a T-shirt. His hair looked longer than when I last saw him, but I knew it probably wasn't. He brushed the hair from his eyes as he saw me and a smile crossed his face that matched mine. When he reached me, he didn't say anything but gave me a big hug that I returned. We both held on tight, probably because once the embrace was over, someone was going to have to say something. Henry was the first to pull back and he looked at my face.

"I'm so sorry, Jane."

"Me too."

He gave a brief nod. We both looked around and knew that we were standing in the way. Henry picked up his bag that he dropped. "I've got some luggage." We turned and stepped on the escalator next to us. The conveyor belt had just started moving when we found the baggage carousel for his flight. There was a little awkwardness as we stood back from the crowd waiting for the luggage to start down the chute. Was that it? Were things back to normal?

Henry turned to me. "I really am sorry, Jane. I didn't mean the things I said. And the religious stuff…I know it's important to you. It's just that I didn't always feel like I could be myself around you. That you judged my relationships." He shook his head. "Anyway, that's no excuse. I should have talked to you about it."

"I'm sorry you felt that way. It wasn't my intention. I'm glad you found Daniel." The first bag slid down the chute and hit the end with a thud. We turned our attention to the conveyer belt as we continued talking.

"How was Hawaii?"

Henry slumped his shoulders. He looked at me as I watched more luggage hitting the bottom; none of it was Henry's. "I'm sorry I went without you. It was supposed to be our trip. Everything I did, I thought you should be there."

I met his stare. "I'm not mad about missing out on the trip. We can go again another time, or we can go somewhere else." As the suitcases continued to fall, Henry recognized one of his bags. He weaved his way through the crowd to grab it.

After we collected the luggage and we were on the road, Henry started with the questions. "Is Grace a better roommate than me?" That was his first one.

"Well, she does clean Prince's litter box, so there's that."

"How is Prince William? I miss him. Does he miss me?"

"He only cares if he misses a meal. Come over and you can see if he remembers you."

"I didn't know if you ever wanted to see me again. I was surprised that you picked me up today after those texts you sent. And you didn't respond to the one I sent you."

My face grew warm. "I didn't see it until yesterday. It was buried in an avalanche of texts, mostly from Grace."

"Yeah, why were you at a motel with Grace puking?"

"Daniel hasn't told you anything?" I glanced at Henry. He shook his head. I turned my attention to the road. "It's an interesting story. It started with a funeral and ended with dinner," I said with a smile, thinking about Nick.

"What does that mean?" I knew Henry was staring at me.

I told him about the last two weeks. As I pulled into the parking spot in front of Daniel's condo, I finished telling him about Nick and Olivia having dinner at the house.

He was unusually quiet.

"What? Do you think I made it all up?" I asked him.

"No, no, I believe you."

"Did Daniel tell you that he picked me up on Saturday night?" I shut off the engine.

"He just said he gave you a ride home. He didn't tell me it was from the hospital."

"I asked him not to say anything to anyone. I was an emotional wreck that night."

"It sounds like it worked out okay. You like this Nick? I guess Todd is out of the picture then?"

Todd. The mention of his name made me feel slightly sick. He hadn't responded to my last text. I wasn't sure what he thought when I suddenly stopped texting him. I never fully explained why I was in an emergency room instead of Hawaii. I wondered if I should reach out again or let it go. Maybe I would ask Daniel what he thought.

"I'm not sure I'm ready to talk to you about boys." I unbuckled my seat belt and opened the car door, effectively ending the conversation about my love life. Henry followed and we grabbed his luggage from the trunk.

I had been to Daniel's place only a few times. It was a very grown-up space. No hand-me-down furniture. A lot of dark wood and leather. *Sophisticated* was the word that came to mind when describing it. I could see why Henry might be insecure. There was the age difference. Henry wasn't immature, but he wasn't going to be rolling whiskey in a glass and then putting it to his nose to smell the oak or the honey or whatever.

Two things were out of place in the large, open living room of Daniel's condo. A pool table filled a large portion of the space, not exactly in the middle of the room, but a little off-center. The former occupant of the Straight & Narrow was Scott's Sports Bar and Billiards, where Daniel had worked as a bartender. He bought the place from Scott and now I know it was with Maxine's help. Daniel sold most of the pool tables when he renovated the bar but kept one. It was initially at the Straight & Narrow but was taking up valuable space, so he brought it home.

The other out-of-place piece was a treadmill. It sat in a corner in front of the bank of windows, and that was where Daniel was running when we walked in. Just inside the door, we piled Henry's bags. Daniel ended his run when he saw us. He wrapped a towel around his neck and walked over to Henry, giving him a quick hug and kiss. "Welcome home! Beach life agrees with you," he said, still looking at Henry.

"But it's nice to be home." He had a big smile on his face while I looked everywhere but at them.

"Well, I should be going. Glad you're back. Come visit Prince. I'm sure he misses you," I said to Henry. Looking around the room again, I turned to Daniel. "Too bad you're allergic to cats, or else Prince William could come live here. I think he'd fit right in." Daniel's eyebrows furrowed and Henry shifted his weight while looking at the floor.

"I'm not allergic to cats, Jane," said Daniel convincingly. I turned to Henry, who now had an innocent look on his face, his eyes wide with his hands stuffed in the pockets of his shorts.

"That's interesting. Henry told me that you're allergic to cats and that's why he couldn't take Prince."

Henry spoke up. "No, I said he has a reaction to cats. His reaction is that he doesn't like them."

"Are you kidding me, Henry?" My voice expressed my exasperation. Daniel stepped in to head off my potential rebuke of Henry's dubious stretching of the truth. Daniel's life was easier if Henry and I were on speaking terms.

"Thanks for picking him up at the airport, Jane," Daniel said, moving his eyes from Henry's to mine.

There was no point in saying anything else to Henry about the cat. "You're welcome. But I'm beginning to regret it," I said under my breath as I looked at Henry.

"What?" That was his only response.

A long sigh. "Daniel, if I don't see you before, I'll see you on Friday. I'm looking forward to seeing everyone from work."

Technically, I was back from Hawaii too, so I could show my face around the office.

"I'll be there."

Thankfully, Henry kept his mouth shut and I showed myself out.

When I returned home, I was greeted at the laundry room door by Prince. I was glad to see him. He let me pick him up and I put his neck up to my face. "Maybe I'm becoming allergic to Henry. Lately, I always have a reaction when he's around." I cradled the soft cat in my arms like a baby.

"Let's go get you something to eat."

| TWENTY-THREE |

Grace was gone all day and I hadn't decided when I should go back to the office. I thought of Maxine and scrolled through the messages on my phone until I found her text.

Maxine: Wi-Fi spotty. Heard about Hawaii. Sorry.

There wasn't a lot to respond to. She left her itinerary, but I forgot it at work, so I had no idea what country she was in. Maybe other people have heard from her. I should have asked Daniel. I wasn't sure what I was going to tell Sarah and Jeanne about Hawaii, but the truth with minimal details was probably the best option. Things between Henry and me were for the most part back to normal. After the last two weeks he couldn't accuse me of being boring.

I busied myself with a long run, followed by a shower, then I decided to visit my aunt. It was about a thirty-minute drive from my house to the nursing facility without traffic. I pulled into the parking lot close to eleven. When I would visit in the afternoon, she seemed less responsive and was more likely to be tired or asleep. After I signed in at the front desk, I took the elevator to the third-floor nurses' station. I recognized only two of the nurses and aides. For so long the staff remained the same, but now there seemed to be a new face every time I came to visit.

"Hey, Jane," said Mary, one of the nurses I did recognize. "I know Alice will be happy to see you. You can head down to her room and I'll be there in a minute. It might be a nice day to be outside."

"Sounds good to me." I walked down the long hallway. The door was ajar, and I lightly tapped with the back of my hand, so she knew someone was there. The room was small, but it had everything she needed. There was a bed and a sink, and a bathroom with a wide door. My aunt was sitting up in her bed and I walked over and put my hand on hers.

"Good morning, Alice."

There was no visible or verbal response. A knock at the door diverted my attention from my aunt's face and I turned to acknowledge Mary as she walked in. She arranged Alice in her wheelchair and I pushed my aunt down the hall to the door leading to the patio and garden, so she could feel the sun and breathe some fresh air. I wasn't sure how often she went outside. I navigated between the chairs and flowerpots to a bench. I turned the wheelchair so Alice could see the garden and I sat down. Her face didn't change and her gaze seemed distant.

My relationship with my aunt was complicated. She moved in to help us after my mom's cancer returned, but she could be cruel to me. My mom loved to cook but usually wasn't hungry or was too tired to enjoy her efforts, so she would go lie down rather than eat with us. My aunt would make comments about the amount of food on my plate or tell me I was getting fat and no boys would like me. There were unkind comments about my clothes, my hair, and my makeup. Nothing I did pleased her. I felt like I had to take her abuse because I couldn't burden my mom with anything else.

When my mom died, my aunt became my legal guardian and was the trustee of my trust. After the funeral, she spent long hours away from the house and I didn't see much of her. At first, I was fine with it. But then I broke up with Mitchell and I was alone most of the time. My friends didn't understand what I was going through, and all the people who checked in on us after my mom died stopped reaching out, including my mom's real estate friends, who had been like a second family.

My aunt didn't object when I told her I offered Henry the spare bedroom. She had never said anything about Mitchell essentially living with me before I asked him to leave, although Mitchell didn't sleep in the spare bedroom.

Maybe she thought her long hours away from home wouldn't be as noticeable if Henry was around. A few months after Henry moved in, we found out what my aunt was doing in the hours she was away.

It was a March afternoon—sunny but cold. I pulled into the driveway after school. Henry went into the house to make a snack, and I went to the mailbox. I had lost my wallet with my driver's license and debit card when I forgot my purse and pizza on top of my car. I didn't tell my aunt, and I didn't want her to see the new license or debit card in the mailbox. I quickly flipped through the mail as I walked into the house, not seeing what I was looking for. I noticed that some of the envelopes had "Past Due" across them.

I walked into the kitchen and sat on a bar stool at the island. Henry was in the middle of making a sandwich. I mentioned the past due notices and he suggested I open them. I hesitated. None of this mail was addressed to me. Henry wiped the peanut butter from the knife and used it to open all the envelopes.

As I slowly unfolded each letter, Henry chewed slower until he put down his sandwich. There were seven past-due invoices, but it was the notice of a late mortgage payment that left me dazed. My mom didn't have a mortgage on the house, which meant that my aunt had taken one out and now she was behind on the payments. Henry asked me if I thought my aunt was taking money from my trust. I had no idea, but I couldn't imagine it.

She had stopped the insults after my mom died, but that was mostly because I rarely saw her. She had started working the night shift a few months prior. She was asleep when I left in the morning and she was gone when I came home. Once a week, she would leave a couple hundred dollars on the kitchen table for food.

Henry asked me if I knew where my aunt kept a copy of the trust or other documents. I assumed somewhere in her room. After Henry used a paperclip to unlock the bedroom door, I stood behind him as we looked around the darkened room. All the window blinds were closed. There was a noticeable odor of mildew and old food.

Henry turned on the light and started searching. I did the same. Neither one of us said anything. Henry searched the dresser, cluttered with food wrappings and soda cans, and I moved to the walk-in closet. Dumbstruck, I stared at the shelves in the closet and the hangers with my mom's clothes shoved to one end. I didn't know where to look first.

Henry called my name, jolting me back to the task at hand. I found him next to the bed, the green-and-blue paisley comforter falling mostly on the floor, along with a pile of wadded-up clothes. He held an accordion file folder in one hand with papers in the other. It was the trust my mom had set up for me. A business card fastened with a paper clip covered the corner of the document. Henry grabbed the card and crammed everything back into the file folder and shoved it back under the bed. He grabbed the mail and his backpack, and the next thing I knew, we were two blocks from my house waiting for the bus to downtown. We didn't say anything as we slid into a seat near the back. I looked out the window. Henry was on his phone.

After stepping off the bus, we made our way to the Fernwell Building. When we were in the elevator, I remember Henry looked at me and said that everything would be okay, but I wasn't sure he believed it. It was probably a small miracle that when we walked up to the front desk at McMahon & Wright, the receptionist didn't dismiss us immediately. When we asked to talk to Mr. Etter, the name on the card that Henry held in his hand, she didn't seem concerned that we didn't have an appointment and told us to take a seat in the waiting area.

At this point I couldn't sit, so I paced while Henry, much calmer than me, sat. I walked to the windows that spanned a large part of the waiting area and looked out, but my view was blocked by the dark steel and cold reflective glass of the building across the street. I knew there was open sky and a view of the water behind it, but in that moment, all I saw was the obstacle in front of me.

Mr. Etter came out and introduced himself as he extended his hand. He walked us back to a conference room, pointing to the chairs across from him as he sat. I didn't want to, but I dropped into the chair. Henry did the talking, explaining the situation to Mr. Etter, who asked a few questions and then excused himself. When he returned, he wasn't alone. Behind him was a middle-aged woman with short dark hair and glasses. It was Maxine. She was holding a copy of the trust.

We learned that Mr. Etter had prepared the document because Maxine was named as an alternate trustee. Maxine had first met my mom when she represented her regarding my father's estate. She asked us some questions and reviewed the mail we had brought. I watched her face—the lines on her forehead deepening and her mouth pulling tighter. She had questions about why Henry was living at the house with me. She asked me if I felt safe at home. After we answered her questions, she assured us that she would figure out what was going on, and she gave me her cell phone number.

Two weeks later, my aunt was arrested. She had been stealing from her employer and had been fired two months prior. She had been gambling with the money that she had stolen, including the money from my trust.

They found eighty thousand dollars under the mattress in my mom's room. Using that money, Maxine was able to pay off the loan my aunt had taken on the house, but the money set aside for college was gone along with most of the other money from my trust. Maxine became my guardian after she resigned as trustee. A week after my aunt was sentenced to four years in prison, I dropped out of high school, took the GED, and started working at the law firm.

It was while my aunt was in prison that she suffered the stroke. They initially ignored her symptoms and when they finally realized that she needed immediate medical attention, the damage had been done. McMahon & Wright represented my aunt and sued the prison, winning a multi-million-dollar settlement. The money was used for her care after paying back the money she stole from her employer.

It all seemed so long ago, and I was surprised that the memory didn't stir any feelings of anger or betrayal. It wouldn't change anything. I pushed the thoughts away and reached down, pulling a book from my bag.

"So where did I leave off?" I fanned the pages until I found the turned-down corner midway through the worn paperback. "Oh, Darcy is visiting Elizabeth in Hunsford." I started reading, relaxing in my seat, enjoying the words and the heat of the sun. Reading was a comfort and I'd like to think that my aunt enjoyed it too.

///

After I returned home, a text message from Nick popped up.

Nick: Are you free Friday afternoon? Olivia wants to go on a picnic at Grand Park.

I quickly replied, giving no thought to whether I was free or not.

Me: Sounds like fun. What can I bring?

The plan was to pick me up at one o'clock and I would bring dessert. After we finished texting, I remembered I was supposed to go to the Straight & Narrow on Friday, after stopping at the office. I was surprised by how little I had thought about work. The only thing needing attention was the new probate we filed before Maxine left. Maxine told me not to check in at work while I was in Hawaii, but after I returned home, the plan was for me to go into the office a few times a week to deal with the mail and email. I pushed all work-related thoughts to the back of my mind and instead concentrated on Friday's picnic. If I had to, I'd blow off Friday night and go into the office on Monday.

///

When I opened the door to Nick on Friday, he was alone.

"Olivia is in the car," he explained. He was wearing dark jeans and a short-sleeved button-down shirt, partially un-tucked at the waist. He had a pair of sunglasses in his hands.

"I just need to grab the cupcakes." I went back into the kitchen.

He followed me.

"I need a second to ask you something," Nick said from behind. I turned around from the counter with the cupcakes in my hand.

"I'm taking Olivia up to the farm after the picnic. Are you free for dinner tomorrow night?"

I hoped my face didn't show my surprise. "Yes." It was the only thing I could manage to say.

"Good. I'd rather not mention it to Olivia, though, if that's okay."

He must have his reasons and I could think of a few myself, so I didn't object. "Of course."

He nodded. "I'll call you later and we can figure out the details."

Olivia was excited about the picnic. After a thorough vetting of the spot where we ultimately laid the blanket, we all sat down.

"I wish I could take my shoes off," Olivia lamented.

Nick's mouth tightened. "Olivia, I only agreed to this picnic idea because you agreed to follow the rules. That includes keeping your shoes on the whole time." I noticed that her skin was mostly clear, with just a few faded red spots.

"I know. I just said I wish I could take them off." There was some sass in her voice and I was glad. It meant she was back to her old self.

"Should I know the rules?" I asked looking at them.

Olivia sat up straight and, with a deep voice, she said, "Shoes must stay on. No dillydallying when we eat our lunch. All leftover food and trash must be thrown away immediately after we are done." She sank down, shifting her weight to one side. She was Olivia again.

"Got it. All good rules. Should we eat and then swing?" I looked beyond Olivia to the set of empty swings behind her.

"Yes!" Olivia opened up a large paper sack and started pulling out food—egg salad sandwiches, carrot and celery sticks with hummus, green grapes, and chocolate cupcakes. I helped arrange the food on the blanket.

"I like your necklace," said Olivia as she took a bite of a baby carrot.

I found the cross necklace with my hand. Instinctively, I was going to tuck it back beneath my shirt but then stopped and rolled the cross between my thumb and fingers out of habit.

"Thank you. My mom gave it to me." As soon as I said it, I wished I hadn't. I couldn't figure out why Nick didn't talk about Olivia's mother, but I sensed it was a subject that wasn't spoken about.

"It's pretty."

Olivia didn't seem to be bothered by my explanation, and I tried not to focus on it, but it rattled in my head as we ate. Eventually, I was able to push it to the back of my mind as we talked about all the things we could do at the park. With minimal dillydallying, we disposed of the remains of lunch and walked over to the swings. Olivia made sure she was between us as we walked. She sat down on a swing in the middle and was already climbing in altitude.

"It's been a long time since I've been on a swing. I hope it's like riding a bike," I said as I pushed off and pumped my legs, trying to catch up with Olivia. Nick stood and watched us. "No swinging for you?" I asked him. "There's an open one." I used my head to point to the swing on the other side of Olivia.

"I think I'm too tall for these swings. They're for short people like you and Olivia,"

"They're probably just for kids," explained Olivia. "But you're not very old, Jane, so it's okay if you swing. Actually, how old are you?"

I should have seen that question coming, but I wasn't prepared, and I didn't know what to say. Nick must have assumed I was younger than him, but maybe he didn't realize the age difference.

"How old do you think I am?"

"Twenty-nine?" she guessed. I should have been offended, but I wasn't.

"Close."

"My dad is thirty-three," she offered.

"He doesn't look a day over thirty."

Nick had been suspiciously silent. He smiled as he leaned against the metal frame of the swings. I wished I knew what he was thinking. I wondered if Olivia was trying to play matchmaker. It wouldn't surprise me. It's something I would have done as a child. I didn't want my mom to date just any-one after my dad died.

After the swings, we walked over to the playground and spent an hour playing tag and sliding down the slide. Nick decided he needed a break and I determined I could use a few minutes to catch my breath, so I joined him after he told Olivia he was going to sit down. Olivia headed back to the swings.

We sat on the grass far enough away that Olivia couldn't hear our conversation, but she was still within our sight.

"She has a lot of energy," I said as I took a deep breath in and exhaled.

"Usually she has a brush in her hand or her nose in a book, so I'm glad she's running around like a regular kid. I'm hoping she can make some friends this school year. I think she real-izes that hanging out with kids her own age is different than hanging out with your dad and grandparents."

"Well, she's not an ordinary kid. She's lucky that she has so many people who love her."

"True. It was just you and your mom after your dad died?"

"Until my aunt came to live with us when my mom's can-cer returned."

"That must have been difficult. Was it lonely?"

I was surprised by the question. I wondered if he asked because he knew the feeling all too well. My head was down, and I was picking at the grass. "It was." I looked at Olivia on the swings. "But life is hard sometimes."

"'Life is pain, Highness. Anyone who says differently is selling something,'" said Nick.

I turned to look at his face, surprised to hear him say those words.

"*The Princess Bride* was Olivia's favorite movie when she was four or five. It was the one line that stuck in my head after watching it a hundred times."

My chest swelled as I drew a breath in. I wanted to push him to the ground and smash my lips onto his, but I didn't. I exhaled. "Yeah, it's one of my favorite movies too. And a very relatable line. Life is hard, but it's also not fair."

He nodded at my observation and then a smile appeared on his face. "That's where Olivia learned the word 'inconceivable' and she would say it all the time." He looked at his daughter on the swings and the smile widened, making it even harder not to maul him.

"It's been hard trying to be a mother and a father to her. I don't know what I would have done if I didn't have the help of both her grandparents." He looked at me. His eyes softened and he smiled. After a moment of looking at each other, he looked back at Olivia. She had hopped off the swing and was skipping toward us.

I wanted to say something before Olivia joined us. "I'm sorry you lost both your wife and brother." I put my hand on his.

He swung his head back to me and I couldn't place the look on his face because I was distracted by the music coming from behind us.

I moved my gaze to Olivia, who was now within ten feet of us, and I understood why she had ditched the swings. As I looked behind me, the ice cream truck pulled into the parking lot.

| TWENTY-FOUR |

Listening at Grace's door and hearing nothing, I busied myself with a word game on my phone. She finally wandered into the kitchen at a quarter to ten to make some coffee.

"I haven't slept that good in a while," she said, yawning and scratching her head. I was sitting at the table, still looking at my phone. I was thinking about last night. Nick had called while I was at the Straight & Narrow. I found a quiet corner by the restrooms to talk, and we made plans for this evening.

There was a bachelor party at the bar that had kept Daniel busy for most of the night, so I didn't get a chance to talk to him about Todd and Maxine. Henry showed up later and shared stories about Hawaii. There were questions—mostly from Sarah—about why I didn't go, but after my vague explanations, she stopped asking. People stayed later than usual. It was nice to see everyone. I missed my work family.

"What are you doing today?" I asked Grace, wanting her to ask me what I was doing, so I could tell her about Nick. A little childish, but it had been a long time since I'd been in this situation.

She sat across from me. "A whole lot of nothing. I don't even work tonight. Do you want to do something? Watch a movie? Play a game?"

"Actually, I have a date. With Nick."

Grace's eyes opened wider and she sat back in her chair. "Really? When did this happen?"

"We went on a picnic yesterday, with Olivia, and before we left, he asked me if I wanted to go to dinner tonight."

"That's cool. Do I need to make myself scarce tonight?"

"It's just dinner. I haven't known him that long."

"Well, I hope there will be some details tomorrow." She took a sip of coffee. "And you're welcome. If I didn't drag you to a funeral, you never would have met him."

"That's true. Thank you."

"No problem. I'm taking a shower." She got up from the table and walked across the house.

Early in the afternoon, I started getting ready. As I looked in the mirror while fixing my hair, my gaze fell on the cross around my neck and I immediately remembered Olivia's comment about my necklace while we were eating lunch. A singular thought flooded my brain and I hurried to my closet. I pulled down my mother's jewelry box that was sitting on the top shelf and took out another necklace with a cross, I put it around my neck, fastening the clasp. It hung a few inches longer than the first necklace.

I heard the doorbell from my bedroom and panicked, thinking it couldn't be Nick already. As I looked through the peephole, I felt my stomach turn when I saw it was Henry, wondering if I said something last night I shouldn't have. I opened the door.

"Hey, what's up?" I asked as I stood back to let him in.

"I forgot my key. Or have you changed the locks?" he said, stepping through the doorway.

"No, I haven't changed the locks."

"Well, I'm here for moral support and to help you figure out what you're going to wear on this big date." He gave me a quick hug. I told Henry last night that Nick and I had made plans for dinner. He was excited for me.

"I mean, this is a big deal. When was the last time you went on a date?"

"A few weeks ago. Todd?"

"Yeah, but Todd was a setup. You found Nick on your own. There must be an attraction."

I didn't confess anything. "Well, I'm glad you're here." We started walking toward my bedroom.

"Is he picking you up? Can I meet him?" Henry asked as he stopped by the refrigerator to grab a soda.

"Is that why you came over?"

"It's not the only reason, but it's one of them." He took off his light jacket, folded it neatly, set it on a chair, and walked into my closet. He started sliding the hangers across the metal rod, occasionally pulling something out to give to me saying, "This might work."

Grace wandered into my room with Prince in her arms. It looked like she just woke up from a nap. "Look, it's your daddy who abandoned you."

Henry stopped what he was doing and removed Prince from her grasp.

"I didn't abandon you. Don't listen to that mean lady." He put his face in Prince's fur.

Grace figured out what we were doing. "Isn't this a cliché? The gay best friend with fashion sense helping the straight friend pick out an outfit?" She plopped down on the end of my unmade bed.

"Maybe," said Henry. "But there are worse things than being a cliché. Like looking like crap. I don't care about labels and trends. I just like put-together people. It was the first thing I noticed about Daniel. And the last thing I noticed about you." He looked at me.

"Hey, I think I do okay," I said, defending myself.

He smiled. "I'm kidding—mostly. I want to be a part of your big night, Jane, and this is how I can help. I miss hanging out with you." He let loose a breath. "There, I said it. Are you happy?" He had a sweet look on his face. "And if Grace was going be the one to help you pick out what you're going to wear, I at least wanted to see what she picked out."

"Well, no worries there," said Grace. "I'm all about comfort. But maybe you can help me now that I have to dress better for work. I've gone through all of my work tops this week, so I need to buy some new ones or start borrowing stuff from you, Jane."

"I'll check out your closet next," Henry assured Grace as he handed Prince back to her. He turned back to my closet and the task at hand. Grace, now completely comfortable on my bed, put some music on. She started locally, with Macklemore's "Thrift shop."

"This reminds me of that movie you made me watch the other night. Crazy people? Where the gay character and the best friend pick out an outfit for the girl to wear because her boyfriend's mother hates her."

Henry stopped what he was doing and stared at Grace. "Are you talking about *Crazy Rich Asians?*"

"Yeah, that was it. This is your montage scene, Jane."

Henry laughed. "It's going to be warm tonight, so what about this skirt and this top? Go try it on."

I did as I was told. I tried on multiple outfits in my montage scene. In the end, we kept the skirt but found a different top and added a white denim jacket with a pair of flat sandals that I had forgotten I had. Henry found them in the back of the closet still in the box. As I looked in the full-length mirror attached to the closet door, I was satisfied with Henry's work, and Grace approved. I promised Henry that he could stay when Nick picked me up with only one ground rule—he had to stay out of sight, only looking out a window discreetly when Nick came to the door. The best place to do that was in the spare bedroom or the tall window in the bathroom off the entry hall.

When the doorbell rang later in the evening, I was surprised at how nervous I was, considering how much time I had spent with Nick over the last week. Last weekend was a roller coaster of events and emotions, and I didn't have much time to think—only to react. And now all I was doing was thinking. I was hyperaware of everything I did and said. I hoped the evening wasn't reduced to awkward small talk.

I knew Nick was paying attention that night when Grace, uninhibited by more than a few drinks, shared that I had slept with my high school boyfriend. I briefly thought about the conversation we had by the pool. Nick must know that I'm not interested in hooking up. And since he asked me out, I assumed he also wasn't looking for that.

As we stepped out onto the porch, I stopped. Nick started to say something, but I wanted to say my thing first. "Hey, before we go, I wanted to give you something." I reached up around my neck and fumbled with the clasp of one of the chains I was wearing. "Yesterday, Olivia mentioned that she liked my necklace and I want her to have it. Especially after she gave me one of her paintings." I pulled the chain down in front of me.

"That's not necessary, Jane."

"I know, but it would mean a lot if you gave it to her. My mother used to wear three cross chains around her neck. If anyone asked her why, she would offer to give them one. That's how I got this necklace. If you decide you would rather not give it to her, I totally understand but I hope you'll still take it." I was talking faster than normal.

"Okay." He held out his hand and I placed it in his palm. "I'm sure she'll be happy to wear it."

"Was there something you wanted to say before?"

"It can wait."

///

I didn't ask where we were going to dinner. We headed downtown and found parking close to The Market. As we turned the corner onto the brick street, with vendors and shops lining both sides, I unintentionally slowed my pace. Nick noticed my hesitation.

"Have you been here before? It just opened a few months ago and I heard good things," he said as we stood near the sign for Al Tavolo, the same place where Todd and I went on our date. You've got to be kidding me.

"I have eaten here. They have good food." If he was disappointed, he didn't show it, and I thought it didn't matter because it was my first time with Nick.

He had made a reservation and I viewed it as a sign that we were seated in a quiet corner. We were told the specials as we were handed the menus and then we were left alone.

"This is nice," I said as I looked around, appreciating a different view. I opened the menu, still carrying some residual nerves.

"Everything sounds good," he said as he looked at me and then the menu.

We started with an appetizer of grilled prawns and scallops and we each ordered a glass of wine after a brief discussion about getting a bottle. When the server returned with our drinks and the appetizer, we ordered our entrees. We closed our menus, handed them back to the server, and focused on prawns and scallops.

Looking down at the table, Nick put his napkin on his lap and moved his utensils around. "What did you order the last time you were here?"

"I had the risotto. It was good. I thought about ordering it again." I took a sip of wine.

"And what did your date order?" He looked at me with a smile on his face.

"I don't remember. But yes, I did come here on a date." With the benefit of hindsight, I proceeded to tell him about my date with Todd, finding humor in it and not necessarily at Todd's expense. I made fun of myself and how I overreacted to the situation. There was a dramatic retelling of me exiting the car at the stoplight and slamming the door with my "It's not called a Beamer, it's called a Bimmer" line. By the expression on his face, I could tell he found the story amusing, especially the part where Todd confessed that he had borrowed his mom's car.

"I'm sorry. I'm trying not to laugh. I'm sure it wasn't funny at the time," he said.

"In his defense, not many guys would have confessed to borrowing their mom's car after driving it like they just robbed a bank. I appreciated his honesty. I found it…" I didn't finish the sentence because I didn't want Nick to think that I had feelings for Todd.

"Charming? Attractive?" Nick attempted to finish my thought.

"Refreshing," I said. "I don't think I could be attracted to someone who wasn't honest."

"But he did try to deceive you—by telling you the car was his. It was only later he confessed."

I thought about it before I responded. "I don't remember him flat-out saying it was his car, that he owned it. I may have assumed it was by the way he talked about it, but I also wondered if it really was his car. He was fixated on it for the first part of dinner, kind of like how we're spending so much time talking about a date I had with another guy."

Nick didn't say anything. I wasn't sure if he still wanted to dissect this or if he was trying to think of a new topic. His face could be so easy to read sometimes and other times it was a mystery. I changed the subject.

"How long is Olivia staying with her grandparents?"

"She'll be there for a week. I fly to Miami on Monday."

"For work?"

"My parents asked me to go. They need to decide what to do with Ryan's place. I was supposed to go last week. I'm sure there are bills to pay. I should probably talk to a lawyer. Isn't this your area of expertise? Do you have any suggestions?"

I hadn't given Ryan much thought, and I felt guilty that my happiness at meeting Nick and Olivia was because someone close to Nick had died. People had to deal with the emotional fallout of losing a loved one, but there was also everything else the person left behind. It could be overwhelming for a family to deal with, especially if the death was unexpected.

"Every state is different when it comes to probate. I would look for a will first. No ex-wives or dependent children?" His body tensed and he looked down at his plate, seemingly uncomfortable with the question.

"No, no, I don't think Ryan was the marrying kind."

I wanted to ask Nick why Olivia didn't know her uncle, which was odd in my mind. I'm sure there were plenty of opportunities for her to see Ryan, but that seemed like a second-date question. I decided to ask him the question I asked in the car when we went to pick up Olivia from her grandparents—the one he didn't answer.

"Why didn't you want Olivia to go to Ryan's funeral?"

"Ryan's death was a shock. I needed to focus on the funeral arrangements and making sure my parents were okay. I didn't want to have to worry about Olivia as well. It was better that she was with her grandparents at the farm." He stared at his wine as he held the stem of the glass in his hand. I didn't ask any follow-up questions because our dinner arrived. Nick used the interruption to change the topic.

"Do you go back to work on Monday?"

"Yeah. Maxine, the attorney I work for, won't be in the office until the end of August, so things will be slow until then. Technically, I'm supposed to be studying for the LSAT while she's traveling."

"Law school?"

"Possibly. I'm not sure."

"Keeping your options open, then?"

"I'd do it if I could be the kind of lawyer Maxine is. She's generous with her time and she cares about people. She's a good person and a good attorney. I've learned a lot from her. In the back of my mind, I wonder if she's planning on retiring soon and wants me to have a plan, which is why she's pushing law school so hard."

"Well, there are worse things than being a lawyer." He smiled. "I'm kidding. Lawyers get a bad rap. And from what you said, Maxine seems like one of the good ones. How long have you worked for her?"

"I've been her assistant for five years. But I've worked at the firm for close to ten."

"She's a probate attorney?"

"Estate planning, general business, and probate are her main practice areas. She's started the law firm a few years out of law school."

"Did you and your friend patch things up?"

I smiled a little. "He's responsible for this ensemble you see me wearing." I spread my arms out wide and leaned back. "I picked him up at the airport and we talked, so things are back to normal for the most part."

"Was he at the house when I came to get you? I thought I saw someone looking out the window as I walked up to the door."

"Yes, that was Henry," I said. I could feel my cheeks getting warm. It seemed a bit like middle school.

After our server removed our dinner plates, she tried to convince us to try the cannoli, but we decided against dessert. No altruistic benefactor picked up the check. I told Nick the next dinner was on me.

Still early, we walked through The Market, enjoying the warm evening with a slight breeze. I looked up to see if there were any dark clouds, but only the wispy kind filled the sky and there weren't many.

Nick stopped in front of one of the flower vendors and picked out a rainbow bouquet comprised of sweet peas, sunflowers, asters, and lilies, handing it to me as he pulled cash from his wallet. I immediately inhaled the smell of summer. We continued to walk through the covered market looking at the wares of the vendors. After a few brushes, Nick took my hand. We didn't talk as we strolled. The silence wasn't awkward, but at the same time, I wondered why he seemed so distracted.

| TWENTY-FIVE |

We decided to drive back to my house even though it wasn't late. Nick was quiet and almost missed my exit off the freeway. Henry's car was still in the driveway, and I mentioned that Grace was home, so after we parked, Nick suggested another walk. There was a small neighborhood park not far from my house and I deliberately headed in that direction. The sun had set and the stars were faint in the sky.

"It's a nice night." Nick looked up. "Have I said that before?"

"You mentioned it earlier." We stopped at the edge of the park, which was deserted. We followed a worn path that lined the perimeter of the open space, neither one of us saying anything. I held the bouquet of flowers in my hand, pulling it up to take another sniff, then dropped my arm to my side. I had no idea what he was thinking, but after staring at him from across the table for an hour and a half, I knew I wanted to kiss him.

He suddenly stopped and turned to face me. But before he could do or say anything, I reached up and put my hands above his shoulders, the flowers brushing the back of his neck as I moved closer to him. I closed my eyes and found his lips with mine. After a few seconds, he pulled back. I opened my eyes to see an unreadable expression on his face. Remorse? Regret? I stepped back. I had assumed too much.

"I think there's been a misunderstanding," he said.

"I'm sorry. I'm so embarrassed." I felt my cheeks burning and I couldn't look at him.

"It's not the kiss." His words rushed out. He must have realized that I was mortified. "I've wanted to kiss you too. But I need to tell you something first. Let's sit down." He led me to a nearby bench under a young tree.

"After our conversation yesterday at the park…I realized that you think my wife is dead. Did Grace tell you that?"

"Yeah, she told me at Ryan's funeral."

"Jane, I had no idea you thought my wife was dead, but…"

I realized what he was saying. I stood up. My words measured, I asked, "Your wife is still alive?" Wife. If she was still alive, why weren't they together?

Nick stood up to face me. "I've never told anyone that she was dead. I don't know why Grace, or anyone, thinks that. But you have to understand—I have to think about Olivia."

"Are you divorced?" My mouth went dry and my shoulders tightened as I clenched the stems of the flowers in my hand.

"Shortly after Olivia was born, Kate, Olivia's mom, left us. She suffered from anxiety and depression and struggled to take care of Olivia. She moved to France, cutting off all contact with me and her parents and Olivia."

I took a deep breath. I ran my other hand through my hair, looking at the ground letting this sink in. I took a few steps away to gather my thoughts, but Nick moved in front of me.

"Jane, I have no intention of ever getting back together with Kate. She lives in Paris. I haven't seen her in almost nine years. Your kiss tells me you have feelings for me. Has that changed?"

"My feelings haven't changed, but you're married." I was trying to leave any emotion out of my voice, but his confession left me unsteady. "I don't see me dating a married man, even if your wife lives on a different continent. I don't see it as a technicality."

He swallowed hard. His eyes narrowed as deep creases crossed his forehead. "I know this is a shock. And I can understand why you would be upset."

"And what about Olivia? Doesn't she want to see her mom?" She didn't have contact with her uncle or her mom? There was something wrong here and confusion, mixed with my rising frustration as to why I was on a date with a married man, made me take a step back.

"When she was little, I would talk about her mom and how she had to move to Paris and how one day she would come back, but a few years ago, Olivia asked that we not talk about Kate anymore. So we don't. She told the kids at school that she didn't have a mom, just a dad. I didn't ask for a divorce because I was worried that Kate might try to seek some kind of custody agreement."

He grabbed my fingertips and stepped closer to me. I searched his face, not knowing what I was looking for, but the fact remained that he was still married, and it did change everything.

"You could have told me sooner. Before we went out to dinner tonight. Before you bought me flowers, before I kissed you." I slipped my fingers out of his grip. "I don't think we can see each other anymore." Maybe my reaction was impulsive, but it would be better to get out now.

He reached his hand up and grabbed the back of his neck and slowly exhaled. "Olivia is going to be crushed. She really likes you. And so do I. What about friends?"

I started walking back down the path toward my house and Nick followed. "I'm not sure." Truthfully, I was worried that my heart would be broken by both of them. A silence settled between us. Any intimacy that was there before was gone as we walked farther apart than two strangers.

At the end of the path, I could see Nick's car in my drive-way. Grace had turned on the outside light. Walking up the stairs, I turned to face him with my back to the closed door. He stood at the bottom of the steps staring at me with his hands in his pockets. He pulled the chain out from one of them.

"Do you want this back?" He held it up.

"No, of course not. I want Olivia to have it."

"Can we talk after I get back from Miami? It will give both of us a chance to think about things."

"I don't know. Maybe. I hope everything goes okay." I looked down at my hand. "Thanks again for the flowers." I walked into the house and closed the door behind me without looking back.

Emotionally exhausted, it took everything inside me not to sink down to the floor. My hand, cramped and sweaty from clutching the stems, hit the back of the door as I leaned against it. Henry and Grace were sitting on the carpet with a game board on top of the ottoman.

"You're home kind of early. How was the date?" asked Grace. I couldn't decide if it was good that they were here or not. I moved slowly to the big room and fell onto the couch.

"Maybe I'm destined to die alone."

Grace sat back on her knees. "What happened?"

I didn't want to say the words out loud and it took me a second to speak. "Nick is still married."

"What?" Her eyes widened and her mouth hung open.

"I thought his wife was dead?" Henry sounded equally surprised.

"That makes two of us." Lifting myself up off the couch, I walked to the kitchen finally setting the flowers down on the counter. Grace and Henry followed me. "She lives in Paris. She left right after Olivia was born." I moved around the room on autopilot, filling the kettle and turning on the stove.

"So, what happened?" asked Henry.

I sighed. "We had a nice dinner and then afterward we walked around The Market, but he was distracted. I thought he was nervous. We drove back here, and he suggested another walk. He obviously was trying to figure out a way to tell me." I pulled myself up and sat on the island counter while waiting for the water to boil. I looked down, inspecting my hands, rolling my fingers over the impressions from the stems on my other palm.

"Do you think you're going to see him again?" asked Grace.

My head shot up to look at her. "He's still married, Grace. I mean, it's not like I expected to marry him, but it's kind of a bad sign when it's not even an option," I said louder than I intended. "Maybe being married is something you mention before you ask someone out."

"Okay, that's true." She seemed surprised by my reaction.

I looked around the kitchen. "And Olivia. It's weird that I have literally known both of them for a week and yet it seems a lot longer." I could see Olivia's painting from where I sat. "He's flying to Miami on Monday. He wants to talk when he gets back."

The room went quiet. Grace turned off the stove and walked to the cupboard. She pulled out a bottle of rum and grabbed a can of Coke and mixed me a drink as Henry and I watched. She handed me the glass and handed Henry the half-full can without saying anything. I took a gulp of the drink.

"There were signs," I said as I stared at the brown liquid in the glass. "I searched his in-laws' house for any photos of a woman—his dead wife—their dead daughter. I thought it was weird there were none. No portrait of Olivia's beloved mother. Just dogs." I took another drink.

Henry was the first to speak. "Well, I know this isn't how you thought the night would go. At least you looked great."

I knew he was trying to make me feel better, but it was going to take a lot more than that. I gave him a weak smile for his efforts.

"Yeah, and you went out while Henry and I sat around and played games. At least you put yourself out there," Grace chimed in. "The last thing I wanted to do is go out tonight. I can see the appeal of staying in on the weekends and watching movies or just hanging out at home after working all week. I didn't realize how tedious a nine-to-five job would be."

"Not really helping here, Grace," Henry said, "but I kind of know what you mean. It was hard hanging out at S and N on Friday. Everyone drinking and me sitting there with a Diet Coke."

I was surprised Henry admitted that out loud. He wouldn't want us to make a big deal out of it though, so I didn't say anything in response to his confession.

"I promise you won't die alone, Jane. You have me," said Henry.

"And me," said Grace.

My smile grew as I looked at them, grateful that I had two friends to cheer me up. "Thanks," I said and let out a deep sigh. "You know, I could really go for some cake."

Henry stood up straight. "On it." He grabbed his keys and headed out the door. Grace and I looked at each other, surprised at how fast he moved.

I hopped down from the counter and moved to the table, bringing my drink along. Grace joined me. Resting her chin in her hands, with an intent look on her face, she asked, "So what's the deal with you and cake?"

I cupped the glass in my hands. "Who doesn't like cake?"

"But you really like it. There must be a reason."

I sat back in my chair. "My dad died on his birthday. I didn't know that until I was seven or eight and my mom and I were visiting his grave. While she was pulling out the dead flowers and replacing them with the ones we brought, I wandered around the cemetery looking at the other headstones figuring out how old people were when they died. When I looked at my dad's grave, I saw the day he was born was the same day he died. The idea that someone could die on their birthday traumatized me. It just seemed so wrong."

"Yeah, that does seem wrong," Grace said.

I took another drink. "Birthdays were a big deal when I was little. My mom would make me my favorite chocolate cake. It was my dad's favorite too. After my discovery, I told my mom I didn't want to celebrate my birthday, worried that I might die too. She must have figured it out. The day after my birthday, she made me a chocolate cake with buttercream frosting and sprinkles. She told me that we don't know what the future holds, which was her way of saying that we don't know when we're going to die, and that we should eat cake whenever we wanted, not just on special occasions. Sometimes we would just eat cake for breakfast. She said if I never wanted to have cake on my birthday ever again, I didn't have to, but I could any other day."

"It all makes sense now," said Grace. "So do you eat cake on your birthday?"

"Not since I was seven."

| TWENTY-SIX |

As I crawled into bed, I played the evening with Nick over and over in my head. Maybe it wasn't such a big deal that he was married. She did live across an ocean, and a big ocean at that. I remembered Nick's accusations about seeing everything in black and white. Was this a gray area?

Sleep was filled with unpleasant dreams. A faceless woman was kissing Nick. I couldn't tell if it was me or some other woman—Kate? Eventually, I managed to get a few hours of sleep before getting up to go to the early Mass.

Grace wasn't up when I arrived home. I made some tea and found something to eat. I thought of things to do to occupy my mind so I wouldn't dwell on the last twenty-four hours. Work would be a distraction. I texted Sarah to see if she wanted to go to lunch tomorrow. It was still relatively early on Sunday to expect a quick reply, but Sarah shot back a text saying she was in. Eight minutes have passed since I came home and made tea. It was going to be a very long day. Grace wandered into the kitchen holding Prince, who lately spent a lot of time in her room.

"Hey, I forgot to mention it yesterday, and there's zero pressure, I promise, but my mom invited us over for dinner tonight to celebrate that I have a *real* job." She grabbed a yogurt from the fridge and sat at the table.

"Sounds good to me. Count me in."

"Cool." Grace seemed surprised by my answer.

That takes care of the evening; now I just needed to fill the time between now and then. I looked at the clock on the microwave again. Two more minutes had passed.

///

This time I didn't come empty-handed to Grace's parents' house. Grace kept telling me that it wasn't necessary, but after I explained it was for Jack and Zac for feeding Prince when we went to the cabin, she didn't say anything more about it. When the boys opened the brown paper bag and saw the six-pack of Mountain Dew and a bunch of candy, they said in unison, "Awesome," then scurried back downstairs. Dinner was takeout from Grace's favorite Asian restaurant and her dad had gone to pick it up.

We sat in the kitchen chatting with Judy until Charles returned with two large bags. We helped open the containers and put them in the middle of the table. There was a lot of food.

The pressure was off to monitor Grace and her parents' conversation for any job talk now that she was gainfully employed. As we passed the containers of steaming food, there was an easy flow of conversation—no buffer needed. For a brief minute, I wondered what it would be like to sit around a table with Nick and Olivia, eating dinner and talking about random, inconsequential things, like our day or making plans for the weekend. Someone asked me to pass the rice, and I pushed the scenario out of my head. I liked Grace's family, and it was nice to be included in her celebration dinner. I did stop mid-chew when Grace's dad asked about her job. But then I quickly resumed eating. It was a fair question.

At the end of the evening, as Grace and I were standing in front of the door saying our goodbyes, Charles gave Grace a hug and then he wrapped his big arms around me. Grace's mom followed right behind. I had forgotten they were huggers.

"You girls—you too—Jane, you know if you ever need anything, anytime, you call me," Charles said, looking at both of us. "Grace, make sure Jane has our number," he added.

"Sure, Dad." Grace turned to me and in a low whisper said, "Now you're in trouble."

///

The first few days back to work didn't go as planned. Maxine had fifty or sixty boxes in the basement of the building and I was informed by Jeanne, five minutes after I sat in my chair on Monday morning, that they all had to be moved as soon as possible. Building management had eliminated all on-site storage. No one knew why. With the sixteen attorneys at the firm being told a week before I found out, I didn't have many options for storing our boxes. There definitely wasn't any room in my office. Maxine's office could probably house twenty or thirty boxes while she was gone, but that left at least twenty that needed to be sent somewhere else. To determine which ones should stay meant I had to go through each of them. Instead of catching up on mail and email, I spent my first day back in the office hauling fifty-four boxes up fifteen floors on the freight elevator. Looking on the bright side, I was so busy emptying out the storage space that no one asked me about Hawaii.

After a quick lunch, I sat on the floor and went through each one, matching the files to the index that was created when the box was sent downstairs. I determined what needed to stay on-site and what could be sent to off-site storage or could be shredded. Most contained files that were archived before I started working for Maxine as a legal assistant. It was a tedious process that took longer than expected. The second day back to work was a lot like the first, except I didn't have to haul boxes up the freight elevator.

As I holed up in Maxine's office with the door closed and some music playing low in the background, I sat up on my knees, moving boxes around, pulling a new one toward me. Opening it, I found the index sheet and started matching the files, flipping through the labeled tabs. I stopped when I saw the label on the next file, slowly pulling it from the box. The Estate of Robert Bell was across the top. My father. My parents weren't married. I never thought to ask why. My dad, along with his brother and sister, owned and operated a small chain of high-end grocery stores throughout the Seattle area. That's where my parents met. When my dad died, my mother hired Maxine knowing that he had intended to provide for both of us. My dad's family have never reached out and I have never tried to contact them. But now I know if I ever wanted to know their names, I'd know where to look. I slid the unopened file back in the box and decided to get a cup of tea.

///

It wasn't until Thursday that I was able to do real work. In fact, it was the first time all week that I had actually spent any time in my office. I moved the huge pile of mail off my chair and onto my desk and sat down. I took a minute to look around the room. It seemed smaller, different. Or maybe it was me.

My eyes fell on Todd's still-blooming orchid. I had forgotten it, but it looked like it didn't mind the neglect. I scribbled a note on a post-it reminding me to take it home while simultaneously wondering if Todd thought I was a complete jerk. I felt bad that I didn't really explain anything to him. The precarious pile of mail suddenly cascaded to the floor, and I held my hand out to try and catch some of it, bringing my attention back to all the work I had to do.

I logged into my email and revised my out-of-office response to indicate that I would be checking email Mondays, Wednesdays, and Fridays, and if it was urgent, to contact Marcy Davis. She had agreed to respond to anything that needed immediate attention while I was on vacation as well as for the last few days as I dealt with the basement situation. I made a mental note to find her to see if anyone had reached out while I was gone. I planned on keeping my door closed for most of the day so I could focus on everything that had piled up the last three weeks. At least things were in good shape when I left.

The morning was spent sorting through emails. Nothing appeared to be urgent, but one caught my attention. Hilary Smith wanted to change her will again. I responded to a few messages and flagged those that needed further attention. I pulled out a legal pad and started making a list. The next thing I knew, Sarah was knocking on my door. We had postponed our originally scheduled Monday lunch to today.

When we ate at the Straight & Narrow for lunch, we usually sat at some random table that the host led us too. I caught Daniel's eye as we were sitting down and, after he finished talking to another patron, he walked over to our table.

"Just the person I wanted to see. Do you think you'd have a few minutes to talk after lunch?" I asked him.

"That shouldn't be a problem." He turned to say hi to Sarah and they exchanged a few words before he excused himself to check on other tables.

After we ordered and Sarah caught me up on the general office gossip, she said, "I think there's something else going on at the firm." She leaned forward in her chair and her face looked as serious as her tone.

"What do you mean?" My eyes narrowed.

"A lot of closed-door meetings. Like for the last week."

"Who?"

"The attorneys. Sometimes it's all of them in one office or just a few of them. I've thought about listening at the door."

"Well, if it's all of them, I wouldn't worry. Why don't you ask one of the family law attorneys about it? Ask Kelly."

"She already thinks I'm nosy. But maybe while you're in the office, you can keep an ear out."

"I can try, but I want to keep a low profile this week." The server put our food down in front of us.

We talked about possible scenarios regarding the many closed-door meetings for a few more minutes but then moved on to Derrick. Sarah no longer seemed as concerned about whatever was going on at the firm. When we finished our lunch, I told her I would see her back at the office and went looking for Daniel. I found him sitting at his desk.

"What's up?" he asked, turning away from his computer.

"First, I wanted to ask you about Todd. He texted me while I was waiting for you to pick me up at the hospital. I responded to his texts at first, but then Nick came out to talk to me, and then you showed up, and I left Todd hanging. I did reach out later, but he never responded. Do you know anything?"

"Nancy hasn't said anything, but I'm not sure she would. Do you want me to ask her?"

"No, no. I just wondered. Also, I'm beginning to think that Maxine is avoiding me. I haven't heard much from her. Have you?"

"Just a few random texts with a few random photos. I think she's having too good of a time to keep us up to date on her adventures."

"Okay. That was it. Thanks."

"Sorry, I didn't have better answers."

/ / /

When I returned to my office, I turned my attention to the big pile of mail. A lot of it was creditors' claims in the new probate we filed before Maxine left. I wondered if she knew about this potential debt and if the estate really was solvent. I looked for the file, but it wasn't in my office. Marcy wasn't at her desk, but the file was. I left a sticky note telling her that I took it.

Back in my office, I scanned the intake notes. There were a number of assets, including a house and two cars—and, it looked like, another property. There was a question mark after "life insurance policy." I hadn't sent out the notice to individual creditors because the client hadn't provided that information.

It was weird that so many creditors had filed a claim without getting a notice sent to them directly. I looked back at the notes again and looked for the estimate of debt. It was blank. I wasn't too worried about it. We'd have four months to deal with any valid claims, and I decided I needed to talk to Maxine before I did anything else.

I went back to the file and found a copy of the will. She left everything to her spouse. It looked like this was the first marriage for the deceased, but the second marriage for her husband. He had four sons, all of whom were adults. I added up all the assets of the estate and it was in excess of three million.

I pulled out the legal pad and started writing down questions. The more I looked through the file, the longer the list grew.

My phone pinged.

Nick: Can we talk?

After some soul-searching over the last few days, I decided I wasn't willing to bend my beliefs to be with Nick. My thumbs hovered over the keyboard on my phone. Finally, I typed.

Me: Yes

My phone immediately rang.

"Nick," I said trying to keep my tone even.

"Hi, Jane. It's nice to hear your voice."

"Are you back from Miami?"

"I came home last night. Can I see you? I need to tell you something and I want to say it in person."

I hesitated. I didn't know if it was a good idea to stand face-to-face with him. I tapped my pen on my desk.

"Are you still there?" he asked after my prolonged silence.

"Yes, I'm thinking." I worked hard all week to not think about Nick. I went into the office every day, reviewing documents and scanning old files, anything to keep my mind busy. This seemed like a step backward. Finally, I ignored everything I felt. "Sure. When?"

"Whenever is good for you. The sooner, the better." There was an urgency in his voice. We settled on a time and a place, and I ended the call.

Looking out the large window in my office, I wondered what Nick wanted to tell me. My shoulders tightened as I thought about our date. I grabbed my purse and headed out, shutting the door behind me.

| **TWENTY-SEVEN** |

The Starbucks where we planned to meet was a ten-minute walk from the office, but I knew I'd be almost a half hour early when I started out. The short walk over gave me time to think. I didn't know what he wanted, but my feelings for him were so new that I wasn't sure if they were even real. Olivia was trickier. I wondered if we could still be friends, like a big sister–little sister situation, but I didn't know how that would work.

As I approached, I was surprised to see Nick waiting in front of the coffee shop. He must have been downtown when he called me. He was looking in my direction, though I couldn't tell if he'd spotted me.

As I drew closer, he waved his hand. I stopped in front of him, but his expression was hard to read as usual.

"Thanks for meeting me."

"Sure, what's up?" My casual reply didn't match the churn in my stomach. He opened the door and we stepped inside. It wasn't busy, so we ordered and seated ourselves at a table as soon as we had our drinks. Nick's demeanor reminded me of our date.

"I don't know where to start," he confessed as he shifted in his seat. I didn't say anything. He took a breath. "I've had a lot of time to think the last few days. Going through Ryan's things brought up a lot of memories I hadn't thought about in a long time because they're ones I wanted to forget. I also thought a lot about you. You deserve to know the whole story about why Kate left."

My stomach churned again. I hoped he wasn't going to tell me something that would make me hate him. Suddenly, I wished I hadn't agreed to meet him.

"Kate had an affair. With Ryan." He blinked a few times as he stared at me, waiting for me to respond.

I let out a deep breath. I leaned back in my seat and took a sip of my drink. I didn't see that coming.

When I didn't say anything, he continued. "We didn't think Kate could have kids because of a childhood accident. She told me about the affair and the pregnancy and asked for a divorce. She assumed Ryan was the father and that they would be together and raise the baby." He looked down at his hands. "But Ryan had no intention of marrying her, and he definitely didn't want to be a father. Kate was devastated when he left her. But because this was Ryan, I knew the affair was his plan all along. He purposely sought Kate out, told her everything she wanted to hear to convince her she married the wrong brother, then left her, ruining our marriage. Except he didn't count on Kate getting pregnant. That wasn't part of his plan."

This explained why he didn't like to talk about Ryan. And it explained why Olivia didn't know him. I remembered Nick's eulogy. "When you spoke at the funeral, you made it sound like you and Ryan were close," I said, trying to understand his relationship with his brother.

"Everything I said about Ryan was true. Like the story of how he covered for me when I snuck back into the house.

But after that night, he used it against me anytime he wanted something from me. He said he could even make up stuff to tell our parents to get me in trouble. The stories didn't have to be true."

"So, he blackmailed you?"

Nick nodded. "After a while, I realized they were mostly empty threats. I thought about telling our parents, but I didn't want them to think their own son would blackmail his brother. And there was the possibility that they wouldn't believe me, and that seemed worse, so I usually went along with whatever he wanted when we were growing up."

Now I looked down at the table. "Grace mentioned something about Ryan. Something that happened in high school." My eyes found his face again. "Celeste told Grace that Ryan was accused of sexually harassing a female trainer. That he pulled his shorts down while she was sitting in front of him."

His face tightened and he sat back in his chair. "That was Ryan's attempt to screw with my college scholarship, except that didn't work out as he planned either."

"Were you there when it happened?"

"I was in the room. He made sure of it. But I didn't see what happened because Mike knocked on the door and I turned around to open it. Mike walked in and started laughing. He's the one who saw everything. I didn't know exactly what happened until later. When they investigated her accusations, I didn't have to lie, which is what Ryan wanted and the whole reason he did what he did—to put me in a position where he could threaten me if I didn't do what he wanted, except Mike knocked on the door." His voice was hard as he recalled what had happened. "I knew that Ms. Hicks was telling the truth when she told the principal what Ryan had done, even though he denied it. He could talk his way out of anything. He fooled a lot of people."

"They believed Ryan over Ms. Hicks?"

"Ryan claimed that his shorts were loose, and they slipped off but that he caught them. He basically said she was lying, and Mike went along with Ryan's account. They did suspend him, but not for long. Ms. Hicks left the school a few weeks later. It didn't occur to me that Ryan would use other people to get to me until that day. And then Kate." His voice trailed off. "I never told her any of the things Ryan did. I tried to keep him out of my life. After the affair ended—it only lasted a few months—Kate and I worked things out and she moved back home. We were excited to have the baby, but the guilt of the affair and the depression Kate suffered after Olivia was born was too much. My parents don't know anything, but Kate's parents know everything."

So many questions swirled in my head, already full after spending the afternoon trying to make sense of that file. I wished I had a legal pad to help me organize my thoughts about what Nick had just told me. But there was one big question left unanswered.

As he looked at me, his face softened. "I know it's a lot. You must have some questions."

"Well, there is the obvious one." I didn't want to ask it.

"Who's Olivia's biological father? Wasn't that what you want to know?" asked Nick.

My eyes must have betrayed my face. "I guess from what you told me, I assumed that Ryan is. I wanted to know if Olivia knew."

"We had a DNA test done after she was born. We decided to wait to look at the results and then we decided it didn't matter. Olivia was our daughter. We didn't know exactly when Kate became pregnant. She took a pregnancy test when she noticed she was gaining weight and wasn't feeling well."

"How could she not know?" I asked.

"Because of the accident she had as a child. The doctors told Kate it would be unlikely she would ever have children," Nick said.

"And you're sure Kate doesn't know if you're the father?"

He looked down at his coffee. "Kate thought that Ryan was Olivia's father. I had no idea that she was having an affair because nothing had changed between us. Something was off emotionally, but we still had a physical relationship, so there's no reason why Olivia can't be mine."

"Then why does Kate think that Ryan is Olivia's father?"

"We had never gotten pregnant in the three years we were together. And then suddenly it happened? To her, it just made sense that Ryan was the father."

"But Nick, shouldn't Olivia know who her father is?" I was suddenly concerned for Olivia and how her world could come crashing down. "You need to find out. That's not a secret you want to keep."

"You have to understand that if Ryan knew he was her father, he would have been able to take her away from me. That he never asked for a paternity test made me realize that he didn't think he was, or he didn't want to be. What better way to screw with me than take away my daughter?"

"But you don't know that. Maybe he just didn't want to raise a child. It doesn't matter why. Only the truth matters and now Ryan is dead and if he is Olivia's real father…"

"I'm her real father, Jane." There was an edge to his voice and his eyes narrowed.

"I apologize. That came out wrong. If Ryan is her biological father, then when she finds out—because she will find out—she'll want to know why you kept it from her. And are you really going to tell her that Ryan was a terrible person, and that she was better off not knowing him? Nick, this won't end well. Trust me. You need to find out."

"Look, I know you think you know what's best, but I've raised her for the last nine years. I understand what you're saying, but it's my decision."

"That's true. But it seems to me you're only thinking of your feelings. And you're not being honest with yourself—or Olivia." I stood. "I need to go. I hope you do the right thing."

I didn't understand why he would keep that secret from Olivia. The emotional rollercoaster with Nick was taking its toll. I needed to get off the ride.

| **TWENTY-EIGHT** |

The great office mystery was solved when the attorneys called a firm-wide meeting on Friday morning. We all crammed into the conference room, where we were told that the Fernwell Building had been sold and the firm was now in the midst of looking for new office space. The move wasn't imminent—within the next year—but it had brought up talks of merging with another law firm. Nothing was set in stone. The reason for the meeting was to avoid rumors floating around the office and an announcement would be made when a decision had been reached.

We all filed out of the conference room, no one saying anything. I went back to my office. My brain had been in a fog since my last conversation with Nick. I was hoping that work might clear my head, but so far that wasn't working. I realized that in a year or so, I wouldn't be sitting in this office. Where would I be?

For so long now I had made this little life—with work, Henry, and a few friends—and in a matter of weeks, it had been systematically broken down. First with Henry leaving, and now the changes to this place, where I met Maxine, where she picked up all the pieces and put them back together so I could keep my childhood home.

My world was imploding, and I felt alone. I let the feeling sink into my bones and then I walked down to the deli a few blocks from the office and ordered a piece of carrot cake with cream cheese frosting.

When I returned to the office, I was feeling better. Todd's orchid still sat on my desk and the sticky note reminding me to take the flower home was still stuck to my computer. I moved it to the back of my office door so I wouldn't forget to take it home tonight.

As I sat swiveling in my chair, my mind wandered. I wondered if Maxine was aware of the changes within the firm—the sale of the building and the potential of a merger with another firm. Overcome with the need to know immediately, I jumped from my seat and tracked down Steve, finally finding him in the kitchen. I told him I hadn't been able to get ahold of Maxine, with the time change and her spotty reception. He assured me that she was aware of everything that was going on. I felt better knowing she wasn't being squeezed out of the firm she built. These were lawyers, after all.

I considered skipping the bar tonight, but the alternative seemed worse, so I ended up walking down with Sarah and Jeanne. A few others from the firm were a few steps behind us.

"Do you think that's why they made everyone clean out the basement?" asked Jeanne.

"Probably," answered Sarah.

"It's a thought that crossed my mind after we were told that the building was being sold," I added.

"Are you worried that Maxine is going to retire, Jane?"

"That's also crossed my mind," I said. It seemed other people had an easier time getting ahold of Maxine. I wondered if she was avoiding me because she didn't want to answer any questions about her future plans. The other thought was that she was keeping her distance so I had time to figure out things on my own.

"I wonder if we'll have to find a new bar to go to on Friday nights. I doubt we'll move just a few blocks. And as much as I love the Straight & Narrow, I doubt all of us would jump in an Uber to get there," said Sarah.

This was something I hadn't thought of when I was wallowing earlier. Sarah's observation overwhelmed me and I felt tears forming in my eyes.

"Are you going to tell Daniel, Jane?" asked Jeanne.

I swallowed and tried to control the pitch of my voice. "Not tonight," I squeaked out.

"Hey, we should all go dancing. Derrick is in Portland visiting his mom, so I'm a free woman this weekend." Sarah reached her hands in the air in an attempted dance move.

"Sure, I'll go," said Jeanne. "Jane?"

"Uh, maybe. I'm not sure I'm up for dancing."

I made a beeline for the restroom when we made it to the bar. I checked my face to see if it was obvious that I was emotional and thought again about going home. Instead, I took a deep breath and walked back out to our usual booth.

A lot of people from the firm showed up and we took up multiple tables. When I saw Grace heading our way, I instantly felt better.

The place was busier than usual and Grace limited her chit-chat so she could take care of her other tables. There were so many of us and because I was on the end, I only caught part of the ongoing conversation. I ended up half-listening. I started looking around the bar and was surprised when I saw Todd walking toward our booth. Crap, I forgot his orchid again. He smiled when our eyes met. I thought I was the last person he wanted to see.

"Hey," he said as he stopped in front of the booth. "I forgot you hang out here on Friday nights."

"Yep, some things don't change," I said, but then thought that's not really true and my throat felt thick. I could tell Sarah, who was sitting next to me, was actively listening to my conversation with Todd.

"Where's your cake?" He gestured at the empty spot in front of me.

"Grace is bringing it." Without thinking I said, "Hey, pull up a chair and join us. You can sit on the end." I pointed to the front of the booth.

"Maybe next time. I'm taking my mom to dinner. It's her birthday."

"Oh, that's nice of you. Tell her happy birthday." That was a thing, right, telling a guy you've been on a date with once to wish his mom a happy birthday? That wasn't weird, was it?

Sarah, no longer just listening, interrupted our conversation. "Hey, we're all going dancing later at Fancy's on Capitol Hill. You should stop by."

"Yeah, maybe," he said as he looked at Sarah. He turned his attention back to me. "Are you going, Jane?"

Before I could say anything, Sarah put her arm around my shoulder. "Yep, she's going." I didn't confirm or deny, but it must have been enough for Todd. "Well, maybe I'll see you there." He smiled again and walked toward Daniel's office. Turning in my seat, I watched him walk away.

"Was that Todd?" asked Sarah.

I nodded.

"Damn. He's cute."

And he's nice and honest too, I thought.

Around ten, we crowded into the backseat of an Uber. I had texted Henry earlier to see if he wanted to meet us at the club. He was going to pick up Grace after she was done with work, and they'd be there around eleven. Henry assured me that he would be fine just dancing.

The club was loud, cast in bright neon lights that moved with the music. The muscled bartender behind the angled backlit bar was pouring drinks while swaying to the Latin beat. We waited our turn and I ordered a shot as did Jeanne and Sarah. Booths and tables lined the perimeter with a railing separating the elevated area with the dance floor below. The DJ booth sat even higher, overlooking the crowd.

Sarah grabbed my hand, as she followed Jeanne out to the dance floor. The DJ played an eclectic mix of Latin and EDM with a splash of Hip Hop. The pulse of the house music made it easy to dance. I had consumed more than my usual number of drinks at the Straight & Narrow, and cake was my dinner, so I could feel the effects of the alcohol.

Around eleven, I started scanning the room for Grace and Henry. I was surprised when I saw Todd. He had seen me first and was heading my way. Sarah elbowed me when she noticed him next to me. He nodded toward the other bar in the back of the room. Trying to talk over the music, he said he was going to get a drink. I followed him.

After we each had another shot, we made our way back to the others. As we danced, I remembered the night at the bar with Grace and her high school friends. The thought disappeared when I felt a tap on my shoulder and turned to see Henry and Grace. I threw my arms around both of them in a group hug. The more I jumped, twisted and turned, feeling the heavy bass thumping in my chest, the more I forgot about the events of the last few weeks.

Eventually, Todd pointed to the front bar and we headed in that direction, leaving everyone else behind. He took my hand as we weaved through the crowd. I had to focus on where I was walking. I was on the hairy edge of being drunk and I told myself no more drinks.

"Do you want to take a break?" he asked as we stepped further away from the dance floor.

I nodded. My hand that was holding Todd's was sweaty and I was hot from dancing, my face flushed. We stopped in the corner to the left of the doors where we had walked in hours before. I leaned my back against the wall. We stood facing each other, still holding hands.

"How's your mom's birthday dinner?" I asked as the music pulsed behind us. I realized my sentence wasn't grammatically correct but decided not to ask again lest he think I was drunk.

"I think she enjoyed it. We brought her a piece of cake from the Straight & Narrow, so she was happy. It might have been her second piece today. I think Daniel surprised her with one earlier."

"Cake is good. I like cake," I said. I winced knowing that I wasn't making sense. I willed myself to sober up by narrowing my eyes in an effort to concentrate. My gaze focused on Todd's face. "You are cute." I put my hand on his shoulder.

He smiled and as I stared at his perfect white teeth, he moved toward me. The next thing I knew, his lips were on mine. I kissed him back.

///

A wave of nausea hit and I opened my eyes but didn't move. Lying on my back, I briefly stared at my ceiling as the room spun. I closed my eyes again and took a deep breath, trying to control my stomach and the increasing ache in my head. I knew I wasn't alone in my bed. I opened one eye and quickly shut it. Henry was peering over me.

"She's alive." His voice was crisp and clear. I was aware that in the past, our positions were reversed. I envied his state of mind and body.

"Why do I always wake up next to you after I spend the evening with Todd?" I wanted to move to my side but was worried about my head and stomach.

"Would you rather wake up next to him?"

"I didn't say that." I moved my arm to cover my eyes and exhaled a breath.

"Well, after last night, I wasn't sure. You guys were all hands and lips. Then you barfed in that potted plant. Do you remember that?"

"I didn't blackout. I remember the evening. Maybe just not in the order things happened." I tried to keep my voice steady and my breathing even.

"No judgment. Been there, done that."

A small moan escaped from my lips. "I never want to feel like this again."

"I don't think people plan on drinking so much that they feel like shit the next day. It just happens. I'm sure you had a reason to drink more than usual. At least I did when I drank too much."

"I was feeling sorry for myself—not a good reason," I said. I could tell that Henry had rolled onto his back.

"You knew why I was drinking too much. You told me when I came over here to tell you that I didn't want to go to Hawaii with you. You were right—I was insecure about my relationship with Daniel. I thought we had to spend all our free time together otherwise he'd realize I was too young and too dull and dump me."

I listened to his confession and knew it was my turn. "You were right too. I was jealous of your relationship. I guess I didn't want anything to change. It just seemed so easy for you to leave. But if you were going to leave me, I'm glad you left me for Daniel."

"I didn't leave you; I'm just not living with you. I'm still here for you."

"I know that now." I kept my eyes closed, fending off another wave of nausea. "Oh, I really don't feel well." I knew my stomach was empty. I remembered stumbling to my bed from the bathroom after we came home. There was a knock on the door.

"There she is. That was a side of you I'd never seen before. You're quite the partier. You've got some dance moves too. We'll have to do that again." Grace's voice was much like Henry's. I guess I was the only one who drank too much last night. As I opened my eyes, I gently pulled myself into a sitting position, my back against the headboard. Grace, standing next to my bed with a tray in her hands, gently placed it on my lap. It had a piece of dry toast and a cup of tea along with a small glass of water and two Tylenol.

"Thank you, Grace."

"Are you sure you wouldn't rather have a slice of cake?" Henry's voice was overly sweet, and I could tell he was enjoying my discomfort.

"Ugh. Why are you so mean?" I asked.

"I'm not mean. I'm sober."

I rolled my eyes and took a sip of tea, the warm liquid soothing my scratchy throat. Henry was now lying on his side next to me, his hand propping up his head and Grace was sitting on the end of my bed.

"Why do you think they call it a hangover?" I asked.

I didn't care why they called it a hangover. I just wanted to hear Henry and Grace's voices to help distract me from my head and stomach. Thankfully, neither one pulled out their phone to google it. As I listened to their unscientific etymology of the word, I thought having my friends here with me was totally worth feeling this bad.

| TWENTY-NINE |

I finally reached Maxine. She was exploring Germany and promised to send a few photos after our call. We discussed the new probate. There was a one-million-dollar life insurance policy that was taken out shortly before the woman died and the insurance company had requested medical records prior to paying the benefit. She said there wouldn't be any issues paying valid claims.

We talked briefly about the firm moving next year—planning would begin in earnest when she returned to the office. Before she hung up, we made tentative plans to go out to dinner once she was back. It sounded like she was having a great trip.

The amount of time I spent thinking about Olivia and Nick diminished each day. But my mind wandered there, especially when I sat in my reading chair—I could see Olivia's painting. I wondered if Nick had found out if he was Olivia's biological father.

Putting things I had no control over behind me, I made the decision to actively study for the LSAT and signed up for a prep program and registered for the August exam. It felt good to have a goal and a plan. Grace and Henry were on board and assured me they would help in any way they could. Todd and I texted during the week and he mentioned he would stop by on Friday night. Even though I wanted to be excited by the idea, I could only muster warm feelings of friendship. But friendship can develop into something else. I never could figure out how someone could go on one date and know they weren't a good match. Feelings can grow over time. I didn't want to be too hasty.

/ / /

After an intense week of studying and a few days of work, I was ready to relax and hang out at the Straight & Narrow on Friday afternoon. Todd showed up shortly after Jeanne, Sarah, and I sat down along with a few others, pushing the booth to capacity. Everyone had exhausted their witty quips about last Friday and my overindulgent drinking episode during the week so thankfully I didn't have to contend with that. Todd was telling me about his recent trip to Southern California. I was trying to listen, paying attention to his words, but as hard as I tried, I realized that I would probably never have romantic feelings for him. He wasn't…

"Nick," I said. He was standing next to the table. I wasn't prepared to see his face. He seemed agitated, but it was obvious he was trying to remain calm as he took a deep breath. He briefly glanced at Todd and then back to me.

"I need to talk to you." I noticed he was sweaty, and his breathing was uneven. The expression on his face—I had seen that look before. Olivia. He was here because something was wrong.

As I looked at Todd, I felt a rise of panic in my chest, but pushed it down. "I'll be right back." I slid out of the booth and quickly walked to the back of the bar with Nick close behind. We passed Daniel. I stopped.

"Can I use your office for a second?" I asked him. He cast a sideways look at us both, and then turned on his heels as he unlocked his door without saying anything. We stepped inside.

"What's wrong?"

"It's Olivia, she's gone. I can't find her."

"What? Have you called the police?"

"I don't think she's in danger. She left on purpose. She was mad at me."

I pulled out my phone. I saw four missed calls and three texts from Nick. "You need to call the police. I can call Grace's dad. He's a detective."

"Is there anywhere you can think she might go?" He wasn't listening.

I shook my head, still holding my phone with the contact information for Grace's dad. Then I thought of one place. "The treehouse."

"I've already looked there. Do you think she could get into your house?"

I hesitated, not sure if I should say it. "Is this because of the DNA test?"

"No. I think she's upset that you and I aren't friends anymore."

"Is that what you told her?"

"Can we talk about this later?" he asked as he ran his hand through his hair.

"The police. You need to call them."

"Can we go back to your house to see if somehow she got in? If she's not there, then we'll call Grace's dad."

"Okay. Where are you parked?"

"On the street, a block west. Can we go now?"

My purse and Todd were both back at the booth. For Nick's sake I decided to leave them behind.

"Okay," I said. He followed me as I led us out the back of the building, through the kitchen.

Once we were in the car, Nick and I were quiet. He drove efficiently but above the speed limit. I didn't say anything. I knew he was only focused on finding Olivia. My house was about twenty minutes away with no traffic. I pulled out my phone, wondering what I could possibly say to Todd in a text. I couldn't call him with Nick in the car. I started typing.

Me: I'm so sorry Todd, something serious came up. I'll call you later

I hoped Todd saw the look in Nick's eyes. He quickly replied.

Todd: Are you okay?

Me: Yes, I'm fine. I promise I'll explain later

I texted Daniel and Grace and said the same thing. I asked Grace to bring my purse home. I hit send and hoped they saw it. I texted Sarah and Jeanne to cover all the bases.

Putting the phone down, I thought about Olivia. I wanted to ask Nick more about the DNA test, but I decided to let it go until we found her. I found the cross around my neck and remembered the conversation I had with Olivia about the painting.

"Nick, there's another place she might be."

"Where?"

"Saint Mark's. Isn't it close to your parent's neighborhood?"

"I've already been to my parents. They're in California. Why do you think she might be at the church?"

"Can you just go there? It's not that far out of the way."

He didn't say anything but changed lanes to get off at an earlier exit. The church was only a few minutes from the freeway. As we pulled up in front of the doors, we could see a bike on its side near the concrete walkway that led to the back of the church.

"She's here." He went to open his car door.

I put my hand on his arm. "Wait. Can I talk to her first?"

"Why?"

"Please, I won't say anything her real dad doesn't want me to say."

"I'll give you a minute." He leaned back in his seat. His breathing was back to normal and his eyes no longer held the fear that was there a few minutes ago.

Walking into the worship space, I saw Olivia sitting in a pew a few rows back from the altar. As I walked down the center aisle, I said a quiet prayer of thanks and sat next to her.

Olivia looked up at me. Her face didn't show any surprise. "Is my dad here too?" she asked in a low whisper. I could see she was wearing the necklace I gave Nick to give to her.

"He's very worried, Olivia."

"He wouldn't tell me why we couldn't see you anymore."

"So instead of the silent treatment and a hunger strike, you went with running away?"

"I didn't run away. I came to pray that you would come back and I thought my prayers would be louder if I did it in church. It worked." She smiled at me.

I decided not to argue with her. "I guess it did. Listen, I like you and your dad very much." I struggled for words, not sure what to say. I didn't want to promise her anything that I couldn't deliver. "Things are just complicated right now."

She stared at me. Her face told me that this wasn't a good enough explanation.

"What if you and I hang out sometime?" I asked.

She turned away from me with her eyebrows furrowed. "You mean without my dad?"

"Maybe you could come over to my house and we could bake something, or we could read or draw in the treehouse."

Her head jerked back to my face. "Really? We could do that?"

"If it's okay with your dad we can."

Olivia quickly stood up. "Let's go ask him."

I took her hand and we walked out of the church. "Thank you for my necklace," she said as she moved the cross back and forth on the chain with her other hand.

"You're welcome."

Relieved to see Olivia, Nick assured her that she could hang out at my house. After we loaded her bike in the back, there was a discussion about what to do next. Olivia suggested going out to eat somewhere followed by some ice cream.

"We're going to drop Jane off at her house. Then we're going home, where I will make you a peanut butter and jelly sandwich and then you will spend the rest of the night in your room. And you're getting off easy, Olivia." He was looking in his rearview mirror as he spoke to his daughter, seated in the back.

Olivia crossed her arms and put her head down. She muttered under her breath, "I didn't run away and I can make my own sandwich."

Nick didn't say anything.

We rode in silence to my house. Now that we had found Olivia and relief took over the fear, I wondered how this new plan of me and Olivia being friends would work. Until Nick could say for certain that Olivia was his biological daughter, I didn't want to engage with him. Otherwise it felt like I was part of the deception.

When Nick pulled into my driveway, Olivia announced that she needed to use the bathroom. It seemed to me that Nick wasn't convinced but didn't want to argue with her. He let out a big sigh. "Quickly, Olivia."

We exited the car and I pulled my keys from my pocket, opening the front door. Olivia went straight into the bathroom.

"Let's go out on the deck," said Nick. Surprised by his suggestion after the silent car ride, I followed him as he headed toward the kitchen.

Outside, with the sliding door closed, he turned to face me. "So, were you with the BMW guy at the bar tonight?"

I had to think for a second about what he was asking me. "Yeah, that was Todd."

"Are you two dating now?" His arms were crossed and there was a sour expression on his face.

My brow furrowed. I didn't want to talk about this. "I'm not dating anyone. Not that it's your business."

He sighed and dropped his arms and the look. "You're right. Sorry." He ran his hand through his hair. "I want you to know that I have thought about what you said and I've decided to look at the DNA test. The bank doesn't open until Monday. Will you go with me? For moral support?"

I never expect whatever comes out of Nick's mouth. This was no different and I felt like I couldn't say no. I was the one who made such a big deal out of him not knowing and potentially keeping the truth from Olivia. "Sure, I can do that." As I looked at him, all the old feelings flooded back.

"Good. And I'm glad you and Olivia are going to hang out together. She loves spending time with Sylvie and Richard, but grandparents are different from friends. I hope we can be friends too, Jane."

"It might be hard for me to be your friend."

"Because you have feelings for me?"

"Of course, I have feelings for you," I said, exasperated. "What do you want from me? You're still married."

He struggled to find words. "Only on paper. I don't feel married. I don't know what it is. I haven't felt like this in a long time. I feel like there's more now than just Olivia and work. I want more than that. I want you, Jane."

I stared at his face, unable to respond. I needed a better reason for why I should care about him without the real possibility of getting my heart stomped on.

"I like to watch you sleep," he confessed. "That night by the pool, and even at Olivia's grandparents. I didn't want to wake you. It just felt so familiar, like I had done it a million times before." His eyes were soft and a smile was beginning to form on his lips. I felt my resolve melting and I took a step back.

"I'm sure you've watched Olivia sleep a million times," I said. "I don't need a father figure. Someone to give me a kiss on the forehead as I drift off to sleep."

"What if I start with your forehead and work my way down?"

I lifted my arms from my side and sighed, but I wanted to scream, *That's why we can't be friends.*

"Look," I said, trying to get the visual of Nick kissing me out of my head, "it doesn't matter that your wife lives in another country. Even if she was locked in an attic, she's still your wife. Not just your wife, she's Olivia's mother. I don't want to do anything to hurt Olivia. I said I would meet you on Monday. And I will. But that's all." Out of the corner of my eye, I saw Olivia walking toward the sliding door. "Here she comes. Text me later what time you want to meet on Monday."

Olivia didn't want to leave until we made plans for her to come over. We decided on next Saturday. Then I thought about Monday. What will Nick do if she isn't his biological daughter? Will he tell her?

/ / /

It was hard to fall asleep on Sunday. I was going to meet Nick at the bank at noon the next day. I didn't know why I was nervous. Until I did. I sat up in my bed, clutching the sheets with my hands. Did Kate know that Ryan was dead? I was sure that was one of the reasons she left and moved across the world. Ryan is—was—an extension of her family. I was sure she never wanted to see him again after what had happened, and yet the odds of that were slim when you were related, even by marriage.

My mind put the pieces together of a scenario that I hadn't thought of before. While I had never asked Nick to get a divorce, he must understand that was the only way I would consider dating him. I understood why he was hesitant to ask Kate. He didn't want to rock the boat, thinking that she could ask for some kind of custody arrangement or try to take Olivia from him, even though that seemed unlikely.

But if Nick was Olivia's biological father, and now that Ryan was dead, maybe Kate would want to try again. Would I stand in the way of that? I broke out in a cold sweat. I fell back down on my bed and let this thought rattle around in my brain, until another scenario occurred to me. That woman at the funeral who was talking to Nick as Grace and I left—was that Kate? Did she go to the funeral, and Nick didn't tell me?

I stumbled out of bed and paced for a few minutes, trying to control my breathing. I forced myself to climb back under the covers, thinking I would ask Nick tomorrow, finally calm enough to fall into a fitful sleep.

| THIRTY |

Nick was standing out front as I approached the bank, and he acknowledged me with a nod and a smile. He pulled out an envelope from his pocket and gestured to a sandwich shop next door. He asked if I was hungry.

"Are you hungry?" I asked, surprised. Wouldn't he want to know what's in the envelope first?

"I could eat," he acknowledged. I couldn't believe he was so nonchalant.

"Are you going to open the envelope first?" This seemed like something I would want to know before I ordered a sandwich.

"If you insist. Let's go sit down." We walked to the sandwich shop and found a place by the window. There were four or five empty tables and while there was a line to order, the seating area wasn't busy.

"Will you open it?" He held it out in front of me.

"Nick, I don't know," I said, staring at the white envelope.

"Whatever it says, I promise it will be okay," he said. His face softened and he took his hand with the envelope back. Sliding his finger under the top fold, breaking the seal, he pulled the paper from the envelope. He looked at it and then handed it to me.

I scanned the page and looked at him with a relieved smile on my face. "I'm glad you were right. What made you so sure?"

"I'll admit for the first few years of her life, I would look for any sign she might be Ryan's. A mannerism, the way she said something, but nothing stood out. And then one day, when I picked her up from my parent's house, my mom said, 'She looks like Kate, but she acts like you.' That was the day I stopped looking at ways she wasn't my biological daughter. I understood why you thought Olivia should know if someone else was her father, Jane, but I didn't think it was a secret I was keeping from her. I guess because, in my mind, it didn't matter."

"Would you have told her if Ryan was her father?" I shouldn't have asked the question, but I wanted to know the answer.

He sighed. "It's not that simple. I would have to explain why. And it wouldn't have been fair to Kate. I don't blame her for what happened. Yes, I would have told her eventually, but not until she was older."

I had taken his wife—Olivia's mother—out of the equation. Someone that Olvia didn't remember or know. "I didn't think of that. I guess it wasn't as black and white as I thought. I'm sorry I butted in."

"You were protecting Olivia. I appreciate that."

I let out a deep breath before I asked him the questions that kept me up last night. "Does Kate know that Ryan passed away? Was she the woman you were talking to at the funeral?" I asked as the words rushed out.

The lines on his forehead deepened. "What woman? Kate wasn't at the funeral. And yes, she knows about Ryan. Sylvie told her."

The seating in the restaurant was filling up and the tables around us were now full. The noise level had risen, and we could no longer speak quietly. Someone behind me jostled my chair as they sat and I scooted closer to the table, cutting the distance between me and Nick.

"Do you know how she reacted?" I asked, no longer looking at Nick's face.

"I didn't think to ask. Why?"

I shook my head, trying to find the right words so I could hear the answer I wanted to hear. "No reason. Just my curious nature."

"Are you wondering if Kate will come back now that Ryan is gone?" he asked.

I straightened up. "The thought has crossed my mind," I admitted.

"Kate isn't coming back. She has a life in Paris. She talks to her mom occasionally and it sounds like she's living with someone. We're both different people now." He shifted in his seat. "But Sylvie has mentioned that she may go visit and Kate seems open to it." He cleared his throat. "And maybe Olivia and I will go too if I can convince Olivia and if Kate agrees to it."

"That sounds like something that you should do. That would be good." I stumbled with my words, not really knowing what I wanted to say even though two seconds ago Nick assured me that he didn't have any feelings for his wife.

I leaned back in my chair as far as I could without hitting the person behind me and thought about why we were here. "Why did you do this?"

"Look at the DNA results?"

I nodded.

"Because I want you to know that you can trust me."

"I do," I said as I stared at him. He was still married though. I glanced at my phone. "I should head back to work.

I'm glad that you were right about Olivia." I scooted my chair back to leave.

"Are you sure you don't have time for lunch?" he said as he reached out and caught my hand.

"No, I should get back to the office."

He slid his hand to my fingers, holding them for a second before letting go. "But I'll see you Saturday when I drop Olivia off at your house."

I brightened at the thought of hanging out with Olivia. "Yes, definitely."

"I'll walk you back."

I didn't object.

| THIRTY-ONE |

For some reason, I couldn't quite get into the spirit of the Friday night hangout. We were sitting in our usual booth. Everyone was in a good mood. Grace had been over several times to fill drinks and drop off food. Her shift ended at nine, so I decided to hang around until she was done so we could leave together. I mostly listened to the surrounding conversation and watched Daniel as he checked on guests and helped staff.

There was no sign of Todd, and I was sad that I didn't take better care of that friendship. He acknowledged my apology, but I guess he was done with being ghosted. I couldn't blame him. I hoped it hadn't made things weird between Nancy and Daniel. I looked at my phone to see how much longer it was until it was time to leave.

Olivia was coming over tomorrow and I had a few activities planned. I figured if we ran out of things to do, we could just sit and read. My mind wandered to Nick, even though I tried to avoid thinking about him. I was never very successful at it. I nursed my drink and when that was gone, I stuck with water. Sarah was the first to leave. I hadn't heard a Derrick story in a while. Maybe they had figured things out.

I texted Henry while I sat in the booth. I understood why hanging out with us on Fridays no longer worked for him. We made plans to go out to dinner next week, maybe even see a movie. After Grace dropped off the check, we settled the bill and everyone else headed home, leaving me alone.

///

When I opened the door Saturday morning, I was surprised to see Olivia and Sylvie standing on my porch. I looked over their heads to see if Nick was sitting in the car. I didn't see a silhouette through the tinted windows. I turned back to the pair in front of me.

"Sylvie, it's good to see you. Come in."

"Nick asked me to drop Olivia off this morning. I'm in town to do our Costco shopping for the month and to run a few errands," she explained.

Olivia was looking around the house, no doubt searching for Prince. "Well, thank you for bringing her over." I hesitated and then asked, "Are you going to pick her up as well?" I hoped I didn't sound too obvious.

"Yes, I'll be back around four. Olivia is coming back up to the farm with me."

"Great, we'll see you then." I tried to hide my disappointment.

"See you in a little bit, Olivia," Sylvie called out. "Be good."

"Bye, Grammy." Olivia didn't turn around but threw back her arm in a halfhearted attempt at a wave. As I shut the door, I wondered if Nick was avoiding me.

"Look."

I turned around to find Olivia with Prince in her arms, his legs dangling as she had a grip around his middle. He didn't seem to mind.

"He likes you. So, what should we do first? We could play a game or make cookies. I have some modeling clay too, if you want to do that," I said as I waved my arms to sell my great ideas. The last time I hung out with a nine-year-old was when I was nine years old. Grace suggested most of the activities I rattled off to Olivia. She had more experience with the under-ten crowd, with her siblings and with babysitting when she was a teenager—something I was never interested in or had the opportunity to do. As much as my mom wanted me to have a normal childhood, her cancer diagnosis and treatment seemed to get in the way. Olivia plopped down on the couch with Prince.

"Can we dress Prince up in doll clothes?" Her eyes were big, along with her grin.

That wasn't one of the options, I thought. "I think Prince would object, most likely with his claws." But thinking quickly, I added, "We could build him a fort out of couch cushions."

Olivia was excited by the idea and she bounced in her seat. "With a bridge he can climb over to another part of the fort!" She had an imagination.

"Of course," I answered. "What's a fort without a bridge?" We spent the next two hours rearranging the furniture and building a fort using cushions, blankets, chairs, and a broom. The flattened ironing board, which I had used only once, was the bridge between the two.

Olivia told an elaborate story about a prince locked in a tower and the fort became a castle. Prince indulged Olivia for a few minutes by wearing a red scarf around his neck as a cape and even posed while I snapped a few pictures with my phone to preserve the moment.

We ate our lunch in the castle, even though the prince had left on a long journey in search of treasure.

"Dogs would wreck this castle in a minute," Olivia observed as we sat with our legs crossed. I was hunched over. Our ceiling needed work.

"Especially if there was food in it," I said. We sat and snacked in the quiet.

"Do you like my dad?"

The question came out of nowhere and I wasn't prepared. It seemed like her dog comment was to make me comfortable before she hit me with the dad question. I took a few seconds to chew the apple slice I had put in my mouth.

"I do like your dad," I said, stating it as a fact.

She seemed to be ruminating on my answer. "He said it would be better if just you and I saw each other." She took a bite of her apple slice.

"Well, that's true," I confirmed.

"He said that it's because he's still married to my mom."

I tried to think of a way to end this conversation. "It's getting hot in the castle. Let's go out onto the balcony." Olivia insisted on a balcony so the people in the castle could see all who approached—friend or foe. The balcony was the back of the couch with a bench pushed up against it. We exited the castle and perched ourselves on the balcony. The backyard was visible through the back windows.

"Did you think that my mom was dead when you met my dad?"

My plan didn't work, and I decided to let her ask her questions.

"Yes, someone told me that your mom had passed away."

"But my dad told you that she lives in Paris."

"Yes," I said, but didn't elaborate.

"My dad asked me if I wanted to go to Paris with him and Grammy to see my mom. Do you think I should go?"

I thought about the first time I met Olivia in her studio. I should have known there would be more questions today.

"I don't know. Have you thought about meeting your mom?" I asked.

"Don't tell, but sometimes I sneak into Grammy and Pop-Pop's room and look at my mom's picture in their nightstand drawer. I think I look a little like her." She dipped her carrot stick in some ranch dressing and took a bite as she looked at me. I wondered what Kate looked like.

"Why don't you ask your dad or your grammy for your own picture of your mom? Maybe that will help you decide if you want to go to Paris to meet her."

"My dad said that if we went and I decided I didn't want to meet her, that would be okay too. That we could just go to art museums and travel around, so I think I'm going to say yes."

"That sounds like a good idea."

Now that her questions were answered, we sank into another round of quiet and my eyes fell on Olivia's painting.

We spent the remainder of our time outside, although I was hesitant at first. I may or may not have spent an hour on the internet searching how to administer an EpiPen. But Olivia didn't seem to be afraid and she showed me the EpiPen she carried in her backpack. We were painting rocks on the deck when we were surprised by the sound of the sliding door. Nick stepped out.

"Grace let me in," he said, explaining his presence. "It looks like you guys have been busy." He glanced back inside at the still-constructed castle. "Olivia, you'll need to help clean everything up before we go."

"Oh, it's fine. I can put everything away. I might keep it up for a while. It's a great fort."

"Well, next time, Olivia, you need to make sure that you help. Okay?"

"Okay. When can I come back?" She blew on the rock she had painted to look like a ladybug to speed up the drying process.

"I'll talk to Jane about it, but you should start cleaning up this mess." Olivia put down the rock and we both put the lids back on the paint. I stood and shook out my legs, cramped from sitting in the same position for so long.

"Thanks for letting her come over," he said.

"We had a great time."

"She was really looking forward to it."

The small talk was annoying. "I thought Sylvie was picking her up?"

Olivia started lining up the freshly painted rocks on the railing of the deck.

"She finished her errands early, so I told her I would bring Olivia up tomorrow morning. Plus, I wanted to talk to you." I felt my stomach drop. I couldn't tell if it was dread or excitement. Olivia was now putting all the unpainted rocks back in the yard.

"Olivia, why don't you wash the brushes off with the hose when you're done with the rocks," he called to his daughter. He turned to me. "Let's go inside for a minute." I glanced back at Olivia and then followed Nick into the house. I had to say something first.

"Nick, I can't take any more revelations, like you're really a secret spy for the government or Nick isn't your real name." I felt weak at the thought of some new information I would have to process.

He took a step closer, and I forced myself not to take a step back.

"I have no more secrets, Jane. Well, maybe one. But I think you'll be okay with this one. I met with Father O'Brien this morning about an annulment. I explained my marriage to Kate, and he seemed to think because we were young, didn't get married in the church, and our families didn't attend the ceremony, that there was a good chance the marriage could be annulled. It's a complicated process though, and Kate and I would still need to get a divorce first. I have a ten o'clock appointment with an attorney on Monday."

I was shocked. I didn't know what to say.

"Olivia seems open to the idea of going to Paris with me and Sylvie. Jane, I think you should go with us. You have the time off and I promise there will be no pressure on my part. Don't say anything now. Just think about it."

I still didn't have the words, so it was an easy thing to do. I heard the sliding door open and Nick and I both turned to face Olivia. Her shirt was soaked with water.

"I got a little wet." She was holding her arms away from her sides, looking down at the puddle forming at her feet.

"Let me get you a towel." I hurried to the linen closet in the hallway, glad to no longer be standing in front of Nick. When I returned to the kitchen, I helped Olivia dry off, wiping her face, arms, and legs of the water spray, then wrapping the towel around her little body. "That will soak up the rest."

"Thank you. And thanks for the fun day. I can't wait until I can come back."

"I had fun too, and your dad and I will figure out a time for another visit." I looked at Nick.

"Okay, Olivia, let's get you home and into some dry clothes." He steered her toward the front door.

"Say goodbye to Prince for me," Olivia said as she walked to the car.

"I'll call you later, Jane."

And then they were gone. I stood by the door convincing myself that what just happened had indeed happened. Had Nick actually said he was going to try and annul his marriage and he wanted me to go to Paris with him, Sylvie, and Olivia?

| THIRTY-TWO |

Henry and Grace were sitting in the big room watching me. I felt the situation called for pacing on my part. Henry was sitting in the big chair with Prince on his lap and Grace was on the couch.

"He said he's going to ask for a divorce and try to get an annulment and he wants you to go to Paris with him?" Grace summed up the long, convoluted explanation as to why I called them here to help me figure out what I should do.

"Yes," I confirmed. Nick and I had already had several conversations about me going with them to Paris. He answered all my questions: Where would we stay? An Airbnb with three bedrooms. Olivia and Sylvie would share a room. How long will we be gone? Nine days, two days of travel and seven days in France. Why do you want me to go? Sylvie and Olivia will spend time with Kate, and I need someone to explore the city with. I need a friend. Because you make everything better. Then he had confessed something else, asking, "Do you remember that night at the motel pool when you asked me if I thought this was fun?"

I nodded.

"I didn't say anything because the truth was, I was so intrigued by you and how you talked about the things you believed. It had been so long since I'd had a conversation about something real. I think about that night a lot."

Grace asked a question and the memory evaporated.

"Is he paying for your ticket?"

"I told him I would pay my own way." I stopped pacing and stood in front of them. Henry, reclining in the chair and petting Prince, had been unusually quiet.

"Should I go?"

Henry sat up. "I don't know, Jane. You barely know this guy and you're going to fly across the ocean with him? Have you thought this through?"

"His daughter and his mother-in-law are going too. It won't just be us." Although we probably would be spending a fair amount of time alone together. I was annoyed that Henry was pushing back when he moved in with someone after dating them for only six months. "I'll be gone for nine days. Less time than when you were in Hawaii. And if things go south, I can always fly home early."

"What about Todd?" Henry asked.

"What about Todd?" I shot Henry a look. Why was he bringing up Todd? From over Henry's head, I could see the orchid I finally remembered to bring home. I stared at it for a second before turning my attention back to Henry.

"I'm just saying Nick has baggage. Todd doesn't."

"Are you saying that Nick's daughter is baggage?" My voice rose higher and I folded my arms, shocked at what Henry was saying.

"No, that's not what I'm saying. But a wife is. And not an ex-wife, either."

Grace chimed in. "Yeah, I think I'm Team Todd too. For the superficial reason that he's hotter."

"Hotter?" I could feel a rise in my chest.

"Yeah, and Nick is a little on the boring side and kind of old for you," she said.

"Well, then Daniel is too old for Henry," I sputtered at Grace.

"Hey, let's leave me and Daniel out of this."

Grace sat forward. "Jane, I'm kidding about Nick being boring and old. It's true that Todd is hotter, but I think you make a good couple. And judging by your reaction, you clearly like Nick. But doesn't it bother you that your meet-cute was a funeral?"

I laughed at Grace's observation and my body relaxed. "Well, at this point Nick and I are just friends." I noticed that Henry didn't laugh at Grace's little joke. He wanted to say something else. "What?" I asked, looking at him.

"Just because he met with an attorney and a priest doesn't mean his wife will agree to any of it. And what if there is a custody dispute? Maybe Kate will see how well Olivia paints and decide she should live in Paris with her. There are so many things that could go wrong here."

I fell onto the couch next to Grace and grabbed a pillow to hug. I was looking for validation, and I wanted to be mad at them for ruining this for me. But they had good points—at least Henry did. I sighed. I was making this decision with my heart, and I needed to use my head too.

Henry stood up, cradling Prince. "Hey, I'll support whatever decision you make. I'll even fly to Paris to pick you up if you need me to." He put the cat on Grace's lap and bent over to give me a hug. I sat up and hugged him back. He whispered in my ear, "Have a great time."

| THIRTY-THREE |

I made the leap. But not before Nick and I discussed our relationship—as friends. I reframed the whole trip in my mind as two friends going to Paris together. Were there still sparks and romantic feelings? Definitely, but friendship is what I offered and it's what he accepted. Harry and Sally became friends first—I made him watch the movie.

Nick would decide whether to bring up the divorce to Kate when we were in Paris, knowing there was no pressure.

There were a few bumps trying to coordinate the trip. Sylvie had already booked her ticket when Nick realized he couldn't leave the same day. He booked a ticket for Olivia, and Sylvie and Olivia flew out the day before us and were in Paris waiting before they met Kate. We were taking a red-eye, just the two of us.

I moved my LSAT prep online and packed my laptop in my backpack. We had close to ten hours of flight time and I could use some of them to study.

I followed Nick down the narrow aisle of the plane. He let me in to my seat while he put our carry-ons up in the overhead bin. "Maybe we'll be able to get a little sleep, so we won't be so jet-lagged," he said, sitting and shoving the backpack under the seat in front of him. Leaning my head back, I could feel exhaustion seeping through my body. I've had a hard time sleeping the last few nights.

Once we were in the air, I looked out the window at all the lights below. I adjusted my gaze and I noticed the shiny reflection of my necklace. Instinctively, I clutched the small cross. After trying so hard to stay awake, my eyelids fluttered and fell. Nick must have been watching me.

"Rest your head on my shoulder," he said.

And I did.

|Epilogue|

The sun warmed my face as I sat under the red awning at a small table for two at a quaint French café that Nick and I had discovered the first day we arrived in Paris. He was going to meet me after spending the morning with Olivia, Sylvia and Kate.

Setting my bag on the seat next to me, I pulled out the postcards and rummaged for a pen. After writing to Henry, Grace, Daniel and Maxine, I stared at the backside of the last postcard. It was addressed to me. My pen hovered and then I scribbled something. I gathered the cards, putting them back in my bag knowing that I would be home before they were delivered.

My phone pinged. It was my group chat with Henry and Grace.

Henry: When are you coming home? Prince William misses you.

Grace: Henry misses you. What are you bringing me from Paris?

Henry: What do you want for your birthday?

Grace: When's your birthday?

Grace: Did Nick's wife sign the divorce papers? Henry's too afraid to ask you.

Grace: Do you think the pasta in the fridge is still good?

The divorce papers. I couldn't figure out why Nick hadn't asked Kate to sign them unless he decided not to ask her. Every day we were here seemed like a missed opportunity. Paris is after all, the City of Love. I was grateful for so many distractions, the museums, the art, the architecture, and the food. Spending so much time with Nick, even as friends, did feel dream-like. Reality was two days away.

I glanced at my phone and reread the texts. A smile moved across my face. I missed my friends. I thought about that Friday night, jumping out of Todd's car, and walking to the bar. I remembered Daniel asked me if I wanted to get married and have a family. I realized that I do want that. Henry moving out wasn't a door closing. It was an opportunity to try a different door.

I nodded at the waiter as he put a croissant and a cappuccino in front of me. Facing the building across the narrow street, the façade checkered with windows and balconies, I glanced down the street, watching a group of cyclists and looking for Nick. And there he was, turning the corner walking toward me, his satchel flung across his chest. As he drew closer, I could see a smile on his face and I could feel the corners of my mouth turning upward, my eyes fixed on him.

"Hey. Sorry I'm late," he said before sitting down.

"How was your morning," I said.

"It was good. Better than good. Kate agreed to a divorce. She signed the documents that the lawyer gave me before we left." He patted his satchel. "I'll have them filed when we get home.

"That's great," I said as I lean forward, closer to Nick, with my arm resting on the table.

"Jane." He reached for my hand. The smile on his face faded. "What's your middle name?"

"Elizabeth."

The smile returned. "Jane Elizabeth Bell. Do you want to date me?"

"I do."